The Major gr_____ner,
and bundled h_____d of
him. He push_____first
floor, and they_____uch
a wild fashion_____len
had it not been

'I won't see _____ Not
tonight, at least_____, I won't! So please let go
of me, and *leave me alone*!'

'Now, you listen to me!' he ordered. 'I don't know
what all this is about, but you hardly seem to be behaving
as one might expect. That dress'—he pointed at the wet,
muddied rose silk—'is not my idea of mourning! Believe
me . . .' his voice sank so that it was very quiet and even,
more frightening than any shouted threat, 'you will
behave as befits a widow, or I shall personally throw you
back on the streets of Vienna where I found you, and the
next time, Gabriela, *no-one* will rescue you!'

Ann Hulme was born in Portsmouth and educated at the Royal Holloway College—part of the University of London—where she took a degree in French. She has travelled extensively, and it was the fascination of the various countries in which she made her home—France, Germany, Czechoslovakia, Yugoslavia and Zambia—which made her begin to write. She now lives in Bicester, Oxfordshire, with her husband and two sons. THE HUNGARIAN ADVENTURESS is her seventh Masquerade Historical Romance.

THE
HUNGARIAN
ADVENTURESS
ANN HULME

MILLS & BOON LIMITED
15–16 BROOK'S MEWS
LONDON W1A 1DR

All the characters in this book have no existence outside the imagination of the Author, and have no relation whatsoever to anyone bearing the same name or names. They are not even distantly inspired by any individual known or unknown to the Author, and all the incidents are pure invention.

The text of this publication or any part thereof may not be reproduced or transmitted in any form or by any means, electronic or mechanical, including photo-copying, recording, storage in an information retrieval system, or otherwise, without the written permission of the publisher.

This book is sold subject to the condition that it shall not, by way of trade or otherwise, be lent, resold, hired out or otherwise circulated without the prior consent of the publisher in any form of binding or cover other than that in which it is published and without a similar condition including this condition being imposed on the subsequent purchaser.

First published in Great Britain 1985
by Mills & Boon Limited

© Ann Hulme 1985

Australian copyright 1985
Philippine copyright 1985

ISBN 0 263 75295 X

Set in 10 on 10½ pt Linotron Times
04–0186–70,750

Photoset by Rowland Phototypesetting Limited
Bury St Edmunds, Suffolk
Made and printed in Great Britain by
Cox & Wyman Limited, Reading

CHAPTER
ONE

For two whole days the weather had been oppressive, and still it did not thunder and clear the air with a storm. Leaves hung limp and motionless on the trees, the streets and pavements sweltered, and people were listless, irritable and nervous, as if they all awaited something which should have happened, but hadn't. Against such a background, the gleaming black horses of the funeral procession seemed strangely out of place. They, too, were feeling the heat, shaking their jet plumes and rattling the harness trappings. Their smooth flanks were marked with patches of sweat, and a white froth clung to the bridle rings as they chewed on their bits.

Seeing so much splendour unexpectedly pass by, workmen and shop assistants in the airless interiors seized a welcome chance to lay down their tools and crowd into the doorways to watch. On the pavements, pedestrians stood still, the men to doff their hats, the older women to sign themselves with the cross, while leaning forward to scrutinise the cortège. Probably none of them knew whose mortal remains were borne in the glass-sided hearse, but it was clearly the funeral of someone wealthy, and in Vienna of 1880, fashionable, lively and snobbish, that was enough. Pallid shopgirls, brawny brewers' draymen and plump housewives all peered with naked curiosity into the carriage which followed the coffin, anxious for a glimpse of such a distinguished grieving family. Even the pert nursemaids lifted up their small charges to see the fine horses, and the older children stood on tiptoe or jumped in the air in their efforts to have a better view.

Gabriela, heavily veiled and sticky in her black crape, stared back at them, despising them all for their shallow pretence at sympathy and respect. A Society funeral and a Society wedding were perhaps not so dissimilar, she thought. So much expense and pomp, and so many people, swamping with elaborate ceremonial and vulgar curiosity what should be a deeply touching and personal experience. Her parents-in-law, with whom she shared the carriage, fixed their eyes impassively in front of them with aristocratic disdain, as if nothing outside existed at all. The envy of the less fortunate was something they accepted as natural and no more than their due, in life or in death. Occasionally Countess Clemenz put a handkerchief to her chin. The two women, in their tightly laced corsets, their veils and gowns with high, boned collars, were suffering particularly in the unbearably stuffy interior. Whenever the Countess made the gesture with the black-edged handkerchief, her husband inclined slightly towards her and enquired courteously, 'My dear?' To this, the Countess only nodded. Once or twice he remembered his daughter-in-law, and asked, 'Gabriela?' To which she replied automatically, 'I'm all right.'

They had lost their son, their heir, their only child. Gabriela had lost a husband, but that was of secondary importance and her grief was not to be allowed to compete with theirs. She was not the wife they had wished for their son. She was the penniless daughter of a dissolute father with whom their son had unfortunately fallen deeply in love on a visit to Hungary. That it had been a love-match on both sides was something they hardly considered. They had never allowed the Hungarian adventuress into their hearts, and had no intention of allowing her into their grief.

The cortège arrived before the fashionable baroque Karlskirche. The tolling of its funeral bell filled the heavy air with a dull, muffled sound and its portals were draped in purple and black curtains. Gabriela had entered this church three years previously as a nineteen-year-old bride. She entered it now as a twenty-two-year-old widow. What epitaph could say more? Then, as on the present occasion, Max had arrived first and awaited her; that is to say, he was borne into the church now by the pallbearers ahead of her. Max, who had been so light-hearted and full of life, and who, in going to the help of a perfect stranger caught in a drunken brawl in the street, had received a fatal stab wound to the heart. When they had brought the news, her mind had been unable to comprehend it at first. It had seemed so meaningless, a kind of macabre joke played by the Fates.

It was just as airless in the church, with an overpowering scent of lilies and freesias. Gabriela's hair was damp with perspiration beneath her large black hat. She found herself repeating in her brain, 'I won't faint!' like an incantation, and fearing the humiliation of giving way before them all, sought some distraction to take her mind from the stuffiness and the sickly flower odours. She fixed her attention on the choristers, a well-known boys' choir, sitting in disciplined ranks, their bright-eyed, rosily healthy, snub-nosed faces twisted into a forced solemnity under the hawkish eye of the choir-master. She could see that two of them were playing some game in the back row under cover of their music sheets. One of them had what looked like a matchbox, and probably contained a beetle or some such insect.

Her mind drifted to when she had been a child, growing up in a rambling, decaying house on the Hungarian *puszta*. It had been a happy childhood, and a healthy one. Her father had seen no reason why a girl should lead a life less active than a boy. His daughter had been taught to ride, to shoot, to swim and to row a boat, and to play at newly fashionable tennis across a net strung between two trees. The more sophisticated feminine accomplishments then considered necessary for young ladies had been almost entirely neglected.

The choristers' voices were filling the Karlskirche now with an angelic music, but their earnest, freckled faces only reminded Gabriela of the ballboy, all those years ago, in attendance at those merry country 'tennis parties' of days past. Her eye fell on the black-draped coffin within its circle of flickering candles. She closed her eyes to blot out the sight, but it could not blot out the sensation of having been left quite alone. They were all gone, her father, her happy childhood—now her husband.

The pure treble voices of the choristers soared into the roof, and hung there motionless like the flight of humming-birds. There was a silence. The priest was climbing into the pulpit. He shuffled his sheets of notes, cleared his throat and carefully balanced his spectacles on his nose. A feeling of melancholy swept over Gabriela. The priest's mannerisms would have amused Max, whose sense of humour had ever been disrespectful and who had been an accomplished mimic. Max had taken nothing seriously—not even his marriage.

Yet it had been impossible not to love her enthusiastic, charming and happy-go-lucky husband. Max had been a true 'coffee-house man', as the Austrians call it, always out with friends, bubbling with good humour and goodwill towards all men. Yet such youthful charmers make unsatisfactory husbands and she, Gabriela, should have known it, because Max had been, after all, a young version of her own father.

The figure of her father had dominated her childhood, a handsome, energetic and beloved papa seen by a child's eyes in an aura of adoring hero-worship. Much later, in her teens, she had realised that however indulgent he might be as a father, as a husband he was feckless, improvident, even cruel, in the unintentional and uncaring way of those who are entirely self-centred.

The first sign of this she had noticed had been her mother's continual pallor, and the lines which marked a face which had once been beautiful and belonged to a woman not yet forty. Then there were the quarrels, overheard late at night when they thought she slept. About money, mostly. There was never any money. Papa was always promising to pay, and Mama and herself hid from tradesmen, crossing the street so that they should not walk past the baker's door, lest he dart out and 'remind' the honourable lady. Eventually the country estate had been sold, the beloved old house, the stables, the pet pony, the overgrown garden and even the uneven 'tennis court', scene of many a doughty and hilarious battle. They had gone to live in Budapest, in a mean, narrow house owned by some distant relative of Mama, who kindly forgot to ask any rent. He would not have received it, anyway.

Then Mama died. Worn out, she had simply slipped out of life. Her bereaved husband had wept real tears. But by then Gabriela was fourteen, and beginning to understand that when Papa wept, he wept for himself. She and he had stayed on in the house, despite the threats from the owner.

At nineteen, extraordinarily pretty, the lively, if dowerless, Gabriela had found herself often invited to the homes of former schoolfriends, even though she could not reciprocate their hospitality. Her early upbringing had given her an unsophisticated charm and unspoiled naturalness, which spoke of the open *puszta*. She had never dreamed that, behind their kindness, many of these friends had felt sorry for her. Or that watchful fathers warned their impressionable sons that they should not 'get fanciful ideas about Gabriela Varady, who hasn't a penny, and is burdened with a disreputable father as well. A pretty face and country charm do not replace a good dowry.'

Perhaps it had been inevitable that she should one day meet a young man who had received no such warning; in other words, that she should meet Max, on a visit from Vienna. He had been so shy before this blue-eyed Hungarian beauty, and so tongue-tied, that he had almost stammered. In love for the first time in his life, he had proposed marriage. Gabriela, captivated by the exuberant charm and obvious admiration of this well-born stranger, who had so clearly lost his head, promptly lost her heart and accepted him.

His father had come to Budapest to meet her and, faced with an unexpected obstinacy in his son, given a reluctant consent to their marriage. Even then it had not occurred to Gabriela that anyone should find it unsuitable that Max should marry her. If only there had been someone to warn *her*, that she was being quite unwise to marry Max. But her own father, by now a dying man tormented by an uneasy conscience, was delighted to know his child so comfortably settled—and without a dowry, too.

So it had been left until she came to Vienna for Gabriela to make the humiliating discovery that everyone considered she had made 'a catch', marrying far above her expectations—and far better than Society considered she deserved. Worse, the marriage was a source of deep disappointment to Max's parents—and to the young lady whom they had intended he should one day marry, and who would, so they had hoped, eventually 'take him in hand'.

Gabriela put a hand to her black veil. Even now her cheeks burned when she thought of it all . . . of the whispers, of the critical and disapproving glances, of the malicious questions about her family and fortune, which could be answered only with embarrassing truthfulness. Perhaps, if the marriage itself, begun so romantically after all, had been perfect, none of this would have mattered. But it had not been so. She had been prepared to build her new life round her husband. Max had certainly never envisaged building his life entirely round his pretty wife.

Yet, in a way, Max was not to blame. The truth was that she had fallen in love with a man, and found herself married to a charming boy. Max's passion for her had been not unlike that of an adolescent feeling the first fierce pangs of love. He had been far too immature as a person to embark on a marriage, and other distractions had soon replaced the burning ardour of the first weeks together. Love was a forest in which Max was lost. Not that he had ever ceased to love her in his fashion, yet he would be equally capable of showing great affection for a pet dog or favourite horse. Like a child, he loved everyone about him, loved them equally. He had never deceived her with another woman, she was sure, but mainly because he was too busy enjoying life in other ways. He had loved the theatre, and music, dinners with his friends, masked balls and carnivals—all manner of jollity and amiable boyish pranks. The responsibilities of marriage had frankly horrified him, and he had much preferred not to think about them.

In the end their relationship had been less that of husband and wife, still less that of lovers; more that of brother and sister. He had confided in her, played affectionate tricks on her, chattered to her cheerfully of all his doings—but the holiday romance was over. Sometimes, when he came home very late after dining out with friends, he would come and wake her up, and sit on the end of the bed and tell her everything that had happened, often very amusingly. But these occasions seldom ended with his getting into the bed beside her. All too often, he had just yawned and said, 'Oh, well, it's late . . .' and wandered off to his own room, quite happy. The worst of it was that he had really wanted her to be as happy as he was, and knowing how distressed he would have been had he suspected she was not, she had never dared to discuss the matter with him. She had continued to hope that things would change, and in the meantime she had continued to love him. But, in truth, as a marriage, it had been a disaster.

All these troubles had been finally resolved in an instant by a murderer's knife. Poor Max. She had wept for him long and sincerely. But now it was time to think

of her own future, which was ominously bleak. She was
alone. She was penniless. She had not the slightest idea
what would become of her.

After the gloom of the interior, the bright sunlight
outside the church hurt her eyes, despite the heavy
black veil. A warm sultry storm-wind had blown up in
the meantime, flicking maliciously at the women's long
skirts. Beside her, she heard Countess Clemenz murmur
a little plaintively to her husband, 'I had expected to
see Adam. I know he never calls now. But he and Max
were so close once, before . . .' She fell silent and
glanced at her daughter-in-law.

Gabriela knew she referred to a cousin, a relative of
whom Max had often spoken, but whom she had never
met. Many Austrian aristocratic families, such as the
Clemenz, represented in themselves a microcosm of
the Empire. Through marriage, a branch had been
established in distant Austrian-ruled, Polish Galicia.
The cousin, Adam Dubrowski, was an army officer
commissioned in one of the most dashing, renowned
and Polish of regiments, the Uhlans, or Lancers. Gabriela had not known he was in Vienna at the present time
and was not particularly pleased to hear him mentioned.
She had always resented this unknown Polish cousin.
Partly because Max had always spoken of him with such
admiration, and Gabriela had not been married long
enough to be prepared to share her new husband's
affections with anyone, although it had been becoming
daily more apparent to her that share him was what she
had to do, and partly because she had learned that
Adam had opposed her marriage. He had written a
letter which she had discovered one day, quite by acci-
dent, in which he urged Max to reconsider, and
reminded him that he had long been expected to make
an offer for Christiane Vonneck—and that a good deal
of misunderstanding would arise if Max suddenly took
it into his head to marry an unknown Hungarian instead.
Max had never mentioned this letter, but the fact that

Adam had never attempted to make the acquaintance of his cousin's bride suggested that a rift between the cousins had followed it. Such a thing could only be hurtful to Max, himself so affectionate by nature, and his eyes, when he spoke of Adam, had betrayed an inner sadness.

Vaguely, Gabriela became aware that someone was talking to her.

'. . . my condolences, *gnädige Frau*,' said a pleasant voice.

She forced herself to pay attention to the speaker, and her eyes focused on a handsome young man of about five and twenty with a fine, sensitive face, its delicate bone structure almost like a woman's, and a crop of dark, curly hair. After casting about in her mind, she was able to put a name to him. Michael Brenner. She had met him once or twice, and never paid any great attention to him. But here he was now, hovering over her, earnestness in his dark eyes.

'Thank you,' she said tonelessly.

'The loss of a friend is, of course, a small thing compared to the loss of a husband,' he said. 'But I shall miss Max very deeply, I assure you. Good friends are not easily replaced.'

Gabriela frowned slightly. She was not aware that Max had been particularly friendly with Brenner. But perhaps he had—Max had so many friends.

Brenner was still talking, leaning towards her, his expression and voice concerned. 'You won't think me presumptuous if I ask if I may call and express my condolences properly? There are so many people here.'

'Of course not; by all means,' Gabriela told him unthinkingly, anxious to be rid of him. She wanted to be away from here, from all these people.

Brenner sensed it. He took the tips of her gloved fingers and bowed over them, but was not so vulgar as to kiss her hand, before retiring into the crowd.

People were still clustered about Count and Countess

Clemenz. Few seemed to think the young widow worth more than a brief word. They knew her lowly standing with the dead man's parents. Gabriela felt a stab of gratitude towards Brenner for coming to speak to her at all, and her quick Hungarian temper was rising. So, they thought her nothing but a moment's folly on the dead man's part, which had led him to make a thoughtless and unsuitable marriage!

'Well, I'm not staying here so that they may have the pleasure of ignoring me!' she muttered. She picked up her black skirts in both hands and glanced quickly round her. Brenner was walking away from the crowd, and she hastened after him and called impulsively, 'Herr Brenner, please wait!'

He turned round, surprise in his face, and then came back towards her. 'Countess?' he asked. He looked and sounded understandably curious, but also wary. She saw his fine dark eyes flicker over the bystanders, several of whom had noticed this new development and were staring unashamedly.

'Would you be so good as to give me your arm?' Gabriela asked him briskly. 'And help me up into the carriage?'

Brenner raised his eyebrows, but smiled and offered his arm as requested, and leading her to the carriage, helped her inside. The little crowd outside the church had fallen silent and was watching with stunned amazement.

'Thank you!' she said, in the same brisk voice. She shook out her black skirts to settle them. From the corner of her eye she could see an array of blank, gaping faces.

Brenner stooped and tucked the trailing hem of her dress safely into the carriage, so that it should not catch in the door. As he did so, he murmured with mock reproach, 'That was not in your book of etiquette, Countess! Nor in *theirs*. They don't know what to do.'

Embarrassed confusion certainly reigned now in the

crowd of mourners and sympathisers. Now that the widow had left, and so obviously, others could hardly linger. They broke off their condolences to her parents-in-law in mid-speech and began to disperse to their own waiting vehicles, making shrugs of incomprehension to each other.

Brenner hid a grin of malicious amusement by putting one hand, in a pearl-grey suede glove, before his face. Then he made Gabriela a polite little bow and took himself off, walking very quickly, probably to avoid encountering Count Clemenz and his wife who were walking unhurriedly towards the carriage in an attempt to restore some dignity to the occasion.

'Trust that wretched girl to embarrass us!' muttered Countess Clemenz venomously to her husband. She glowered through her black veil at the carriage and the partly obscured figure of her daughter-in-law within, and then, with a mixture of anger and suspicion, at the retreating figure of Michael Brenner. 'Who is that young fellow? I don't know him.'

Her husband was staring thoughtfully in the same direction, through narrowed eyes. 'It looks like . . . I do believe it *is* young Brenner. What the devil has brought *him* here?'

That evening, alone at last in her room before dinner, Gabriela picked up the photograph of Max from the dressing-table and stood with the heavy silver frame in her hand. Outside the window, night had fallen, and a distant thunder rolled. The storm, promised so long, was approaching at last. It flickered on the horizon in little flashes of light, like Greek Fire, as if a battle raged somewhere over there.

She set down the photograph and surveyed herself in the mirror. Clad in mourning black, a slim, pale and embattled figure stared back. Wide-set blue eyes looked straight out of the mirror challengingly. 'I know you all despise me,' said the defiant gaze of those proud blue eyes. 'But I'll show you. I won't be beaten by any of you!'

Glancing down at her black gown, she twitched the skirt scornfully. Max had hated to see women in mourning: 'black crows', he used to call them. How he would have loathed the sight of his pretty Hungarian wife in such dreary garments. Gabriela pursed her lips obstinately. That, at least, was something which could be remedied straight away. She seized the bell-pull, and rang vigorously for her maid.

'You do understand what I'm going to do, don't you, Max?' she addressed the photograph. 'They'd crush me like a beetle if I'd only let them do it. Nothing I could ever do would please them, so I've nothing to lose by doing things my way—and this horrible black dress, you'd be pleased to know, is going first!'

A click at the door announced the maid, towards whom Gabriela cast a mistrustful glance. She had never liked the girl. Countess Clemenz had chosen Arlette to serve her daughter-in-law when Gabriela had arrived in Vienna, and it had not taken her long to discover that Arlette was also her mother-in-law's spy. Even without this, she would not have liked her. The girl had a sharp, shrewish little face, mousy crimped hair and pale, almost lashless eyes. She claimed to be French, and to come from Alsace, a province lost to Prussia in the war of 1870. Prussia was not liked in Vienna, and Arlette liked to play on her claimed nationality, telling spine-chilling tales of Prussian crimes. For all that, Gabriela was fairly sure that the girl really was German, probably a Rhinelander, who had learned a little French somewhere and knew how to adopt the accent. A French lady's maid was able to command a better salary than a German one. Add to that whatever the Countess paid the girl for informing on her young Hungarian mistress, and Arlette probably had a tidy sum set by.

'Lay out my rose pink dress,' Gabriela told her firmly. Arlette's mouth dropped open and her pale eyes popped. 'The pink, madame?' In her amazement, she even forgot the French accent.

'Yes, the pink one!' Gabriela snapped. She sat down before the dressing-table and began hurriedly to pull off her mourning jewellery, the garnet rings and jet beads and earrings, then pushed the articles all together roughly in a heap. 'And put these things away in a box somewhere. I shan't need them.'

'N-not need them, madame?' The maid looked as though she could scarcely believe her ears.

'That's what I said. The funeral's over. Do you have to repeat everything I say? Are you deaf?'

'No, madame,' the maid said stiffly. She scooped up the discarded mourning trinkets, her voice and frame quivering with outraged indignation. 'I'll lay out the rose gown, as madame wishes.'

The gown had been one of Max's favourites. The skirt, banded with handmade Hungarian lace, was tied back by an ingenious arrangement of unseen ribbons, a fashion which had just replaced the bustle. A row of little rose velvet bows decorated the swathes of material behind, and the train gave a tantalising frou-frou as it swept along the floor. Gabriela looked into the mirror again. Had Brenner been there, he probably would have remarked that this, also, was not in any book of correct behaviour, but she had no time for 'correct behaviour'. She would wear no black for Max—she wore this gown for him, because that was how he had liked to see her. It was her own very special way of observing his memory. Wherever Max was now, if he could see, he would understand and approve.

She patted her thick blond hair, which was piled into a simple chignon, and tried to tuck away the unruly little tendrils which escaped from it. Gabriela had hardly slept since the news of Max's death and her eyes seemed enormous in her pale, drawn face, her Magyar cheekbones more prominent than usual.

Pinching her cheeks to colour them, she made her

way downstairs and put her hand on the knob of the drawing-room door. As it swung slowly open, the voices of Max's parents fell on her ear. She entered the room, and closed the door quietly. They had not heard her, and the Countess, who was in mid-speech, continued, heedless of the newcomer.

'Adam's absence today was, to put it mildly, extraordinary. I know he is in Vienna. Half a dozen people at least have told me they've seen him, and I simply cannot understand why he was not at the church today.'

'Some good reason delayed him, no doubt,' her husband observed in his calm way.

'Good reason? Some woman, I don't doubt!' Before her husband could reply to this accusation, Countess Clemenz continued vehemently, 'That womanising Pole takes after his father, who eloped with your sister when she was a girl of fifteen! Don't pretend differently!'

'Adam's father proved a good husband to my sister, none the less,' Count Clemenz said firmly. 'And had my poor sister lived longer and Adam himself been able to know his mother better, perhaps the boy would have grown up showing more respect for women. As it is . . .'

'As it is, he is over thirty and he has never shown the slightest indication of settling down. I always feared that his friendship with Max would lead to some disastrous result, and so it did! Max was tempted to flirt with that Hungarian chit, but because he lacked Adam's hard head and experience, she trapped him into marriage, and now we have the girl on our hands. What's to be done with her? Tell me that!' she concluded, flinging the words bitterly at her husband.

The blood surged into Gabriela's cheeks, where she stood by the door, and she cleared her throat to announce her presence. The other two spun round. Count Clemenz had the grace to show some embarrassment, realising that his daughter-in-law had obviously overheard. But his wife showed not the slightest discomfiture, and advanced on her dead son's wife, with glittering eyes and a vitriolic expression.

'Well, Gabriela, eavesdropping now?' she asked in a voice like a whiplash. 'Perhaps it is the fashion in Budapest?'

In a tight little voice, Gabriela said, 'I assure you . . .' But she was not allowed to finish.

Countess Clemenz darted forward and grasped a handful of her daughter-in-law's rose silk gown. 'And what is this, pray? Do you dress for a party on the day we bury your husband?'

'No!' Gabriela snapped, jerking her skirt from the woman's grasp. 'I am dressing as Max would have wished to see me! He always hated the black crape and long faces at funerals. I know he would not have wished me to wear it for him.'

'You scheming little vixen,' the Countess hissed. 'You trapped my poor son into marriage, and now you haven't even the decency to show respect for his memory! From the moment my poor boy set eyes on you, on that accursed trip to Hungary, he thought of nothing and nobody else. For his sake we were obliged to accept you—*you*! A penniless little Hungariar nobody! Well, young woman, now that your unfortunate, besotted husband is dead, it is for *us* to decide what is to be done with you.'

'That's enough, Caroline!' Count Clemenz interrupted in a tone of voice which commanded her silence instantly. He came towards Gabriela and interposed himself between his wife and daughter-in-law. He was a man of some seventy years of age, but no one would have credited it, so upright and trim was his figure crowned by a head of silvery grey hair, as thick as it had been in his youth, and his sharp blue eyes, fixed now on Gabriela with a piercing but not unkindly scrutiny. 'My dear Gabriela,' he began courteously, 'you will forgive, I am sure, a mother's grief. My wife is distracted. Believe me, I regard you as a daughter. My son brought you to this house, and while I live, you shall have a home here with us.' He glanced towards his wife meaningfully.

'I have never asked anything of either of you,' Gabriela retorted in a low, emotional voice, barely under control. 'I want nothing from you now. I loved Max . . .'

'Liar!' screamed the Countess. There was a silence, in which the shrill echo of her voice resounded in the high-ceilinged room. It was overwhelmed by the crash of thunder, and the threatened storm broke with a savage suddenness. Lightning threw a jagged yellow javelin across the unshuttered window and a flurry of rain pattered urgently on the panes like a hail of bullets. She leapt forward, and before anyone could prevent her, snatched at the topmost layer of lace banding the skirt of the rose gown and wrenched it away. 'Take off that dress, you gipsy, or I swear I'll rip every last shred of material off your body!'

Gabriela gave a cry and stumbled back, as Count Clemenz lunged forward to restrain his wife. The woman was beside herself, screaming accusations, some of them couched in the vilest language. Appalled, Gabriela stared for a moment in disbelief at this wild creature, filled with hatred for her. She had realised that Max's mother had disliked her, but this torrent of obscene and vicious abuse was beyond anything she had ever thought possible in a woman of such high social standing. The Count was still grappling with his wife in an effort to restrain and silence her. Gabriela, overcome with horror and revulsion, seized her skirts in both hands and ran from the room filled with that shrieking hate-laden voice, out of the family apartments, and down the outer staircase to the inner courtyard.

The people there were servants and dependants of the family, who lived, with their wives and children, in the warren of rooms on the ground floor, as was customary in great mansions like this one, built some two hundred years previously. They were clustered together, talking sombrely of the tragedy which had befallen the family on which they all depended and which must inevitably also affect them. They parted before her fleeing, dishevelled figure. Only one man, the little gnarled old doorkeeper, hobbled forward as though he would prevent her.

Gabriela turned on him imperiously. 'Open the door!'

She spoke with such fury and authority that whatever protest he had been about to make died on his lips. Obediently he dragged open the great outer door into the street. Gabriela ran out into the narrow cobbled road, and a squall of heavy rain struck her face and bare shoulders. The darkness was split by a flash of lightning that eclipsed the feeble glimmer of the gas-lamps leading away to her left towards the glittering lights of the Herrengasse, a busy thoroughfare. The other way, to her right, lay in rain-drenched darkness. She could hear her father-in-law calling to the door-keeper to restrain her, and glancing back, she saw that the old man was already moving to obey the master of the house. She did not hesitate. Heedless of the pelting rain and growling thunder, she plunged into the darkness to the right, running headlong down the street, the rose skirts clasped in her hands, neither knowing nor caring where she went, desiring only escape.

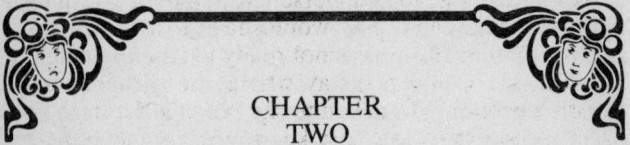

CHAPTER
TWO

At the end of the street, Gabriela's flight brought her into a broad, ill-lit square dominated by a large building which loomed dark and sinister against the night sky, and another flash of lightning briefly revealed the outlines of a church. She made her way towards it, and huddled under the cold wet stone buttresses. In the darkness, the cobbles echoed to the clatter of the feet of servants sent out in search of her. Fearful of being betrayed by the lightning, she crouched down and made herself as small as possible. They entered the square, calling and searching, until she heard someone exclaim, 'She's not here, she must have gone the other way—come on!'

The searchers set off back the way they had come, and she was left alone in the square, eerily dark and silent under the brooding mass of the church. She felt her way along the outer masonry until she came to the doors. They exuded an odour of wet wood, old incense and ancient grime, which recalled the church and funeral service earlier that day. In a useless gesture, she tugged at one of the iron rings, vaguely hoping it would open the door and allow her to seek sanctuary within. But the doors were locked fast. A swinging lamp fitfully and inadequately illuminated a notice nailed to the door. In German and Italian it announced that this was the church of the Minorites, used by the Italian community in Vienna, and gave the times of the masses. Letting the iron ring slip from her hand, Gabriela leaned back against the barred door. Cold and wet, she felt herself near to despair.

Resolutely she forced herself to conquer her panic and to think clearly. She would have to go back, but not yet. Although she was not ready to face them again so soon, she could not stay where she was. She was rapidly becoming drenched to the bone in the light silk dress, so she must at least keep moving and hope to find shelter in some archway.

She set off into a street leading off the square on the far side. The bad weather was keeping most people indoors, and for that she was heartily glad. From behind shuttered windows in the houses on either side, light gleamed in golden strips. Inside, families were sitting down to dine together, and her feeling of utter loneliness increased. She had no one any more, not a single person whom she could love or who cared for her, in the whole of this splendid, sprawling city. Footsteps approached, and a man appeared out of the shadows, hastening homewards. He cast an insolent eye over her as he passed, and said something she did not quite catch. She hurried away from him, and fearing he might follow her, turned into the first alley she came to, and thence into another, until she found herself in a veritable maze of little streets, a surviving corner of old Vienna that had escaped the demolition fever which had swept the city in the fifties and sixties of the century, when the old fortifications and huddled houses had been swept away to make way for the new Ringstrasse. Here the streets seemed even darker because they were so narrow, and the tall, flat façades of the buildings, ornamented with chipped baroque mouldings and nestling against one another, shut out even the night sky. A hundred and fifty years ago this had been a fashionable quarter, echoing to the carriage-wheels of powdered aristocrats hastening to the court of the great Empress Maria Theresa, but the fashionable and wealthy had long abandoned it. Now it was a rabbit-warren of subdivided buildings housing workmen's families and mean little shops, and other shuttered places with doors that

bore no nameplates, behind which the proprietor conducted his business in the strictest privacy. Beneath her
feet the cobbles were ill-repaired and treacherous, and
she trod cautiously, fearing to slip and twist an ankle
on the uneven ground.

Suddenly, and with dismay, she realised she was
hopelessly lost. She stood for a moment, trying to take
her bearings, but she had no idea even which direction
to choose. She would have to ask the way of the very
next person she met, no matter who it was, but what
help could she hope to find in these empty streets?

At that very moment, as if in answer, the unexpected
but familiar sound of gipsy music struck her ear, and
she looked about her in surprise. At the corner she saw
lights which, together with the gipsy music, seemed
to issue from somewhere subterranean. The plaintive,
passionate notes drifting out into the night air recalled
her far-off homeland in a fashion which sent a stab of
pain through her heart and a wave of homesickness over
her. She began to hurry towards the sound. Where there
were gipsies, someone would speak Hungarian and
might take pity on a fellow exile. Stone steps, shielded
by a railing, led to a cellar which had been turned into
some kind of tavern or cabaret. The scrape of gipsy
fiddles issued from this place. Above the door was
painted its name, 'The Golden Fleece'. A curious, pungent odour drifted out from the open doorway compounded of wine, cigar smoke and the overpowering
stench of cheap perfume. With it came the high-pitched
giggling of girls and tipsy male laughter.

Gabriela halted abruptly, and drew back. She knew
what kind of place this was. Outwardly it appeared to
be a drinking-den and cabaret with a small orchestra,
and a singer or two to entertain customers. But an
unusual number of pretty girls, garishly dressed, would
be going in and out of such an establishment, and a
large number of gentlemen, often none too anxious to
be seen. They drank on the lower floor, and listened to

the music, before retiring to a room upstairs with one of the tawdry hostesses. Thankful that she had recognised in time the nature of the place where she had been about to enquire her way, she stood wondering what on earth she could do. Just then there was a noise from below, and figures appeared in the basement doorway of the Golden Fleece. She crouched down quickly, and only just in time, behind the railing.

'Going so soon, Major?' demanded a woman's voice playfully. There was a further movement below, and Gabriela, peering cautiously down through the railings, suddenly saw an astounding sight. A monstrously fat woman, in a tightly corseted, bright scarlet gown out of which rolls of flesh cascaded like the overflow from a dam, had come into view. She was sixty at least, and quite the most grotesque creature Gabriela had ever set eyes on. Her hair was surely a wig, because it was such a strange, unnaturally even, bronze colour. It was parted in the centre and surmounted with a tall wire loop, over which the hair was twisted in the fashion called some forty years earlier an 'Apollo knot', but which was never seen now. Heavy earrings dangled from beneath the coarse bronze bandeaux of hair, framing a bloated, raddled face, heavily powdered and rouged, as if such aids could create beauty on such an unprepossessing countenance. A beauty spot even adorned the topmost of the several chins. This Gorgon seemed intent on barring the door, most effectively, to a customer about to leave.

'Don't delay me, Jetta,' returned a man's voice moodily. 'I'm bored and tired of this place. This is a black day for me, and every moment I spend here makes it worse.'

'Oh, come, Major! You are among friends here. Why don't you come back? We can amuse you, I'm sure, and make you forget your woes. I've a new girl, only started work yesterday. She's Hungarian. You'd like her,' the fat woman wheedled in a grotesquely coy voice.

'A Hungarian?' The man chuckled, a low, throaty sound which sent an odd little shiver along Gabriela's spine. 'Don't lie to me. You mean she's a gipsy! Good night, Jetta!'

Gabricla, listening in the shadows above, flushed angrily at his disparaging tone, and craned her head to try and see who had made the remark, as the fat woman moved reluctantly aside. As she waddled away, a figure stepped forward to take her place.

No greater contrast could have been presented to any watcher's startled view. The speaker was an Uhlan officer, a magnificently resplendent figure, tall and slim, in a walking-out dress of red breeches and polished black riding-boots. He wore the tightly-fitting blue tunic, the *ulanka*, with red cuffs and collar. Slung rakishly across one shoulder and secured by a cord was the second jacket, the blue *pelzrock*, which he chose to wear in this decorative and highly impractical fashion, like the Hussar pelisse. On his head he wore the familiar Polish *czapska* with its high, four-cornered crown, and decorated with a plume of black horsehair.

Whether he knew, or cared, what a splendid figure he cut in this seedy back street, no one could say. He stood in the rain, which was now reduced to a steady drizzle, softly whistling to himself some pretty, melancholy folk-tune she did not recognise, and searching with his thumb and forefinger in one of the narrow flapped pockets of the *ulanka*. He was looking for his cigarettes. Gabriela saw him pull out a flat metal case which gleamed in the light of the gas-lamp over the door. The metal looked like gold, and he was surely unwise to take such a valuable object into a place like this. But if he was a good and regular customer, the monstrous Jetta would have warned her bawds to keep their nimble fingers out of his pockets.

Gabriela watched the Uhlan take out a cigarette, tap it on the case, and place it unlit between his lips while he tucked the case tidily away. His movements were unhurried and capable. As for his face, she could barely see it because of the peaked *czapska*, but there was a rasp and a flare of flame as he struck a match on the heel of his boot, and for a second his features, lean and with an arched bridge to the nose, were illuminated in the yellow glow. The aroma of Turkish tobacco floated into the night air. He tossed aside the spent match and climbed the steps to the level of the pavement, his boots scraping on the worn stone. So fascinated had Gabriela been, that she had almost forgotten she was in hiding and cowered back quickly, but too late. His keen eyes caught the faint movement in the shadows and the pale smudge of her gown in the darkness.

'Come out of there!' he ordered sharply. He took the cigarette from his mouth and beckoned to her.

Gabriela stood up, and took a reluctant step forwards.

The Uhlan hissed impatiently, expelling the sound between his strong white teeth, and clicked his fingers. 'Out here, girl! Come along—that's better. Stand still.'

The sharp order, issued in such a brusque tone, acted like a spur to her fiercely independent Hungarian spirit, and although she knew she was bedraggled and dishevelled and that her hair was plastered to her cheeks and temples in damp, curling tendrils, she stepped out of her shadowy hiding-place and returned his inquisitive scrutiny proudly.

'What the devil?' he exclaimed. He stopped to peer at her more closely. 'You're not one of Jetta's girls.'

She opened her mouth to retort angrily, but then closed it again. He took her for a street-walker! It was a humiliating but natural enough mistake. What other young woman would roam about at night, clad only in a light gown despite the stormy weather? Shivering in the chill air, she hugged her bare arms as she cast about in her mind for some acceptable explanation for her extraordinary appearance in such an unlikely place.

The Uhlan narrowed his eyes and regarded her speculatively and a little perplexed, as if he also were not quite sure what to do about this unexpected encounter. Then, without warning, he stretched out his hand and brushed back a trailing wet curl of her blond hair, and asked softly, 'What's your name?'

Gabriela, who had not been expecting his move, flinched beneath the light contact with his hand, and whispered fiercely, 'Don't touch me!'

The man froze, and in the dim light she fancied she saw suspicion flicker across his face. But, to her relief, he lowered his hand and did not try to touch her again. 'Pay first, eh?' he said in an insolent tone. 'Sorry, my dear, but I'm in no mood.' He half turned aside from her, then hesitated and turned back. 'See here,' he added in a more friendly tone. 'You won't find many clients about on a night like this, but you are well on the way to pneumonia. Why don't you go home, eh?'

Home! Her father-in-law's house had never been that for her, even when Max had been alive.

'I can't,' Gabriela said in a flat voice tinged with misery.

He grunted. 'Ah, I understand.' He fished in his pocket and took out a leather wallet. Opening it, he held out some paper money towards her. 'Here, go on, take it!' he said impatiently when she stared at him uncomprehendingly. 'I don't want anything in exchange. On another occasion, eh? But if it will save you a beating when you get home, you're welcome to it.'

'No!' Shock made Gabriela find her tongue at last. She pushed the money away, deeply insulted. 'I don't want it. I'm not—not what you think. That's not why I'm here. Please go away and leave me alone!'

Though she stammered slightly as she spoke, the vigour and resolution of her tone obviously impressed him. He frowned and put away the wallet.

'Then perhaps you'll tell me just why you are here?' The tone of rough kindness had left his voice, leaving it cold and unfriendly. 'Why can't you go home?' In a lightning movement he thrust out his hand and grasped her wrist tightly. 'Well, well, a wedding ring!' he observed insolently. 'Who'd have thought it? Did you burn his dinner?'

Gabriela twisted her wrist free of his grip, and muttered, 'It's none of your business! I've nothing to say to you.' Prompted by a surge of inner pain, she added emotionally, 'My husband is *dead*!'

'Is he, now?' The Uhlan was staring at her again in that thoughtful way. 'Death always takes the people we should most like to keep, my sweet. Didn't you know that? It sifts out the finest and the best in its sieve and leaves behind the dross.' There was such a great bitterness in his voice that she was too surprised to attempt any reply. 'All right!' he went on briskly, as if he would dismiss whatever gloomy thought possessed him. 'I'll take you home. Tell me where it is, and hurry up—we're both getting unnecessarily wet. Here . . .' He unslung the *pelzrock* and, shrugging it off, draped it rapidly over her trembling shoulders. 'Well, what's the address?'

She pulled the heavy jacket gratefully about her bare shoulders. It was warm from his body. He was right— it was time to go back. In as firm a voice as she could muster, she told him the address.

He took the information in a way she could not have anticipated. 'What game is this?' he snarled. He grasped her arm and pulled her into the yellow circle of light cast on the pavement by the entry to The Golden Fleece. She gasped as he took her chin and forced her to face the glare of the gas-lamp. 'What are you playing at? Speak up, damn you!'

'Nothing! Let me go—please! I want to go back . . .' she stammered, frightened now by the expression on his face.

He released her. 'You'll go back, all right!' he said grimly. He put the cigarette in his mouth and turned, striding off quickly and purposefully down the dark street. He seemed to intend her to follow him, and Gabriela did so uncertainly, not at all sure where he was taking her, and confused by his unpredictable and changing temper.Perhaps he was drunk, or depressed. But, in any case, she had no choice but to trust him.

As they turned the corner, trotting hoofs echoed on the cobbles. He put his fingers to his mouth and let out an ear-splitting whistle, and a *Fiaker*, a closed unnumbered cab drawn by two horses, clattered up. It was the kind which plied for hire freely, not making use of the regular public cab-stands. Such cabs were frequently used for assignations, and perhaps this one was now returning from just such a clandestine journey. Her escort bundled her unceremoniously inside and spoke to the driver, before jumping in and throwing himself down on the seat beside her. The cab-man whipped up his nags and they set off with a jolt, rolling noisily over the cobbles.

'It's very kind of you,' she said, with what she hoped was dignity.

'It's not a kindness,' was the sour reply. 'It's an obligation.'

'You don't owe me anything,' she objected.

'I didn't say it was an obligation to *you*. I owe it to —to someone else.'

Gabriela flushed at his tone and drew back into the corner of the cab, glad of the darkness which concealed her from him. The upholstery smelled of a woman's perfume, perhaps that of some Society lady hastening to her lover. But it was difficult to get far from her companion in the cramped *Fiaker*, which obliged them to an intimacy neither of them seemed to relish, unlike the cab's usual fares. She could sense an aura of ill-humour about the man beside her, as if he really was very angry. His features were hidden by the gloom, and the only glimpse she had was when he drew on the cigarette and the glow briefly illuminated his face, set in a forbidding scowl. Neither of them attempted to speak again until he had finished his cigarette and leaned forward to toss the stub out of the window in a jerky gesture.

'Have you any idea,' he demanded vehemently, and her heart gave a startled leap, 'what might have happened to you out there, on the streets at this hour of the night, alone?'

'I didn't mean . . .' she began defensively, then added angrily, 'It's no concern of yours!'

The cab drew to a halt, and the driver shouted out that they had arrived. Her unwilling rescuer jumped out on to the cobbles and lifted her down. He paid the cab-man and rang violently at the door of the Clemenz mansion.

'I can go in alone,' Gabriela protested hastily.

'No!' The syllable was clipped and definite, and she did not attempt to argue. The door creaked, and the old doorkeeper peered out into the night. To her astonishment, an expression of recognition and pleasure crossed his face as his eyes fell on her companion, and he pulled the door open wide for them both to enter.

'Good evening, Major!' he piped. 'Bless you, sir, it's good to see you again. We expected you earlier. Ah, a sad day, sir,' he shook his head dolefully. 'They'll be more than pleased to see you.' He caught sight of Gabriela, and his expression and tone changed. 'Oh, you found her,' he grunted, as if he had hoped that the girl, after her disgraceful behaviour, had been lost for good. 'Best bring her inside, Major. Everyone's been running round in circles here because of her!' He snorted disdainfully.

'You are Adam!' she cried, staring wildly at the Uhlan, as the stark realisation struck her, almost with the force of a physical blow.

'Yes!' he said, grasping her arm in no very gentle manner, and bundled her roughly through the doorway ahead of him. He pushed her quickly up the staircase to the first floor, and they burst into the family's apartments in such a wild fashion that she stumbled, and would have fallen had it not been for the tight grip he had on her. He seized the first startled servant to come running up, and ordered, 'Go and tell my uncle I'm here—and have brought the Countess Gabriela with me!'

'I won't see them!' Gabriela cried vehemently. 'Not tonight, at least. I can't, Adam. I won't! So please just let go of me, and *leave me alone*!'

She tore herself free of his grasp and ran wildly up to the next floor and along the corridor to her room. He caught up with her, and grabbing her shoulders, swung her round so that he barred the entry to her door.

'Now, you listen to me!' he ordered. 'I don't know what all this is about, but you hardly seem to be behaving as one might expect. That dress'—he pointed at the wet, muddied rose silk—'is not my idea of mourning!'

'You should have told me who you were, when you realised my identity!' she countered stormily.

'You came with me willingly enough, even *not* knowing who I was!' came the swift and biting reply. 'I don't know what crazy idea was in your mind out there, but you won't continue to play the gipsy while *I* can prevent it! Max took you out of obscurity in Budapest and brought you here and into this family. Believe me . . .' His voice sank so that it was very quiet and even, more frightening than any shouted threat. 'You will behave as befits his widow, or I shall personally throw you back on the streets of Vienna where I found you, and the next time, Gabriela, *no one* will rescue you!'

'It's almost mid-day, madame.'

The maid's voice floated somewhere above Gabriela's head, forcing its way disagreeably into her semi-consciousness. She opened her eyes sleepily and pushed herself upright on the pillows. Arlette was drawing back the curtains, allowing the bright sunlight to flood the room, her back turned to the bed. Gabriela eyed her mistrustfully. By now, probably every servant in the street knew what had happened here last night. By the bed stood a tray with a little silver pot of hot chocolate, steam rising gently from the spout. She pushed back her tousled, tangled hair. The memory of her flight lingered as a nagging headache, but in the light of a new day she was able to view it with a certain detachment, and acknowlege it to have been the height of stupidity. She had lost her head and played into their hands.

Arlette came across to the bed to ask, with a slightly spiteful glint in her eye, what madame would like to be laid out for her to wear today. The Hungarian girl's resolution not to wear mourning had set the servants in a fever of gossip. Arlette waited with bated breath to hear whether the lady would bow to convention, or whether she would repeat her scandalous behaviour of the night before.

'The dark blue velvet,' her mistress said calmly, 'with the little bows on the bodice.'

The velvet was by no means 'mourning', but it was discreet. She had been ill-advised in offending her mother-in-law so openly, and the velvet gown was a gesture, an offer to meet Max's mother half way. Whether Countess Clemenz would see it thus was another, and debatable, matter. But Gabriela was beginning to learn—as so many had before her—that it is often far easier to adopt a course of action than it is to explain it—or to abandon it, once chosen. Even if she had wished to go back on her decision not to wear mourning, she could not now have done so. She had nailed her colours to the mast, and so must sail under them.

Arlette, her pale little eyes glittering, went to search in the great carved wardrobe, while Gabriela sipped the hot chocolate. Yes, last night had been a fiasco of the worst kind. The encounter with Adam had been a final touch—proof, if any were needed, that Fate was a joker, of a particularly black and cruel kind.

As soon as she was dressed, she dismissed the girl and stood before the mirror, tugging nervously at her sleeves and turning over in her mind what she should say if they should remonstrate with her about the previous night. Suddenly a light, confident rap on her door made her jump, and to her astonishment and displeasure it swung open to reveal Adam, who strolled in, showing not the slightest hesitation at entering her room.

'What are you doing here?' she demanded coldly.

The words echoed like a challenge, and something flickered in his eyes, as though he took it as one. 'Here in this house, or here in this room?' he retorted with a casual insolence which brought a rush of crimson to her pale cheeks. He was reminding her that he was a blood relative, in this house as of right—whereas she was not.

'Both!' she snapped. She watched him seat himself uninvited on a near-by chair, removing, before he did so, an article of female underclothing with a faint twitch of an eyebrow. She took the opportunity to study him more closely, as this was really the first occasion on which she was able to see him for any length of time. In the street and in the *Fiaker* it had been too dark, and on their return to the house she had been too agitated to mark his appearance. Now she saw that he had a very striking face and one not easily forgotten. It was not conventionally handsome; in some ways it was almost ugly, but of that irregularity which attracts rather than repels. It was too thin, and the lean lines cast into sharp emphasis the strongly marked brows, deep-set, intelligent eyes and the high bridge of the nose. The jaw was a little too long, jutting aggressively, and the mouth, both sensitive and sensual, was too wide. In all it was a disturbing face, clever, determined, shrewd and pleasure-loving. It belonged to a man who lived life intensely, and whose sharp wits would miss very little.

She was interested to note that despite his evident familiarity with the Golden Fleece—and no doubt with similar establishments in other places—he obviously spent much time in the open air, for his skin had none of the unhealthy pallor of some young officers whose time was principally spent in ballrooms and boudoirs. This man's complexion was tanned by wind and weather. She could have wished his face and manner were more friendly. He had thick, curling chestnut hair, too; that faint hint of red in the brown suggesting that there might be a fearsome temper lurking behind the keen, truculent gaze which she saw was now fixed on her.

'I'm here in your room,' Adam said, 'because I came to see how you were after your adventures of last night, and Arlette said that you were dressed. I did ask her that.' The brown eyes mocked her now. 'I'm here in this house because my uncle has asked me to stay here for a while. I've sent for my things.' He stretched out his long muscular legs and crossed them comfortably.

He's a horseman, she thought, quite irrelevantly. Being a Uhlan, that's to be expected, but I dare say he rides for pleasure, too. That's why he has such a healthy complexion. Aloud, she said, 'You're staying *here*?' making no attempt to hide her discomfiture.

'I see you don't care for the notion,' Adam said drily.

'Why should I care?' she exploded with a force which took him unawares and caused him to raise his eyebrows in unfeigned surprise. 'Do what you like—*I* shall not be staying here!' She turned her back on him in an angry swish of skirts.

'Where would you go? You've no money and no family,' he reminded her cruelly. 'You have to stay here. You depend on my uncle.'

'I'd rather starve!' she burst out bitterly.

'Rubbish. You're talking nonsense!' he said coldly. 'And you know it. You're not stupid, girl. There's a brain in that pretty head—use it.'

There was a silence. 'They expected you at the funeral yesterday,' Gabriela retaliated icily.

'And you, did you expect to see me?'

'I never gave you a thought. After all, you've never tried to meet *me*. But you were Max's boyhood friend, and he often spoke of you. Why didn't you come to the church?'

'I did go to the church,' Adam said, after a pause. Thought she still kept her back to him, she was able to see his reflection in the dressing-table glass, and saw that he looked not at her, but at the photograph of Max in its silver frame. 'I arrived early,' he went on, 'before anyone else. It was all tricked out in black and purple and they had put up the bier ready in the centre of the aisle, with the candles set round it.' He looked away from the photograph, staring towards the open window and the sunlight. 'I thought, that's not how I want to remember Max. I want to remember him alive, fishing for stickleback in a stream with a bent pin and a piece of string, when we were children, enjoying himself. Max liked to enjoy himself. He liked to see people happy. I left the church and went—went elsewhere. I'm sure there were plenty of people there without me!' He gazed back towards her aggressively.

She turned slowly to face him, and said fiercely, 'You went to the Golden Fleece, a brothel!'

'What's it to you, my dear? I went there to get drunk, if you must know. But it's a fact that if a man wants to get drunk, he never can. The more I drank, the more sober I seemed to become. I just felt worse in myself.'

'Then, Adam, perhaps you know how I felt,' Gabriela said quietly. 'And I, too, mean to keep happy memories of Max. So if you've come here to ask me to go down veiled in black and sobbing on your shoulder, you're wasting your time. I won't wear black, and I've done all the weeping I'm going to do. If that shocks you, I'm sorry, but I can't help it. I loved Max very dearly. You couldn't begin to understand how much I miss him. But I'm going to behave as I believe Max would have wished,' she concluded with unmistakable stubbornness.

'You made a fool of yourself last night, and there's no need to do so again. Your behaviour was extremely offensive, both to my uncle and to my aunt.'

'It doesn't occur to you, I suppose,' Gabriela suggested equally coldly, 'that your aunt behaved atrociously towards me?'

She fancied that, just for a second, he looked embarrassed, but then an aggressive look entered his face, and he said sharply, 'If you'd just stop and think for one minute, you'd realise that my aunt's behaviour was born of fear!'

Seeing the astonishment on her face, he went on irritably, 'Max was the most dutiful son any mother ever had. He always heeded her advice, and she had no reason to suspect he wouldn't marry the woman of her choice. Then, without warning, *you* appear! Max announces that he's going to marry you, and won't be dissuaded. It was totally out of character. Max hadn't a serious or sober thought in his head, let alone *marriage*! We'd all assumed that Christiane, who had enough common sense for both of them, would eventually take him in hand, and that Max, too, accepted that this would be the case. Suddenly we were all faced with a whirlwind romance, a girl we didn't know—and a Max we didn't know! My aunt knew then that you, a stranger, would be the influence in his life from then on. Can't you imagine what that did to her—the shock to a strong-willed woman who suddenly finds she is weak and powerless? Confound it,' Adam shouted angrily. 'I don't think you have the slightest comprehension of the turmoil your arrival caused in this family!'

'Don't you think that Max had a right to marry as he wished,' Gabriela demanded, fire in her blue eyes, 'and that he might have appreciated your support?'

An unyielding and obstinate expression closed over Adam's face and imbued his whole attitude. In a cruelly dispassionate voice, he said, 'Max was an easy-going fellow, future heir to a considerable fortune, and certainly no ladies' man. He'd very little experience of women. Generally he was shy in their presence. A man like that can always fall prey to a poor but pretty girl with sharp wits and no scruples.'

Gabriela took a deep breath. So, it was at last out and in the open, and spoken. A sense almost of relief mingled with her anger. Calmly she said, 'I see. I am an unscrupulous adventuress, then? Seducing poor Max into the marriage bed? You must have thought him a fool. Max was shy, but not stupid, and not incapable of falling in love. Perhaps it was "out of character", perhaps even Max mistook his own emotions and was not as much in love with me as he thought. You see, I don't delude myself, Adam. But, at the time, he loved me. He told me so, and I believed him. I married him for love, Adam Dubrowski, not for money. Possibly you cannot understand such a thing. If so, I am sorry for you.'

In the quiet which followed, his eyes met hers unflinchingly. 'I had no knowledge of either your character or your intentions, Gabriela,' he said evenly. 'I had, however, known Christiane Vonneck most of my life. She and Max were not engaged, I admit; but, as I have explained, she had every reason to expect . . .' Adam broke off and shrugged his broad shoulders. 'All this hardly matters—now!' he said abruptly. 'I wrote to Max, advising him to caution. Perhaps he thought the advice came ill from *me*. Perhaps, as you say, he had expected my support. He wrote to me very strongly in reply. He was offended. I was obstinate.' In a gentler tone, in which there was a sudden echo of pain, he added, 'You may believe this or not, but on this visit to Vienna I had planned to call here and make my peace with Max, and to meet you. But I'd left it too late . . .' he finished quietly.

'And you blame *me* for that?' Gabriela gasped.

'I meant what I said last night,' Adam replied in a low, hard voice. 'Whether you wear black or not really doesn't bother me. In fact, it's probably better now that you don't. Then, with a little luck, people will assume that you are eccentric, and not just insensitive.'

She flushed.

'But watch carefully what else you do, Gabriela. There are things I won't forgive. And don't make an enemy of *me*, my dear. That would be a serious mistake.'

He smiled, then, and she rather wished he hadn't.

CHAPTER
THREE

THE NEXT day, Michael Brenner called. Gabriela had quite forgotten him, but when he was announced, she recalled his kindness at the funeral and rose to greet him as he entered with a feeling of real pleasure, almost of relief. Here at last was someone who had nothing to do with the family, who would not grumble, who appreciated her loss, who had called just to see her, and —the best recommendation of all—had been a friend of Max. She only wished that she could recall Max ever having mentioned Brenner, but he must have done. She wished she had paid greater attention. Feeling a little guilty about it, she held out her hand as he came through the door and exclaimed, 'Herr Brenner! How kind of you to call.'

Brenner, a handsome, well-dressed figure, with a slight, disarming air of hesitancy which reminded her closely and painfully of Max, smiled. 'I'm not intruding?' he asked anxiously, as he bowed over her hand. 'I'll go away at once, if you prefer.'

'No, please,' she insisted. 'Please stay. I'm very pleased to see you.' She saw his gaze rest briefly on the green gown she was wearing, and added hastily, 'I expect you're surprised not to see me in mourning, but it's a decision I've taken for very good reasons of my own.'

'To tell you the truth,' he said frankly, 'I've never cared to see women, young women anyway, in black. I find it unnecessary.'

'Max used to say that,' she told him, pleased.

'I'm truly sorry about Max,' he said in his soft voice.

'I wanted to tell you so the other day, but there hardly seemed to be time or opportunity with so many people about.'

'It was a very difficult day for us all. I'd rather not talk about it any more, if you don't mind!'

Brenner gave no sign of finding this unusual. He began to discourse pleasantly on one topic and another, and after a while, Gabriela felt herself relax and was soon chatting to him quite freely. She was almost sorry when he rose to take his leave, apologising for overstaying his visit.

'Do come again, Herr Brenner,' she said impulsively. 'You were Max's friend, and, well, I lack acquaintances here in Vienna. It's difficult not to have any family—of my own, I mean.' Hastily she added, 'My parents-in-law are very kind, of course; at least, my father-in-law, but . . .' She fell silent.

Brenner's dark eyes rested on her sympathetically. 'I would be honoured if you would consider me your friend,' he said gravely. 'Please, if there is anything I can do, call on me immediately.' He smiled, an engaging boyish smile. 'You know,' he said, 'my name is Michael, but my friends call me Mischa. I'm Austrian, but I was brought up in St Petersburg, where my father had business. A Russian nursemaid gave me the nickname, which has stuck with me ever since.' He took her hand again, in parting, and this time he kissed it.

He must have passed Adam on his way out, because she heard the sound of men's voices, and a few minutes after her visitor had left, Adam strode in, looking out of humour and more than usually truculent.

'What was Brenner doing here?' he demanded without preamble.

Gabriela's hackles rose. 'He called to see me and express his condolences. He was a friend of Max.'

'It's the first I've heard of it! Max probably knew him, but I wouldn't take it further than that. Brenner makes himself known to everyone.'

'Perhaps, as you didn't see much of Max these last three years, you don't know his friends,' Gabriela suggested silkily.

Adan scowled at her. 'Three years of marriage must have changed my cousin out of all recognition if he'd begun to make a friend of a plausible rogue like Mischa Brenner!'

'Three years of marriage to *me*, you mean?' Gabriela, white with fury, threw the words at him. She drew a deep breath and asked in a voice which trembled with anger, 'You have some reason, I suppose, for calling Mischa a rogue?'

'*Mischa*, is it? Then I was right—he *is* plausible!' Adam turned on his heel and strode out, slamming the door violently behind him.

Oh, no! thought Gabriela furiously, You shan't leave it at that! She ran to the door and wrenched it open. 'If you have something to say against him, then say it— if you feel I should know. Or perhaps you just dislike him because he was here, and not everyone despises me!'

Adam stopped in his tracks, and without turning to face her, said stonily, 'I don't trust him. He was born and grew up in St Petersburg, and is more of a Russian than an Austrian, for all his parentage. Sometimes he has money, and sometimes he doesn't, and where it comes from, when it comes, no one knows. He's everyone's acquaintance, and nobody's friend. If you ask me to specify something against him, I can't. I hear rumours, as does anyone. I don't repeat them, unless I know them to have some foundation, so I won't repeat the rumours I hear of Brenner to you.'

'So, all you really have against Mischa is that he has a Russian background! You're Polish, so I don't suppose you like any Russians. You don't care very much for Hungarians, do you? And I'm certain that, for all that Austrian uniform you wear, you don't have much time for Austrian Germans! Tell me,' she asked him in a dulcet voice, 'Do the Poles like anyone, other than themselves?'

She knew, even as the words left her lips, that she ought not to have spoken them. Adam whirled round, his expression so savage she almost thought he was going to attack her, and she stepped back automatically.

'What do you know about *us*?' he demanded. A fierce light burned in his dark eyes, and there was a passion in his voice she had not heard before from him, or perhaps not from any man. 'Have you ever been in any part of my country—dismembered as it is in the flesh, but always united in our hearts? Were you ever in my home, Cracow, where the kings of Poland were once crowned? Let me take you there, and I'll show you one of the most beautiful cities in Eastern Europe, and one of the oldest universities in the whole of Europe! I'll show you its great cathedral, where lie buried King Jan Sobieski, who drove back the Turks and saved Vienna and Europe, and brave Poniatowski, who was one of the most gallant of Napoleon's marshals, and great Kosciusko who defeated the Russians and liberated Warsaw less than a hundred years ago! Our heroes are not dead—they live in our hearts and in us. We breathe our history and our past in our air. We see it about us. If you want to know what all that means to us, ride with me for half an hour out of the city, and we'll come to a small hill, built not by nature but by the bare hands of the men and women of Cracow to remember and honour their hero Kosciusko, forced to die in exile like so many Poles. From its summit I'd show you a view no Pole ever forgets and you would not forget: the spires of Cracow floating in the haze like the setting of a fairy legend, and the mountains beyond, which are always capped with snow and so beautiful that their majesty takes your breath away, and the river Vistula, winding like a silver ribbon thrown down by the angels themselves!'

There was an interminable silence in which his voice

seemed to echo in the high-ceilinged corridor. Perhaps he regretted his outburst, which had allowed her a glimpse into his innermost emotions, because the enthusiasm died abruptly in his eyes, as if a veil had been drawn across, and was replaced by a sardonic glint. 'As for not liking others,' he said, 'I have no objection to pretty women of any nationality!'

'I can believe that!' she snapped, finding her tongue at last, but badly shaken in the face of such an over-whelming passion, and the bitter pride with which it had been expressed.

'Then believe what I said yesterday,' he said softly. 'There are some things I wouldn't forgive—and we have long memories and a patient talent for vengeance, we Poles. So just take care, Gabriela!'

'I shall see Mischa if and when I like!' she declared resolutely, but inwardly she felt a stab of fear, because she knew that he meant every word he had said.

In the minuscule and windowless office to the rear of the Golden Fleece, in which the gas-lamp had to be lit at all hours of the day, the mountainous Jetta eased her bulk in her whalebone stays and fixed her little button-bright eyes on the perspiring tradesman who dared to argue with her. The unfortunate was beginning to wish he'd held his tongue. Jetta, her vast frame encased in emerald satin, stretched to bursting-point at the seams and creased and strained into horizontal folds over her ample bosom, seemed not merely to dominate but to fill the tiny room, like some huge exotic tropical spider brooding in its den. To make matters worse, the procuress was smoking a Havana cigar, and filling the already airless room with a pungent blue haze.

'Do you take me or my gentlemen for fools?' she croaked suddenly, leaning forward so that her wretched visitor stepped back hastily. 'Do you think the kind of fine gentlemen who come to the Golden Fleece don't know the difference between French champagne and *that*?' She pointed the cigar disparagingly at a bottle which stood on the desk between them.

'Tante Jetta,' protested her supplier. 'You can see yourself, from the label . . .'

'Label?' Jetta bit the word off sharply, rather as a mantis snaps its jaws on its hapless prey's head. 'Label? That scrap of paper can say anything. I know French champagne—and I know when someone tries to cheat me!'

'As if I would, Tante Jetta,' he whined unwisely, taking out a spotted handkerchief and mopping his damp brow.

'Dolt!' roared the proprietress. 'Idiot! Get out of my sight and take your undrinkable *ersatz* champagne with you!' She seized the bottle and hurled it at the luckless salesman, who fortunately managed to dodge the missile, and without attempting to protest his innocence any further, turned and fled. The bottle bounced on the floor, miraculously unbroken.

'Weakling!' muttered Jetta scornfully. 'Numbskull! Try to cheat me, would you?'

There was a tap at the door and one of the hostesses, a pretty snub-nosed girl with a mop of henna-red curls, put her head round it cautiously. 'Tant' Jetta? You alone? You've a visitor.' She lowered her voice. '*He's* back.'

'Hah?' Jetta ground out the cigar and dispersed the smoke with her fish-belly-white hand. 'Then show him in. Wait—did that fool of a wine salesman see him come in?'

'No, Tant' Jetta, no one saw him.'

'Good. Well, fetch him, and bring us some coffee and the good schnapps. And tell Friedl there are two cases of that so-called champagne.' She pointed to the bottle lying on its side by the door. 'Tell him to take them to the back of the police station and leave them for Inspector Gruber, with my compliments. It will keep that busybody from poking his nose in here. Go on, girl, move!'

The girl stooped to retrieve the bottle and scuttled away. She could be heard conducting a newcomer along the stuffy corridor which led to Jetta's sanctum. The door opened, and allowed the dapper form of Mischa Brenner to enter.

'So there you are, at last!' croaked Jetta, an unexpectedly indulgent note in her harsh voice. 'I was beginning to wonder when you'd turn up again, like a bad coin!' She chuckled and spluttered. 'Paid your tailor, I see,' she added, eyeing his fashionable appearance.

'Bad but profitable coin,' her visitor returned drily, seating himself across the desk from her. 'For pity's sake, Jetta, when will you stop smoking those vile cigars?'

'The best, my dear, they're the best,' crooned Jetta, not at all affronted by his impertinence.

Brenner wrinkled his nose fastidiously and placed his malacca cane on the desk so that he could pull off his suede gloves. 'It's damn hot in here, Jetta,' he grumbled.

There was a clatter outside, and the henna-haired girl came in with the coffee and schnapps. Both Jetta and her visitor sat silent until she had left and closed the door behind her.

'Do they ever eavesdrop?' the young man asked a little uneasily and indicated the door with a gesture of his curly head.

Jetta chuckled. 'My girls? They know better! Anyhow, I pick them to be trusted. Katy wouldn't go running to inform. She's got no love for the police.' Her expression sharpened. 'Well, my young friend, is it business or pleasure which brings you here?'

Brenner leaned forward eagerly. 'Business, Jetta. Business such as you and I have only dreamed of!' In his emotion, he got to his feet and walked restlessly up and down the little office. 'An opportunity of a lifetime, Jetta. A golden opportunity. The chance to gain access to one of the greatest fortunes in the Empire!'

'When people promise me an easy road to a fortune, I smell danger,' the fat woman said, her eyes as hard as granite. 'If you mean to take risks, take them alone! I'm too old for such foolishness.'

'You don't know what I have in mind. Wait until you hear it, before you refuse me!' he said quickly, and sat down again. 'You'll forget your age, Jetta.'

'So easily?' Jetta heaved a massive sigh. 'Ah, the years pass, we all grow old. Look at me. When I was your age, I was as slim as a reed. Go on, laugh, you rascal! I can see your disbelief in your eyes. But I was a beauty then. Well, that's life,' she added philosophically, and pouring out a generous tumbler of the schnapps, tossed it back in one gulp. 'Only the good die young, as the old Greeks believed, and are beautiful for ever, eh? The rest of us grow old and ugly.' Her beady eyes rested on her visitor with a hint of cruel mockery in them. 'Even you, my young stag! But perhaps you will have the fortune to die young, pretty fellow, and join the immortals?'

He looked away from her. He was more than half inclined to believe that the old harridan had the Evil Eye. She was enough to make a fellow superstitious. If he did not need her, he would not come within a mile of this wretched place. He forced himself to speak in a brisk, businesslike tone. 'You remember, Jetta, that some time ago we discussed a certain wealthy and high-ranking gentleman?' His voice sank, and despite himself he could not prevent a tremor of excitement in it. 'The Archduke Alexander . . .'

'No names!' Jetta said sharply. 'Walls have ears. I trust my girls so far, but not when such names are bandied about. Have a care, my dear.'

'Oh, I'm a cautious fellow,' Brenner told her with his boyish smile. 'Especially when I'm seeking to land such a valuable fish.'

The ingenuous smile had a mollifying effect on Jetta, and something of her former indulgent tone returned, but she still said discouragingly, 'You will need a special bait, and you won't find it easily.'

'But I have found it!' he said swiftly, and was gratified to see that he had taken the woman by surprise. For a moment, she allowed her curiosity to gleam in her little jet eyes. 'I was at a funeral recently, Jetta. A sad affair. The only son of Count Clemenz. He leaves a widow, to whom I introduced myself as a friend of her late husband. She's young, and very beautiful—and has all the right aristocratic connections for what we need. I called on her earlier today—with her permission. She's lonely, and was really quite glad to see me. She lacks a confidante, poor girl, and was only too ready to pour out her troubles into a sympathetic ear. She's quite penniless and without family, totally dependent on her late husband's parents—who would like, I fancy, to be rid of her. She herself is desperate, though she did not say so, to be independent of them. And in case you fancy she is sitting about weeping and wailing, I assure you that she doesn't even wear mourning. I encountered her maid in the street, a girl who will tell you anything for a handful of florins. The grieving widow put aside her mourning, it seems, directly after the funeral, and caused quite an uproar in the household. She ran away, and was gone some time, and had to be brought back in disgrace by one of the family.'

'No way to behave,' said Jetta sententiously. 'Upsetting people you need without cause, very foolish.' She put her podgy white fingers to her rouged lips, a sign of thought. 'I hope this doesn't mean that she's a scatterbrain. If so, she would be worse than useless. To keep the attention of the high-ranking gentleman whose name we do better not to mention—always supposing she attracts it in the first place—she would need character and resourcefulness.'

'She has that. As for *him*, all Vienna knows he falls in love very easily. He can't resist beauty and spirit combined, and she has both. Besides, the girl is Hungarian, and he is inclined to be romantic about anything Magyar. It is an interest he shares with his close friend, the Crown Prince. I'm sure that, if he were introduced to Gabriela, he would become instantly enamoured.'

'He may be all you say,' Jetta said frankly. 'He's a young man like many another, with a weakness for a pretty woman which is no crime. But to use that to our own advantage, as you suggest, could be viewed very seriously by those who are in a position to make their displeasure felt. The young man is close to the imperial family. You meddle in his affairs at your peril. I don't like it.'

'It's worth the risk!' Brenner exclaimed fiercely. 'He's immensely wealthy, and impetuous both in mind and heart. Any woman he's ever loved has spoken of the strength of his passion and declared herself powerless to resist him. Women set great store by that kind of thing.' He shrugged.

'Do they, indeed?' Jetta retorted sarcastically, but he saw that her interest was caught. 'I think you run on too fast, my pigeon. How do you know the girl will co-operate?'

'She wouldn't,' Brenner admitted honestly, 'if she knew what we were about. That's why I shan't tell her anything of it. She has no reason to suspect I'm anything but a loyal and disinterested friend. She trusts me. Later, when she has met Alexander, and he is at her feet protesting devotion and showering her with gifts, she will not be able to draw back. She can't refuse him. He's too powerful a figure to offend needlessly, and she is quite alone and has no one to speak for her. But why should she want to, anyway? She'll see it's to her advantage.' Brenner smiled seraphically. 'And mine.'

'If you are so sure, pretty boy,' Jetta cooed, 'why do you come to me, eh?'

Brenner shifted in his chair, visibly a little less sure of himself. 'There is just one possible stumbling-block,' he admitted unwillingly. 'Tell me, does the gallant Pole still favour the dubious delights to be had here?' His tone was careless, but his long slender fingers picked nervously at the pearl-grey gloves he had thrown on to the table.

'You mean Major Dubrowski, I suppose?' Jetta's little black eyes, sunk in the folds of flesh like currants in dough, grew shrewd. 'What of him? He comes often, whenever he's in Vienna. Mind you, he doesn't always stay long at a visit. Often he just drinks a glass or two of wine and orders the gipsies to play Polish tunes. Then he leaves.'

'He doesn't dally with your young ladies?'

'Oh, occasionally. He likes Katy, who brought the coffee just now. Why?' she added sharply.

'He's a nephew of Count Clemenz, and is the only person who might be clever enough to guess what we're about. He'll go back to his Polish wilderness soon and be out of the way, but in the meantime I need to be able to keep an eye on Dubrowski. I don't think he troubles himself unduly with his Viennese relatives, but a pretty widow might just appeal to his chivalrous Polish instincts. If so, I need to know it. The girl, Katy—you say he likes her. Perhaps he might be persuaded to take a deeper interest in her?'

'He's not a fool,' Jetta said heavily. 'None of those Polish officers is. Sometimes we get a whole group of them in here. They drink enough to put a regiment under the table, and at the end of it they are still as sharp as steel! Drink makes them wild, or amorous, or sentimental, or all three together, but it never makes them stupid. Beware of Dubrowski. He's a dangerous man!'

'He's impressed you, I see,' Brenner said, a little sullenly.

'Oh, I'm old and ugly, but I can still admire a fine fellow like that.' A faint smile crossed her pudgy face at some distant memory, and for a split second the observer could see that incredibly, long ago, this grotesque creature had once been beautiful. Even Mischa Brenner was surprised and fell silent, filled with an unease he could not have explained.

'A man,' Jetta said dreamily, and her sharp little eyes glittered at him mockingly, 'and not a tailor's dummy!'

She took hold of the emerald satin of her bodice, where it stretched across her gigantic bosom, and twitched at it several times to let a little air circulate over her perspiring flesh. A flicker of distaste showed briefly in her visitor's eyes, but he was astute enough to hide it. He rose to his feet and took up his malacca cane and suede gloves.

'I'll come again, Jetta, and tell you what progress I make.'

'Goodbye, my dear,' said Jetta in an absent voice. 'Make eyes at the widow yourself. It would do no harm, and satisfy anyone who was curious as to your interest in her. But mind she doesn't fall in love with you, or you with her, because then what would you do, eh?' She gave a throaty chuckle in which there seemed to be an echo of every sin known to man.

Repulsive old witch, the young man thought. I do believe the old hag has committed every crime in the book in her time.

He wished he could manage this without her, but he needed someone to watch the Pole. The most skilful captain of the finest ship could run into a storm, and he, Brenner, must plot his course carefully if his plans were not to go awry. He certainly didn't mean to have everything ruined because of that great wild devil of a Uhlan. If he could be successful . . . Mischa knew only too well this fashionable Viennese society, with its rigid social hierarchy, its scorn for anyone who could not produce wealth and title. It condescended to grant him entry to its golden ranks only because he was young and good-looking, and knew how to make himself agreeable, and useful—especially if the matter was one to be negotiated with discretion. He knew all its weaknesses and vices, and he knew how to play on them. Now he took the greatest gamble of his life, and if he could bring it off, not only would it ensure that he would never need to hide from his creditors again but it would make him too indispensable ever to be dismissed. But, most of all, it would enable him to take his revenge for all the snubs and insults he had endured at the hands of that privileged, gilded coterie, and which had scarred his sensitive soul.

The young man took his hat from crimson-haired Katy and stared at her critically. So this was the girl Dubrowski fancied. She was pretty and pert, but hardly intelligent, and a whore besides. Some other woman was needed to occupy the Uhlan completely, a woman of his own class and background, of whom he would not tire. A woman who would occupy the Pole so completely that he would forget the widow. Well, Mischa didn't know such a woman—yet. In the meantime, Katy would have to do.

'Seen enough, have you?' Katy demanded with asperity.

Mischa started. 'I beg your pardon, my dear. I was lost in my thoughts!' He pinched her cheek familiarly before running lightly up the steps which led from the basement entrance to the pavement above. Katy shrugged, and went to collect the dirty cups from Jetta's office.

'When the Major comes next,' Jetta said to her, 'be nice to him. He's an attractive man, anyway, and it will be no hardship.' She pushed herself up out of her chair with some effort and waddled to a cupboard. 'Give him some of this,' she said, taking out a bottle of apricot-coloured liqueur from behind a stack of ledgers. 'Tell him it will help his love life,' she chuckled.

'He doesn't need it,' Katy said.

'Mmm, all the same, it has a little something in it,' Jetta said. 'Something which loosens tongues, do you understand? Get him to talk about his family.'

'He doesn't talk about himself, Tant' Jetta,' Katy replied with unlooked-for obstinacy.

'Stupid girl . . .' Jetta said idly, and fear flickered in the red-haired girl's eyes. She picked up the bottle of liqueur and took it with her.

In the stuffy little office, the procuress waddled to the stained gilt mirror on the wall and peered into it ruminatively. 'Yes, Jetta, my dear,' she said affably to the raddled reflection. 'You're growing old, getting along in years—too old, perhaps, for such a dangerous undertaking.' She pursed her rouged lips and touched them with her fingertips. 'But profitable. Worth a pension to me at my age, *mein Gott*!' She nodded slowly, and the reflection nodded slowly back, as if it agreed. 'The boy has his head screwed on the right way,' she pronounced to the reflection, adding indulgently, 'and didn't even try to borrow money from me this time. He *must* believe his prospects to be good!' The reflection, painted, formless and evil, became further distorted by an expression of suspicion. 'Won't do,' Jetta muttered to it. 'Won't do for the boy to go falling in love with the widow. Won't do at all. We intend the widow for a special bed, don't we, eh?'

She tapped roguishly on the glass of the mirror, and it rocked on its nail, sending the reflection lurching crazily.

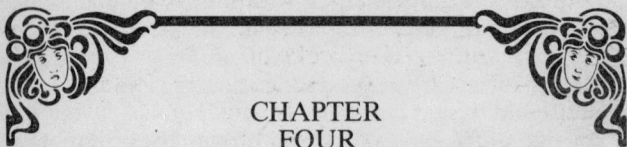

CHAPTER
FOUR

'SO WHEN you turn the cards up, you see,' Brenner said, suiting his actions to his words, 'all the kings come together, all the queens and so on.'

'It's a trick, Mischa, and I don't see how you do it.' Gabriela leaned her elbows on the table, propped her chin in her hands and studied the cards. The pearl droplets in her ears quivered invitingly. Brenner smiled to himself.

'Of course it's a trick! And I've shown it to you twice,' he said patiently.

'But I still don't see how it's done, and I don't *like* to be tricked, Mischa!'

'Don't you?' Brenner darted a quick, furtive glance at her from his dark eyes which, with their fringe of long black lashes, would not have disgraced a girl. 'Then I *shan't* show you again, Countess!' He scooped up the cards deftly with a nimble movement of his long, slender hands.

'Do you play Bezique?' Brenner had called to see her, and the onset of a heavy rain shower had led her to beg him to stay and keep her company. Robbed of Max's cheerful, anarchic presence, the house had become an elegant prison for her, in which she seized eagerly on any diversion to fight off loneliness and its attendant fears. 'If not, I could teach you. Since my mother-in-law has been away taking the waters, I've been playing Bezique of an evening with my father-in-law. He doesn't play cards when his wife is here, because she disapproves! You know, when his wife is out of the way, Count Clemenz is really a very pleasant old gentleman, and I get along with him splendidly. That will all change when *she* gets back. She does detest me. If only I could . . .' She broke off.

'Do you ever play these games of Bezique with Dubrowski?' he asked her casually. He was laying out the cards carefully now in front of him, as for Patience.

'Only once, and *never* again. He, would you believe it, plays a version of it called—naturally—Polish Bezique, with slightly different rules. So of course we got in a muddle and I was so cross, because he was so obstinate, that I threw down my cards. then Adam flew into a temper and got up and walked away from the table, and refused to come back and finish the game, even though his uncle sat by and watched us. After he had stalked out, furious because he couldn't get his own way, Count Clemenz said, "Aha, my dear! Those are not the tactics to use with Adam!" That made me so angry that I nearly threw the cards at *him*, though the poor old man meant nothing by it.'

'How do you think Dubrowski feels about you generally, then?' Mischa was placing his cards with mathematical precision on the table, one by one.

'He disapproves of me thoroughly. I think he'd like to be rid of me once and for all, but hasn't found the way!'

'The man's a bully,' Brenner said decisively. 'You have to stand up to him. Show any weakness, and he'll terrorise you. You won't be able to draw breath without his permission. I know those Poles.'

Gabriela had already realised that Mischa disliked Adam as much as Adam disliked him. There was some deeper cause to their enmity than anything either of them had so far confessed to her, but her inclination was to take Mischa's side in the quarrel, whatever it was, for he had been kind to her, and she deeply appreciated his kindness.

'He wouldn't like it if he knew you were coming to the races with me tomorrow!' Brenner said drily.

'I dare say he wouldn't, but Major Dubrowski's likes and dislikes are not my concern!' she replied sharply. Then, because she did not want to sound curt with him, she added, 'You're not worried about it, are you? Please don't be. Adam is already convinced I'm a low adventuress. Nothing I could do would shock him.'

'Dubrowski doesn't frighten me!' Brenner returned with unnecessary emphasis.

They fell silent for a little while after that. Ostensibly she watched him play out his game of Patience, but in reality both of them seemed preoccupied with other thoughts. Gabriela's were far less assured and untroubled than her words suggested. She had been seeing a good deal of Mischa lately. At first she had met him accidentally, while walking in the park. The meetings had seemed accidental at the time. After a while he had dropped the pretence of coincidence and waited for her openly at an appointed hour. He was a pleasant companion, and there had seemed no harm in it. He had called at the house a few times, when Adam was out. But today was the first time he had lingered over a visit. She glanced at the window and saw that the rain was lessening. With luck it would be a perfect day tomorrow at the Freudenau, where the celebrated Vienna Turf Club was holding a race meeting. Mischa's invitation to accompany him had been his first suggestion that they go elsewhere than the park. Eager for the distraction, she had accepted the idea readily, telling herself that any number of people had already seen her with him, and her reputation could hardly suffer more than it already had. Or could it? Vienna's race meetings were notoriously frequented by fast young men with a great deal of money, and society ladies whose own reputations were founded on their unquestioned beauty and fashion, and highly questionable morals. Gabriela sturdily forced aside any doubts as the natural obstinacy of her character, together with the smouldering resentment for the way they had all treated her, combined to create a perverse wish to shock them all and fly in the face of their displeasure.

She had ample reason for wanting to be out of the house as much as possible. Count Clemenz had obtained the transfer of his nephew from regimental duties to the War Office. Whether Adam appreciated being given a desk job which tied him to Vienna was debatable. But he seemed inclined to accept the change, perhaps to oblige his uncle. For several weeks he had been living in the house, and she could not help but notice that, in a curious way, he had assumed the mantle of head of the family. This was very odd, for Count Clemenz, though elderly, was in full possession of his mental faculties. But a change had come over her father-in-law since the loss of his son, and he had suddenly begun to look his age. A stoop bowed his former upright stance. He no longer showed his former energy, and seemed disposed to refer any decision to his nephew. 'See what Adam says', had become the phrase with which he all too frequently concluded any discussion. Thus, somehow, they all ended up doing what Adam wanted—with the exception of Gabriela, who took every opportunity presented to do the opposite. She and Adam, outwardly polite, regarded each other, as it were, over a simmering emotional cauldron of unspoken accusations and recriminations. Any moment now, the cauldron would finally boil over. In the meantime, Adam grew increasingly tense and impatient, and she defiant and resentful.

But perhaps there was a simple explanation why Adam did not mind being transferred to Vienna, and why he had suddenly assumed a role in the family, which, if it had belonged to anyone, would have been Max's, had he lived. Adam now represented the next generation. There would be no more Clemenz in this line, but he carried Clemenz blood through his mother. The future of the family lay, then, in the hands of this Polish nephew. Count Clemenz had begun to take Adam into his confidence in the matter of his personal and business affairs. His lawyer, Dr Rimmer, a small, white-haired, pink-cheeked man with a gold pince-nez, scurried in and out of the house like a little white mouse, casting furtive and short-sighted glances around him. It was obvious that when, in time, Count Clemenz felt himself unable to handle his affairs, he would pass the direction of them to his nephew.

Where all this would leave Gabriela, if events ever put her own future in Adam's hands, was extremely uncertain, and the prospect was not encouraging. Two things alleviated her worries for the moment. One was the absence of her mother-in-law who, for the sake of her nerves and at Adam's suggestion, had retired to take the waters at Marienbad in Bohemia, and would not return for several weeks. The other was the friendship of Mischa Brenner, without whom Gabriela really did not think she could have managed.

She became aware that Brenner sat silent and still before the upturned cards, apparently lost in thought. 'What's wrong, Mischa? Can't you get the Patience to work out?'

Brenner roused himself. 'Not yet. I do believe,' he went on slowly, 'that the red king is in my way.' He drummed his fingertips on the stack of cards remaining in his hand. 'I shall have to see if I can't do something about *him*!' he said softly.

Gabriela might have enjoyed herself more at the race meeting the following day, had the spectre of Adam not lurked at her elbow the whole afternoon. The sight of the horses themselves, glossy and handsome in the sunshine, reminded her of Adam, as did every army uniform—of which there were a great number. Even the band which played merrily on the racecourse chose to include in its repertory a lively little Polish dance-tune called, she knew, a Krakowiak. The only ingredient missing was the Polish Uhlan himself.

She tried her best to conceal her nervousness from

Mischa, who had set himself to entertain her, and was betting large sums of money, apparently with great success. He bore her off to the nearest refreshment marquee and bought champagne to celebrate his winnings. She was only half listening to him as he raised his glass in a salute to her, and said earnestly, 'You bring me luck, Gaby. I always knew you would. You and I together, we can't go wrong!'

The bubbling wine, the stuffy marquee and the hot sunshine, combined with the jostling crowd and the air of excitement about the finish, made her head sing and confused her. She laughed too much at Mischa's jokes, and clung tightly to his arm for support.

Adam was at home when she arrived back, rather later than she had anticipated, and he was not alone. He was deep in conversation with a slim, handsome young woman in a fashionable tailored costume. She must be Christiane! They broke off their talk as she entered, and something about the glance they exchanged indicated that they had been discussing her. Then the young woman rose to her feet with a sophisticated elegance, and bestowed a cold kiss on Gabriela's cheek.

'Dear Gabriela, I had to wait and see you before I left, no matter how late it got. How are you?' Her grey eyes flickered over her coolly.

'Very well, thank you, Christiane.'

Gabriela caught Adam's eye and glared at him defiantly. In response, he turned his back pointedly and walked to the further end of the room to stare out of the window. It was as if he dissociated himself from any conversation between the two women and did not even want to overhear. In fact, Gabriela suspected that he could hear very well. Christiane, in any case, made no attempt to lower her voice.

She turned her attention back to the girl everyone had supposed—wrongly—that Max would marry. She wondered whether Christiane still saw her as a hated rival. There was a cold gleam in those grey eyes which implied that she did.

'You do look very well,' Christiane said, surveying her. 'Adam says you're making a great effort to get out and about, and I do think it so wise of you, my dear.' Christiane permitted herself a flicker of a glance towards the silent figure of the man at the far end of the room. 'It's so nice to see Adam again,' she went on, raising her voice slightly. 'I suppose you still miss Max? Such a pity that you and he had no child. A pity for his parents, too. A grandchild would have been a great consolation. How long were you married? Three years, wasn't it? Ah, well . . .' She sighed in commiseration.

'Is that why you waited to see me? To remind me that I'm childless?' Gabriela asked her calmly. 'I don't want your sympathy, Christiane, and I don't need your friendship. You don't like me. You don't care how I feel, or whether I'm lonely. Let's be honest, at least!'

She saw the two spots of red stain the girl's pale cheekbones. Christiane came close to her, pushing her white face almost into hers, her grey eyes glittering, and lowering her voice so that it was barely audible, even to her, hissed, 'You stole Max from me! It was always intended he should marry me. And I would have given him children, too!' She seemed to recollect herself, and drew back. In an ordinary tone, she went on, 'I am so glad to have seen you, Gabriela. And now, I really must go.'

At the far end of the room, Adam stirred and walked slowly towards them. 'I'll see you out, Christiane,' he said courteously.

The girl put her hand on his arm and smiled up at him, as if they shared some secret. Gabriela turned away angrily. So, having failed to secure the Clemenz son, Christiane meant to make sure of the dashing Polish nephew. Well, good luck to her, she thought scornfully. She and Adam deserved one another. She went over to where he had stood and threw herself down on a sofa, leaning back and closing her eyes.

She felt nervous and irritable, perhaps the aftermath of the champagne. But the brief meeting with Christiane had hurt—far more than she might have expected. There had been something about the sight of Christiane putting her hand so confidently on Adam's arm, and the way she had tilted her face up towards him, that had been profoundly disturbing and unwelcome. But why should Christiane not be interested? Women, surely, were attracted to Adam. He was a handsome man, Gabriela could not deny it, and he carried a certain reputation as a rake which was bound to make any woman curious.

A faint frown puckered Gabriela's brow as her mind developed this train of thought. It was strange that the two cousins had been so close until their quarrel over Max's marriage. Odd, not only because of some difference in years, but because of such a striking dissimilitude of personality. Max, so easy-going and cheerful, who never worried about any serious matters, always assuming things would 'turn out all right somehow'. If he had ever been aware that anything was amiss with his marriage, he would probably have adopted the same attitude of ignoring the problem, in the hope that it would go away. His quarrel with Adam had been one unpleasant fact that he had not been able to ignore. Yet, loyal in his affection towards his difficult cousin, he had never criticised Adam openly or spoken of him with anything but respect and admiration. For the first time Gabriela found herself wondering whether Max had secretly doubted his own adequacy as a husband, and, while hiding his doubts beneath an outward show of jollity and general merry-making, had envied the cousin he saw to be so virile and confident. She began to wonder if she herself had not been partly to blame, waiting for Max to come to her instead of trying to reach him herself. Well, if was all too late now. Perhaps it was as well she had no child. Penniless and friendless as she was, she would almost certainly have been obliged to surrender the all-important grandchild to Max's parents. It would have been a double bereavement, and one she did not think she could have borne.

She forced her mind from Max and turned it to Adam, comparing him. He was different in almost every way. He was moody, passionate and proud. He had strong opinions, and disliked opposition. He set high standards for himself, and he would set them for his women. To be married to Adam would be a constant challenge, and to be in Adam's bed . . . Gabriela broke off her musings with a shiver, and pushed the thought out of her mind, almost with a feeling of alarm. Just at that moment, she heard the click of the door and footsteps approaching the sofa.

'Gabriela?' Adam's voice asked, from just behind and above her.

'What do you want?' she returned resentfully, refusing to open her eyes. She supposed he was about to deliver a lecture. He must have known she had gone to the races, and was probably going to attack her friendship with Brenner again. She only hoped he was not preparing to sing the praises of Baroness Christiane Vonneck. Gabriela was prepared to be admonished, but not to be compared unfavourably with that steely-eyed Prussian virago.

'A word with you. Are you tired?'

'No.' She sighed and sat upright, opening her eyes at last. 'But if it's just to grumble at me, Adam, I don't want to hear it. I know what you think of me.'

'Do you?' he asked, a little enigmatically. He paused. 'It's not to grumble. In fact, it's to apologise.'

She was so astonished that she twisted round and looked up at him, her lips parting in surprise.

He came slowly round the sofa, running his hand along the curved frame, and sat down on the cushions at the far end, facing her. He looked ill at ease, even a little embarrassed. 'It's about Christiane,' he began, speaking quickly, as if he feared interruption, or that he would not be able to say it all unless he said it in one piece. 'I used to think that Max should have married her. I was wrong. I'm not saying anything against Christiane, but she would have been absolutely the wrong wife for him. It would have been a disaster.'

He fell silent and waited, obviously expecting some reply from her. He had found the admission difficult. The day was warm, but the perspiration on his skin was not due to the heat.

For a moment she could not say anything at all, as the words slowly sank into her brain. 'Do you mean to tell me,' she began at last, speaking very slowly and quietly, 'that you refused to wish Max well on his marriage, to meet me, or even to see Max again before he died, because of something about which you now say airily you were wrong?'

A flush crept over Adam's lean features. 'If you like,' he said in a prickly voice.

'No, I don't like it, Adam.' She took up his words. 'I don't like it at all!' Her voice was beginning to grow louder and shook slightly. 'Max thought the world of you. Have you *any* idea how much that quarrel—which was entirely of your making—hurt him? Your refusal to meet me, your refusal to see him? It was like a slap in the face to him, Adam, a slap in the face from someone he loved! Oh, don't think he grumbled about you to me. Max wouldn't do that. He never spoke of you but as of a friend. A fine friend you were to him, Adam! I know how much your attitude hurt him—your selfish, obstinate, self-opinionated and self-righteous attitude! And now you say you're sorry? Sorry! What am I supposed to say? That it's all right? I forgive you? I understand? Well, it isn't all right. I don't understand how you could behave like that to him, and I'll *never* forgive you!' Her voice rang out in the room. 'I'll never forgive you, Adam, not because of the insult to me, but because of the unhappiness caused to Max!'

'Very well,' Adam said hoarsely. 'I intended my apology in good faith, but if it's to be thrown back in my face, I'll take it back myself, freely! No, I didn't want to meet you. Frankly, I don't think I missed much. If you want to know what I think of you, I think you're a cheap little hypocrite. Don't preach at me about Max. If you gave a damn about Max, you wouldn't be running all over Vienna with that gigolo, Brenner! He specialises in widows, you know. Usually they're more elderly, and they pay him for his services. As you are young and pretty, perhaps he lets you enjoy his favours for nothing!'

'Mischa is a friend of mine, that's all!' she exploded furiously. 'How dare you make such a vile suggestion?'

'A friend? A lover, more like it! Or perhaps you don't confine your activities to Brenner? You've been to the races, haven't you? Did you make your choice among all those rutting stags of the Turf Club? Or perhaps anyone will do?'

There were no words which Gabriela could have found then that could have expressed a fraction of the blind white rage which flooded over her. She lost all control of herself and flung herself towards him, striking at him like some wild creature, scratching at his face. Perhaps she was stuttering incoherent words; if so, she was not aware of it. A mist of pure fury enveloped her. At that moment, if she could have killed him, she would have done so.

He grasped her wrists and forced her hands away as she clawed at him and, imprisoning her, twisting furiously and impotently in his strong grip, he thrust her down on the cushion of the sofa, and trapping her beneath him, pressed his mouth against hers, fiercely and violently, forcing her head back into the cushions and half suffocating her. She tried desperately to escape, but could not. Her arms were pinned to her sides, and the weight of his body across her breast prevented any attempt to struggle up, and almost prevented her breathing. Then, suddenly, a thrill of wild exhilaration ran through her. Every muscle in her body seemed to shudder and lose the strength and even the will to fight. She heard Adam, above her, swear softly beneath his breath. Abruptly his grip slackened. He released her, and stood up.

He looked down at her where she lay across the sofa, gasping for breath, her blond hair, disarrayed in the encounter, spread across the crushed cushions. He was breathing heavily, and his eyes burned with a smouldering anger that lent an expression of indescribable ferocity and scorn to his face.

'Yes,' he said softly, as she stared wildly up at him. 'Anyone will do—even *me*!'

'Get out . . .' Gabriela whispered, though it hurt her constricted throat even to utter these words.

'I'm going! Tell them that I shan't be in for dinner. I'm eating out, and afterwards—afterwards—going elsewhere.'

He was walking towards the door now, having regained some control, and tossed the words almost casually over his shoulder towards her.

She scrambled up, so that she was half sitting and half kneeling on the sofa, her hands clasping its back of the frame so tightly that the knuckles gleamed white.

'To the Golden Fleece!' she shouted after him. 'Isn't that where you intend going? Well, go to your whores of the Golden Fleece!'

'At least *they* know what they are—and don't pretend to be fine ladies!' He looked back at her, his face dark with scorn, and then he was gone.

'And good company for someone who pretends to be a Polish aristocrat and a man of honour, but who is nothing but an ill-mannered rake!' Gabriela cried. But only the swinging door answered her.

The bed had a headboard carved with cherubs and love-knots. Inartistic clients had since added to its decoration by carving their initials. Adam, stretched out naked beneath the sheet, stirred and rolled over on to his front as Katy shook his shoulder vigorously. He mumbled something in Polish from deep within the pillows.

Katy had dealt with this sort of situation before. She dragged the pillow away from his face and said loudly, 'Major? Major—wake up! You've got to go home. You can't stay here any longer. Get up, or I'll tip that water-jug over you!'

At first there was no response. Katy dipped her finger-tips in the water-jug and flicked the drops at his face. Adam grunted, and pushed himself up on the crumpled pillows, rubbing his face with his hands.

'Get me some coffee, Katy, there's a good girl,' came in a muffled voice through his fingers. 'I feel like hell.'

'And so you should, Major!' the girl told him sententiously. 'I've brought you coffee—good, strong black coffee which will clear your head. My, but you were in a state. Friedl the potman helped me to put you to bed.'

'I can't remember a thing,' Adam growled, accepting the coffee. He tasted it and made a grimace. 'Dear God, Katy, what's it made of? Acorns?'

'Indeed it's not! The way your mouth is, I dare say anything would taste like acorns!' Katy told him sharply.

'I was all right,' he said with unexpected clarity. 'I was all right until I had a glass or two of that confounded apricot liqueur.'

Katy avoided his eye, and muttered, 'Well, it's strong stuff.' These Polish Uhlans were never as drunk as you thought they were. Most of the officers were Polish noblemen of one kind or another. However drunk they were, they never forgot they were aristocrats and different from other people. Other, lesser men, Katy thought, would have forgotten. She should have expected Dubrowski—who was a count or something—to remember.

She watched him push the coffee away undrunk and scratch his mop of thick chestnut hair lazily. Perched on the edge of the bed, she could almost read what passed through his mind. It was morning. The sunlight squeezing a single ray through the half shuttered window told him that, and he'd come here early yesterday evening. He was piecing it together, working out what had happened. She twisted her hands together nervously. If he decided in his own mind that he had been drugged, then he might well turn violent. She had never known him strike any of the girls before—but none of them had plied him with laced drinks. The sunlight played on his bare skin, making it glisten, and on the reddish-brown hair on his chest. The gold medallion on a chain round his neck glinted in the light.

'You Poles,' Katy said suddenly, partly to distract him, and partly because the idea had just struck her. 'You're all the same—religion and women. You want both, and generally manage to have both.' She stretched out her hand and touched the gold medallion.

'Best of both worlds!' Adam told her, looking up with a grin. He leaned back on the pillows and stretched out his arm invitingly. Katy slid into the crook of it and nestled her head on his shoulder. He kissed the top of her pile of red curls. 'Will you tell me what's going on here, Katushka?'

'Such as what?' Katy demanded cautiously, her heart giving a little leap of alarm.

'Such as anything I should know. Some men, my sweet, get drunk and pass out for hours. I *don't*. I don't know what was in the liqueur, but I do want to know why I was given it. Don't lie to me, little one. I don't like it.'

Katy was silent for a moment. 'This is a strange house,' she said at last. 'I've worked in some odd places, but this is the oddest, I'll swear. Old Jetta, she really scares me. Do you know what she does? She talks to the mirror—just like the wicked queen in *Schneewittchen*. Honest!' Katy crossed herself rapidly. 'Hope to die. She stands in front of that old mirror in the office and talks to her reflection. It's the eeriest thing you ever saw. Wonder she don't crack the glass, that's what I think! Everyone's terrified of her—all the girls, Friedl the potman, everyone. Even that Brenner is—though he behaves as if he weren't.'

She felt the man's arm about her shoulders tighten its grip. 'Tell me about Brenner,' Adam said softly into her ear.

'Oh, *him*!' Katy's disgust echoed in her voice. 'He's old Jetta's pet. He can't do anything wrong in her eyes. She gets quite sentimental over him. You should see it.'

'I'd rather not!' Adam muttered.

'I never knew anyone give himself such airs. Talk about a high opinion of himself! Fancies himself a regular answer to the maiden's prayer, that one. Mind you, I don't say he isn't a nice-looking boy in his way, but to my mind too pretty. Not how a *man* should look.'

She paused, and gave a little sidelong glance up at her companion. A man like this one, a woman could really lose her heart to a man such as this, even she, Katy, who knew enough about men to warn her off falling in love . . .

'Major!' she said in a low, urgent voice. 'You're right. Something is going on. Jetta and Brenner have been plotting away down in that office as though they were going to steal the crown jewels. And, Major, you come into it somewhere. I overheard your name, clear as anything, when I was in the corridor. I'd taken in some coffee and was going back to see if they wanted any more. I heard Jetta speak your name, and a bit later on, Brenner said it, too. I dawdled for a bit in the corridor, but I was afraid I'd get caught.'

Adam grunted and scowled. 'See here, Katy, keep your eyes and ears open, and I'll see you're well rewarded. But take care! You're right to be afraid of Jetta. The old hag is quite capable of murder. If you ever think yourself in any danger, even for a moment, get out of here and run to Inspector Gruber, or come to me. Gruber is a good man, and will listen.'

'Perhaps,' Katy suggested, 'the best thing would be if you didn't come here for a while.'

'I have to come, or we'll find out nothing. But don't give me any more drugged drinks, Katushka, there's a good girl.' He patted her shoulder kindly to show that he did not blame her for the trick played on him. After that he was silent for some time, staring moodily ahead of him.

'What's on your mind now?' Katy ventured.

'Oh . . . things, Katy. Things you wouldn't understand.' He drew a deep breath. 'I'm thirty-one, Katushka. I'm beginning to wonder what I've achieved in over thirty years. It seems to be precious little.'

'Now, then,' said Katy severely. 'Don't go talking like that. It's not true, and it achieves nothing. Think about something else.'

He turned his head and grinned at her. 'I am . . .' he said, and chuckled, pushing back the sheet and pulling her down on to the bed beside him.

Afterwards, when he was getting dressed, he said, 'Don't forget, Katy. Keep your ears and eyes open, and your wits about you!'

Katy, kneeling on the floor and pushing his boots on to his stockinged feet, said, 'I'll do it.' Privately, as she struggled with the boots, she thought, I'll do it, but only for you, you Polish devil—for you, and not for the money! Then, aloud, 'Last night, before you fell asleep, you were mumbling on about your cousin—and his wife.'

'His widow,' Adam corrected her. 'What did I say?'

'Oh, nothing that made sense,' she said quickly. 'And I won't tell Jetta.' She sat back on her heels. 'Is the widow pretty?'

'No,' Adam said calmly. 'She's beautiful.'

Katy said nothing, but an odd sort of pain struck her, one she had not felt before, a bitter-sweet sensation. She looked down at the floor. Adam put his hands to the nape of his neck, unfastened the gold chain, and hung the medallion round Katy's throat. She looked up into his face enquiringly.

'To help you to think good thoughts, and mend your ways,' he told her, smiling.

'Much you'd like it if I mended my ways!' she retorted sapiently.

'Perhaps,' he said, 'it's time I mended mine.'

CHAPTER
FIVE

ADAM'S BEHAVIOUR had left Gabriela feeling physically sick. Had he struck her an actual blow with his fist, it could not have been worse. Or if there had been any truth at all in his sordid accusations, it might have been different. But it was all so untrue! She liked Brenner. He had been kind, which she appreciated, and his company was a pleasant distraction and an escape route from this hateful house, but she had no other interest in him. It was this very fact—that Adam's charge had been so unjust—which made her stomach muscles churn and contract in a spasm of emotional nausea, and at the same time steeled her determination to stand by her friendship with Brenner, whatever the cost.

Not surprisingly, when she next saw him, Mischa was quick to sense that something had occurred.

'Dubrowski!' he exclaimed almost viciously. 'He's been talking to you! What did he say, Gaby? Was it about me?' He grasped her arm in an uncharacteristic gesture, his fine dark eyes alive with urgency.

'It doesn't matter what he said!' she returned sharply. She moved away from him to oblige him to release her, but he had already realised his error, and was taking his hand from her sleeve.

'You don't have to tell me,' he said bitterly. 'I can guess.' He fell silent for a moment, watching her moodily. 'Do you know why Dubrowski hates me?' he asked her suddenly. 'It's because I *know* what he is like, Gabriela. I know all about him!' He drew a deep breath. 'You've lived long enough in Vienna to understand the people who live here, the people who *matter*! Such

culture! Such aristocracy! Such god-given assurance!'
His voice was drenched in sarcasm. 'It's a great, glittering sham! Everyone knows the truth, and no one speaks
it! Do you want me to describe Dubrowski to you as he
really is? I shall. He's a typical Polish Uhlan officer—
arrogant, quarrelsome and debauched. Did you know
he had fought two or three duels in Galicia, even though
the army frowns on duelling and doesn't care to have
its officers maim one another? It's hardly an enviable
reputation, is it? But here it is quite ignored, because
Dubrowski is an aristocrat who can trace his ancestry
back generations—to the kings of Poland, for all I
know!'

'I know what he is,' she interrupted. 'I don't need to
be told.'

'You don't know, Gaby! To understand the man, you
have to know his background. Oh, I don't mean a list
of his noble ancestors or an account of his wealth! Have
you any idea what it's like in Galicia? I've been there.
It's a wilderness, burnt up by the sun to a dust desert
all summer, and reduced to a swampy quagmire all
winter. It's peopled by illiterate, superstitious peasants,
living—if such an existence can be called a life—in
filthy, ramshackle, wooden huts overflowing with
vermin and lice-ridden children. That is what Polish
nobles like Dubrowski preside over! That is the heritage
of which they are so proud! Do you know what kind of
a fine, upstanding, Austro-Hungarian officer gets posted
to a garrison there? I'll tell you. There are three sorts.'
Mischa held up his hand in its pearl-grey glove to mark
off the points on his fingers. 'First, the Poles themselves,
Polish officers of the Uhlan regiments, whose country
it is and who like the place. Second, Austrian officers
who have blotted their copybooks in some way, sleeping
with the colonel's wife or some such foolishness. Third,
poor unfortunates who have no influential contacts and
are sent there because the decent postings have gone to
those who do have family and friends in high places.

And what do they find when they get there? That there is nothing to do but gamble and get drunk on vodka! More than one poor wretch, driven to despair by sheer boredom, has blown out his own brains!'

Much as she hated Adam at that moment, Gabriela felt an instinctive reaction against Brenner's words. Perhaps because of the passion and fervour which she remembered Adam's voice had held when describing his homeland—so differently—to her. Or perhaps because she felt that Brenner, in speaking so freely of Max's cousin, was permitting himself a liberty to which he was not entitled. There was something else, too. A little stiffly, she said, 'You forget that Max admired Adam.'

But he interrupted her. 'That was when Max was young and easily impressed by a dashing figure such as Dubrowski likes to cut. But as Max grew older—and especially after he met you, Gaby—he came to realise what sort of a fellow Dubrowski really was. You told me yourself that after he married you, Max did not associate any more with his cousin.'

'That's true,' Gabriela admitted unwillingly. 'But, in fact, Mischa, it was the other way round. It was Adam who didn't come . . .'

But he was not giving her time to protest. 'I know it's hard for you to believe anything bad of any member of that family,' he continued urgently. 'But I know Dubrowski, and I know his kind!'

She shook her head irritably, annoyed by the indecision that racked her, and moved away from his side a little.

Seeing that she was unconvinced, Mischa frowned discontentedly. 'There's something else!' he said suddenly. 'Something you haven't told me.'

'No, of course not!' she denied too quickly, the flush on her cheeks betraying her.

'Good God!' Mischa exclaimed, taking her hand in his. 'He's tried to make love to you.'

'Nonsense. Of course he didn't!' she replied vigorously. 'You're letting your imagination run away with you, Mischa.'

He shook his curly head decisively. 'No, I'm not.' His fingers closed tightly on hers, so that she was obliged to stand and listen to him. 'Gaby, listen to me. Please! You can't allow a man like that to make your life a misery. I wouldn't do anything to harm you. You surely know that. Certainly the last thing in the world I would want to do is to damage your reputation. If I thought for one moment that by being seen with you I was doing that, then of course I would be the first to say to you that our friendship must, alas, cease. But what will you do, Gaby? Will you submit every new friendship to Dubrowski for his approval? Do you mean to stay in that house and see no one but those whom Dubrowski thinks fit company for you?'

'Of course I don't!' she retorted. 'You are probably right, Mischa, in everything you say. I know that Adam dislikes me for having married Max. Perhaps he was even a little jealous of me . . .'

'You can be sure he was,' said Brenner energetically, 'and resented that Max had turned away from him to you. Believe me, my dear, that is the root of the matter,' he concluded confidently. 'After Max met you, he wanted no more to do with Adam.'

Gabriela stifled the few remaining faint inner twinges of doubt with resolution. Mischa made sense—and more important, perhaps, what he said corresponded to what she *wanted* to feel.

'I want you to know, Mischa,' she said in a quiet, firm voice, 'that I don't desert my friends. But I don't want to make trouble for them, either. I'm sure Adam can be most unpleasant if he chooses. If, as you say, he has fought duels . . .'

'I don't think he'd call *me* out,' Mischa told her with his boyish smile. 'Major Adam Dubrowski has a very low opinion of me, my dear. I'm sure he would only fight someone he considered his equal, and I don't believe for a moment he considers me that. I suspect there are very few people he would consider his equal. He has a very fine opinion of himself, Count Dubrowski!'

They had been walking in the park during this conversation, near to where some children were bowling hoops. The childish laughter and the rattle of the gravel beneath the running feet formed a joyous and contrasting background to the sober tone of their speech. Gabriela looked with envy at the youngsters' happy, glowing faces. Just then, one of the little boys lost control of his hoop, which rolled, wobbling erratically, towards them, spinning to the ground at their feet. Mischa laughed, and stretching out his malacca cane, hooked up the hoop and rolled it back towards its red-faced little owner.

'You know, Gaby,' he said, 'I had been going to suggest that you come out with me for a drive. I don't keep a horse myself, but I have a friend who will lend me his gig. I'm quite a capable whip, so we shouldn't have any accidents. Wouldn't you like to bowl merrily down the Hauptallee of the Prater? And don't tell me anyone could possibly object. It's very fashionable, and as a result everybody goes there. No one could possibly accuse us of using it for an amorous rendezvous!'

'It would be unwise, Mischa,' she said regretfully. The picture he had painted was certainly an attractive one.

'Ask Dubrowski's permission, if you like!' he snapped, allowing a little of his irritation to spill over in her direction for the first time.

The words stung, as he had known they would. 'Of course I shan't ask his permission!' she replied with a flash of spirit. 'I'll come with you, Mischa, just for an hour.'

'Good. I'll collect you tomorrow, if it's fine—and do stop thinking about Dubrowski. The man really isn't worth worrying about.'

Mischa struck the ferrule of the malacca cane on the ground to emphasise his words, but an almost feverish light glittered in his eyes, and it was obvious that something worried him very much.

Brenner was certainly right in his assertion that anyone with a claim to fashion wanted to be seen driving or riding in the Hauptallee, the broad tree-lined avenue which cut across the vast pleasure area of Vienna known as the Prater. The Prater catered for everyone. Sporting men gambled on the racecourse of the Freudenau. Workmen and their girls, nursemaids and children, shrieked on the merry-go-rounds of the fairground. Lovers met in the discreet little cafés, and here on the Hauptallee, every young blood and every pretty girl seemed to have congregated to hurtle at a terrifying pace in gigs, carriages and traps down the great avenue, three or four vehicles abreast. Wheels missed touching by a hair's breadth, coachmen cracked their whips and shouted warnings as others swept past, even the horses themselves seemed imbued with a special kind of madness, snorting, tossing their heads and manes, and dashing along with such fury that sometimes it was all their drivers could do to restrain them. The noise of hoofs, wheels, harness and whips reduced all conversation to a minimum.

Gabriela was greatly relieved to discover that her escort was the capable whip he had assured her he was. They kept to the outer edge of the throng and trotted merrily along in a pretty, glossily painted gig drawn by an obliging chestnut cob, which, though it snorted noisily from time to time, seemed of a placid disposition and not desirous of joining in the mad race with the showier equipages.

'Aren't you glad you came?' Mischa shouted at her, with an engaging grin, above the tumult.

She nodded, clutching at her hat, as yet another barouche clattered past, bearing two ladies and two young gentlemen out for a spree. Mischa glanced around him and, from time to time, over his shoulder. She assumed that he was anxious to avoid any collision, and was glad to see him so prudent. He had a slightly anxious look on his face, although whenever she spoke to him it vanished to be replaced by his usual cheerful, confident expression. Nevertheless she had the impression that he was enjoying this less than she was. Perhaps it was only the responsibility of driving—but it was almost as if he had something on his mind.

After a while he drew over to the side of the road and reined up. 'Give the horse a breather,' he said. He took out his fob watch and consulted it quickly, before casting a searching glance over the vehicles rattling past.

'Are you looking for someone?' Gabriela asked.

'No, no,' he denied quickly. 'Just wondering how we were doing for time. You said you didn't want to be away long . . .' He broke off, and leaned forward slightly. A new air of intentness showed in his attitude, and Gabriela followed the line of his vision with some curiosity.

A two-wheeled gig, drawn by a dapple-grey horse, was just passing in front of them. It was driven by a young man, presumably its owner, for a liveried groom sat beside him, stony-faced and arms folded. The young man wore a hat tilted over his eyes at a rakish angle, obscuring his forehead, and, despite the mild day, an overcoat which had a high collar that muffled the lower part of his face. As he passed them, he glanced their way, and Gabriela had a brief impression of an intense and rather disturbing gaze. But in a second he was gone, lost in the crowd of other vehicles.

'We can drive on, perhaps,' Brenner suggested. He shook the reins, and the cob moved on obligingly.

'Who was that in the gig?'

'What? I've no idea.' Brenner shrugged. 'I was look-ing at the horse. A fine piece of bloodstock.'

'He's coming back this way!' Gabriela exclaimed
suddenly.

The gig drawn by the grey horse was coming rapidly
towards them. Very faintly, just by her ear, she heard
Brenner exclaim 'Ah!', as if in satisfaction. She had not
realised that he was so interested in horseflesh.

The gig swept past, but this time the driver took a
longer and more deliberate look in their direction, and
she automatically turned her head aside, somehow
embarrassed by such obvious scrutiny.

Brenner now appeared in high good humour. That
faint air of anxiety had quite evaporated. He was hum-
ming to himself as they bowled along, a smile hovering
round his curved lips.

Gabriela was about to comment on his cheerfulness
when an unexpected and undesired encounter effectively destroyed the gaiety of the little outing once and
for all. A horseman was bearing down on them. He had
clearly seen them, and was seeking to head them off.
Even without the sight of the army uniform, she would
have known who it was, and her heart sank. Brenner
muttered, 'Devil take it!,' and for a second seemed to
be undecided whether to try to outrun the solitary
horseman. But then he heaved a resigned sigh and
pulled on the reins, restraining the cob to a walk.

Adam galloped up in a shower of grit and dust, and
leaning from the saddle at a perilous angle with all the
skill of a Cossack, stretched out his hand to grasp the
bridle of the chestnut cob and bring them abruptly, and
rocking dangerously, to a halt.

Brenner rested his forearms on his knees, the reins
held slackly in his hands, and said nothing, waiting.
Adam rode up to the gig, alongside Gabriela. He was
breathing heavily, and his face was contorted with
anger, deathly pale.

'Get down!' he ordered hoarsely.

She stared at him incredulously. 'What?'

'I said, get down from that gig, damn you!' he roared.

His mount snorted and flung up its head, dancing away nervously from the side of the gig. Adam clapped his heels to its sweat-drenched flanks and urged it forward again. He reached out and seized her shoulder tightly. 'You heard me!'

'Your Excellency surely does not wish to leave the lady on foot amid all this traffic?' Brenner demanded coolly.

'You hold your tongue!' Adam snarled. 'I'll deal with you later.'

'How dare you speak to Mischa like that?' Gabriela cried angrily. 'And speak to *me*, too, like that? I may drive here if I wish.'

'Where all Vienna may see you,' he flung back at her, 'with *him*?' He jerked his head scornfully towards Brenner.

'I am aware I do not enjoy Your Excellency's high opinion,' Brenner said drily. 'But I repeat, if you oblige her to descend, she will be almost certainly run down. Or do you propose to throw her over your saddle and carry her off home, as in some Polish legend?'

'You mincing little popinjay,' Adam said threateningly. 'You keep out of this, or I'll leave you to pick up your teeth from the dirt, one by one!'

'For goodness' sake, Adam!' Gabriela cried, horrified.

'Not here, I think!' Brenner retorted surprisingly, almost with a note of triumph in his voice, and a strange light gleaming in his dark eyes. 'Not here, Uhlan! This isn't Galicia. You aren't at home now, where you may do as you please because no one will cross a Polish nobleman. This is Vienna; and over there, observing us closely, is a splendid Viennese gendarme.'

Adam stared at him for a moment. Then he jerked on the reins and rode slowly round to the other side of the gig, so that he was now beside Brenner, who drew back, but was too slow in anticipating the major's next move. With a lightning sweep of his arm, Adam seized the driving whip, dragged it from its socket on the gig, and struck out furiously at Brenner with it. Gabriela screamed, and Brenner threw up his arm to protect his face, but in doing so, lost his balance and tumbled from the gig into the dust of the roadway. He rolled over and half scrambled up before Adam's horse reared up over him, and the whip struck him across the shoulders and sent him sprawling back into the dirt.

'Leave him alone, Adam!' Gabriela cried desperately, as the horseman raised the whip on high again. 'I'll get down!'

The gendarme Brenner had mentioned now came running up. Adam spun his horse round to confront him. 'The lady is my relative!' he snapped.

The man halted and eyed his opponent. A senior army officer—and one in a towering rage, at that. Army officers were a law unto themselves, and most had friends in high places. Any report on the incident would probably get 'lost', once it had been submitted. Besides, reasoned the gendarme, by 'relative' the officer probably meant 'wife'. That's what this was. The Uhlan had discovered his wife out driving with a lover. Interference in domestic matters was always a waste of time. No one ever wanted to bring charges, once tempers had cooled down. Reputations were at stake. All in all, the best thing to do was to issue a warning, and turn a blind eye.

'Very public place, this, sir,' he said blandly, aloud. 'Lots of ladies about.'

'All right, all right!' Adam said irritably. 'There will be no more trouble.'

The gendarme saluted and disappeared rapidly. Brenner, in the meantime, had got to his feet and was dusting down his clothing. He stooped to pick up his hat, and climbed back into the gig. The lash had caught his chin, scoring a red weal, and his eyes burned with sullen hatred.

'Stay where you are!' Adam ordered Gabriela, who was preparing to scramble down unaided. 'You'll be trampled, as he says.' He turned to Brenner. 'Drive her home!' he ordered brusquely. 'I'll follow.' He tossed the whip into the Austrian's lap and rode round to the back of the gig.

'That was barbarous!' Gabriela hissed to Brenner. 'Adam is an officer and a man of honour—I never would have believed him capable of such behaviour!'

He glanced at her. 'Wouldn't you? What makes you think Dubrowski's never done it before?'

He shook the reins and they set off homeward, their unwanted escort following behind.

On arriving home, Gabriela shut herself in her room and refused to see Adam or anyone else. Rather than face a scowling Major Dubrowski across the dinner table, she sent Arlette down to the kitchen to bring up a tray. The maid came back with the tray—and a message.

'The Major says, madame, as he is sure you will want to come down later.'

'Tell the Major that I haven't the slightest intention of doing any such thing! I have a headache.'

Arlette's eyes sparkled maliciously. Madame and the Major had quarrelled. The elder Countess Clemenz—still absent in Marienbad—would be pleased to know of it. She had instructed Arlette to keep her informed.

But after Gabriela had picked at the food on the tray, and pushed it away, mostly uneaten, she grew thoughtful. Adam's order—for such it was, to come down and show herself—was not because *he* wanted to see her. It was to avoid arousing the suspicions of Count Clemenz. She slowly tidied her hair and put on a suitable gown, before making her way slowly downstairs.

Outside the dining-room door, which was not quite shut, she halted. Adam and his uncle were still in there, probably sitting over their brandy. Count Clemenz's voice could be heard, a little querulous but clear.

'She's very young, Adam. You are too severe. She

feels the loss of Max, as we all do. She tries to forget him by letting this fellow Brenner take her driving, and all the rest. But I am convinced there is no harm in it. I confess I don't find him an altogether suitable companion, but I should be a great deal more concerned if she were being escorted by some more high-ranking party. Then the matter would be serious.'

'It's serious now, sir!' Adam's voice replied impatiently. 'She has no other friends here in Vienna, that's the trouble! She would be far better off in Budapest, in her own country, where she could renew her links with her friends there.'

Gabriela stiffened. So he wanted to send her away! She had been expecting this.

'But who would look after her, Adam? She was my son's wife and she carries our family name. I want to keep her here. I want to *know* what she's doing, even if I don't always approve of it! She has far more sense than you credit her with. She would not commit any indiscretion with Brenner. The fellow has no breeding at all!'

'We could pay some suitable woman to be her companion,' Adam suggested.

'To be a spy, you mean!' Gabriela muttered outside the door.

'No, no. I have told her she has a home here while I live, and I stand by that,' replied the Count with more firmness than he had shown in weeks. 'I trust your judgment in almost every matter, my boy, but in this case I rely on my own.' There was a pause, and the chink of a glass. 'Besides, she has no money,' he added.

'We are not short of money!' Adam interrupted. 'The family can well afford to make her an allowance. If the financial aspect could be put to her attractively, I'm sure she would agree.'

She clapped her hand to her mouth to prevent herself crying out. Turning, she ran back upstairs and slammed the door of her room, leaning back against it, panting.

'So!' she said aloud in a strangled voice. 'So, I am to be bribed—paid off! Oh no, Adam Dubrowski. Oh no!'

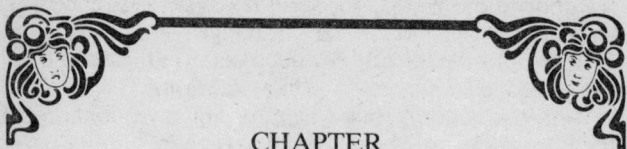

CHAPTER SIX

'YOU CAN go, Arlette.' Gabriela dismissed the maid brusquely. She patted her blond hair and twitched her sleeves. She had spent a sleepless night, turning over and over in her mind what she should do, and had reached a decision. She wasn't tired now, despite her lack of sleep, only very calm and determined. 'Do you know if Major Dubrowski has left yet for the War Office?' she called out after the departing maid.

Arlette, half-way through the door, turned, her pale little eyes flickering over the figure of her mistress. 'I believe not, madame.'

Gabriela nodded, satisfied. Everything seemed quite clear to her now. She knew exactly where she stood, thanks to the snatch of conversation she had overheard last night—and now Adam was about to find out exactly where *he* stood.

She waited until Arlette was safely out of the way, and then made her way down the corridor to the door of Adam's room. Without hesitation she knocked briskly at it.

'Who is it?' came his voice.

'Gabriela. I want to talk to you,' she called softly at the panels, after a second's delay in which she fought and conquered the urge to run.

Footsteps approached the door, and Adam jerked it open, facing her. He was fully dressed to go out, and that he was getting ready to go to the War Office was shown by the sheaf of papers he held in his hand. But he was taken aback by her unexpected appearance in his doorway, and for a moment his usual assurance had slipped.

'Here?' he asked, and the deep-set eyes flickered over her, puzzled, doubtful—perhaps cautious.

'Why not?' she replied calmly, her own confidence feeding on his indecision. 'May I come in?'

Adam held the door open silently and stood aside for her to enter. It was a bedroom like any other in the house at this early morning hour. The windows had been pushed open wide to let in the fresh air, and a pair of city sparrows hopped along the sill outside in the sunshine. The bed was unmade, and a dent in the pillows showed where his head had rested.

'Do you want me to close the door?' he asked expressionlessly behind her.

'Yes, close it.' She turned towards him. 'You look surprised, Adam. Don't tell me you were never alone in your room with a woman before?'

'That's a cheap remark,' he said in a brittle voice. 'And unworthy of a woman of your background. Your association with Brenner is betraying itself.' He walked to a small table on which lay a document case and pushed the papers inside, fastening the clasp with a snap. 'What do you want, Gabriela? I'm in a hurry.'

'You can wait and listen to me for five minutes. It won't take any longer.' She walked slowly and deliberately across to him. 'I'm not one of your Golden Fleece jades, Adam,' she said quietly. 'I'm not to be paid off.'

She saw a flush spread slowly across his face. 'Listening at the door last night, were you, my dear?' he said calmly, picking up the case. 'I thought I heard a scuffling in the corridor.'

'Why did you bother with my father-in-law?' she asked. 'Why didn't you come direct to me, and make your offer to me, if you think it's money I'm after? You do think that's what I'm waiting for, don't you? That I'm waiting for Count Clemenz to offer me money.

That's why I've stayed in this house, and why I behave as I do. So that the family will buy me off!'

'No!' he exploded, and threw the document case away from him with a force which sent it half-way across the room. It burst open as it struck the wall and scattered its contents across the carpet. The unexpected violence of his reply caused the crystal chandelier above their heads to ring, and prevented Gabriela from replying immediately. 'I was not offering to buy you off!' he shouted at her.

'You were!' The words came low and filled with accusation, and she took a step closer to him, her blue eyes blazing. 'Oh yes, you were, my gallant, honourable Pole. That is just what you were suggesting! Well, I don't have a price, Adam. If I ever leave here, I'll go as I came—with nothing!'

Adam was visibly struggling to regain his composure. 'Look . . .' He rubbed his hand over his forehead and seemed to be trying to adopt a placatory tone. 'You misunderstood. I know you're not happy here—why should you be? It's not your home. No! I mean, damn it, it *is* your home, but you'd be happier by far in Budapest. I wasn't suggesting *paying* you. You have a right to an income from the Clemenz fortune. You're Max's widow, and unless you marry again, you have every right to expect his family to recognise your claim.'

'No, I don't,' Gabriela interrupted him. 'I have no rights at all. I'm here because my father-in-law is a charitable man. I'm an object of charity, Adam. But if ever I do find a way to leave here—*not* with Clemenz money—then, you're right—I would leave!'

'But that's the whole point!' Adam exclaimed furiously. Suddenly he seized both her elbows and shook her urgently. 'You're going to make the wrong decisions, Gabriela. You're getting so desperate to get away from here that you're blind to what's going on! You don't see what you're getting into.'

'What am I getting into?' she flung at him. 'Tell me,

Adam, what is this sinister affair which is all around me, and which I don't see?'

'I don't know, damn it!' He had lost his temper now. Perspiration trickled from beneath his chestnut hair which had fallen forward untidily over his forehead, and he hardly seemed to know how to express his evident frustration. 'If I knew, I'd tell you! I'd put a a stop to it. All I know is that if you were fat, forty and plain, it wouldn't matter. But you're not. You're young, beautiful, poor and unhappy. It's a recipe for disaster. Can't you see how vulnerable it makes you? Why I want you away from here—for your own good and safety!'

'Vulnerable to whom?' she cried out. 'In what way?'

A silence fell. Adam drew a deep breath. 'You don't know?' he asked in that low, quiet voice she feared. 'Come over here, my dear. Come on. You marched in here very boldly, so don't hold back now. Give me your hand.' He smiled at her, but the smile was not reflected in his eyes, which glittered oddly at her.

Gabriela looked down at his hand stretched out towards her, palm uppermost. Almost as if mesmerised, she put out her own—it looked very small and white against his broad, brown palm—and touched his fingers.

They closed on hers like the snapping spring of a steel trap. Adam dragged her after him across the room to the bed and pushed her forward so that she had to grasp the bedpost to prevent herself falling across the rumpled sheets.

'That's what it's all about, my sweet—that bed! You're a very desirable woman, or hadn't that thought occurred to your bright little brain? You're the sort of woman men want. Didn't any man ever tell you that? Well, I'm telling you now! Whatever this is all about, there is the centre of the matter! I don't know what Brenner's game is—but that is where it ends up!'

Panting with alarm, her eyes fixed on the crushed pillows, Gabriela drew in her breath with an audible gasp. She tore herself free and whirled round on him, wild-eyed. 'Brenner! You're obsessed with poor Mischa. What harm has he done? Adam—he's a friend, only that! He's not trying to seduce me.'

'No—*he* can't afford you!' Adam said callously. He stepped back, but at the same time gave her a little push, so that she fell back and landed sprawled across the bed, pressed against the feather mattress, still warm and smelling faintly of perspiration. He looked down at her for a moment. 'But there are others who can!' he said harshly.

He turned and walked quickly over to where his document case and scattered papers lay strewn across the floor. He stooped and began to gather them up in rough haste, his back to her, cramming the flimsy sheets into the leather case.

Gabriela pushed herself upright. 'You're mad!' she breathed. 'You're—you're sick. No one in his right mind . . .'

Adam straightened up and turned round, fastening the case. 'I will find out, you know,' he said, glancing towards her and speaking in a crisp, matter-of-fact voice. 'Be sure of it—and you can tell that effeminate little Russian bastard so, from me, with my compliments.' He went out, slamming the door.

As it happened, there would have been no need for Gabriela to give any message to Mischa, even had she intended to. In Jetta's office, a fierce argument was in progress.

'I tell you,' Brenner exploded. 'I've got to get rid of that confounded Pole! He'll ruin everything. What's the matter with that girl of yours—Katy, isn't it? Can't she keep him occupied?'

'Patience, my dear,' Jetta advised him comfortably. 'All you young people need to learn patience. Everything must be done quickly and in hot blood, or you fret. But it's not the way.' She ran a pudgy finger down the columns of her accounts ledger, and frowned.

'I haven't got all the time in the world!' Brenner put his hands on her desk and leaned over her, so that Jetta was obliged to close the ledger and look up, fixing her black eyes on his flushed face. 'Alexander is ours. He's dying to meet her. He's sent an intermediary to me, asking who was the lady I drove in the Hauptallee. He's even enquiring whether she has a favourite flower. I have persuaded him that to send the lady flowers would be premature and extremely unwise. She is shy and very nervous. That, of course, has served to make him doubly impatient. I have to arrange for her to meet him, discreetly, so that she doesn't take fright. And it must be soon, Jetta, or Alexander may take matters into his own hands. What's worse, he may fall for another pretty face and lose interest. I've *got* to find a way of distracting that wretched Uhlan!'

'The Major is not perhaps himself attracted to the lady?' Jetta suggested.

'No.' Brenner shook his curly head. 'But she's his cousin's widow, and he thinks it is not right for her to run about Vienna enjoying herself. He especially dislikes to see her with me. He dislikes *me*!' He touched the red mark on his chin, and scowled.

Jetta's eyes glinted with a spiteful merriment, but then she grew thoughtful, and picking up a bill from the desk, fanned herself with it. It was, as usual, stiflingly hot in the little basement office and the air was choked with stale cigar smoke. Brenner was suffering. He took out a handkerchief and wiped his forehead with it, and then his chin, wincing as he touched the weal with a nervous gesture that was not lost on Jetta. She speared the bill neatly on a wickedly sharp metal spike which protruded from the wall.

'Something else bothers you, my dear,' she crooned, as one encourages a child to speak.

'Well, yes . . .' Brenner stuffed the handkerchief in the pocket of his expensive English tweed jacket. 'Something isn't right. I can't tell you what, but Dubrowski looks at me, whenever we meet, as though he's trying to read my mind. It's as if he *knew* something. That girl—Katy—you're sure she's to be trusted?'

Jetta sat quite still, smiling blandly, her plump white hands folded over her fat stomach, looking like some obese Buddha. 'I'll look into it, my dear,' she said at last reassuringly, and watched Brenner gather up his gloves and malacca cane.

When he had done so, he hesitated. 'Jetta, I'm short of money. Escorting Gabriela around every fashionable haunt in Vienna is costing me more than I have at present. The hire of that horse and gig cost me a small fortune.' His tone became wheedling. 'Come on, Jetta, you know I'm putting it to good use.'

'You always have a good reason,' she commented, but she unlocked the cumbersome wall safe and counted out some money. He took it hastily and it stuffed into the inner breast pocket of his jacket.

Jetta raised one pudgy hand and patted his cheek affectionately. Somehow he managed not to flinch beneath that soft, white touch, though inwardly he could not have been more appalled if the hand had carried the scabs of plague.

'You will see about Katy?' he urged.

'Yes, yes, pretty boy. Don't worry your curly head about it. Jetta will take care of it. Jetta will take good care of *you*, my pigeon!' she crooned.

Brenner backed out of the room with indecent haste, and bolted up the steps to the street.

When he had gone, Jetta called out to the potman, who just then was staggering along the corridor, bearing a crate of bottles. 'Is that you, Friedl? Leave that, and go and tell Katy I want to see her.'

The mirror on the wall rocked slightly as she passed by it, with a soft, grating sound, as if it chuckled at the prospect of mischief.

Brenner had run up the stone steps to the pavement

outside and stood there, taking deep gulps of street air. He put his hand to his cheek and scrubbed at the spot where Jetta's fingers had caressed it. He felt sick. He hated these visits. He didn't trust the old witch. To tell the truth, she frightened the life out of him. If he could only find some other ally . . .

He set off briskly down the street, and as he did so, a closed *Fiaker*, which had been waiting on the other side of the road, rolled forward and began to follow him. At the corner, it caught up with him and halted. The door opened slightly and a woman's voice called, 'Herr Brenner?'

Brenner eyed the dark slit of the open door mistrust-fully, but he approached to within a few feet of it to ask suspiciously, '*Gnädige Frau?*'

'Please get in,' the voice invited. 'I should like to talk to you.'

'Perhaps,' Brenner said coldly, 'I should first know with whom I have the honour . . .'

'It is a matter of interest to us both . . .'

Brenner's eyes narrowed, and he jumped up into the cab. Even as he closed the door, the cab-man whistled to his horses and the *Fiaker* set off again at a smart trot.

'Please don't be alarmed,' said the woman calmly. 'I told the man to drive us round the Ringstrasse. It is the best place I know to hold a private conversation without fear of interruption.'

Brenner leaned back, resting his hands on the silver knob of his malacca cane, and studied his companion. By her voice and figure she was young; by her fashion-able clothes she was wealthy. That she was veiled, and coy about revealing her identity, signified that she was up to no good. Other men than Brenner might have found such a situation surprising, but to him it was perfectly natural. Society gentlemen—and ladies, too —often needed to conduct a little business which they were not anxious to advertise. Frequently they came to Mischa Brenner for assistance.

'Dear lady,' he said, smiling and taking off his hat. 'In what may I oblige you?'

'This is a very private matter,' the woman said. 'I am told that you are discreet. In any case, this is a matter which concerns us both. I fancy we may oblige each other.'

'In that case,' Brenner said gently, 'I need to know with whom I'm dealing.' His tone was courteous, but firm. This was one of his terms.

The woman understood. She lifted her veil and turned it back over her hat. 'You know me, Herr Brenner?'

He nodded, narrowing his eyes shrewdly. Christiane Vonneck. A wealthy and well-connected family. Prussians, of course, with estates in distant Silesia. But they were a cultured family who preferred to reside in Vienna rather than in some barrack-like palace in Berlin. They had made money in Silesian coal, and were to be reckoned with. He waited prudently for her to unburden her mind.

Christiane responded by beginning to speak quickly and fluently, as thought she had rehearsed her speech. 'You are interested in the Countess Gabriela, Herr Brenner. I don't ask what your interest is; that is your affair. My interest is in Major Dubrowski; that is my affair. Major Dubrowski is in your way. The Countess Gabriela is most certainly in mine.'

'Life has many inconveniences,' Mischa said politely. 'But usually they can be resolved with a little ingenuity —and good will.'

A faint dry smile flickered across Christiane's face. She picked up a fat, sealed envelope from the seat beside her. 'I think you will find sufficient good will in there, Herr Brenner.' She held it out.

Brenner accepted it with a bow. 'These matters do, alas, involve certain expenses, dear lady. But possibly the greatest obstacle may not be bought off with money.'

'Leave that to me!' Christiane told him sharply. 'You

just do your part and keep that Hungarian trollop out of the way!'

'You're sure you can take care of Major Dubrowski?' Brenner's voice grew suddenly eager, and his fine eyes, fixed on her pale face, burned with intensity.

'If you will take care of the Countess Gabriela,' Christiane retorted. 'The matter is a simple one, Brenner. I was told you were a clever man. I should not have to repeat myself.'

The insult, which he would normally have added to that mental list of such snubs engraved in his memory, this time flowed over him unheeded. He leaned back, smiling now and quite relaxed. 'Honourable Baroness, you may depend on me. The Countess Gabriela will soon cease to be of any concern either to you or to the Clemenz family. Please don't worry, everything is in hand.'

His confidence was well founded. He had discovered his ally.

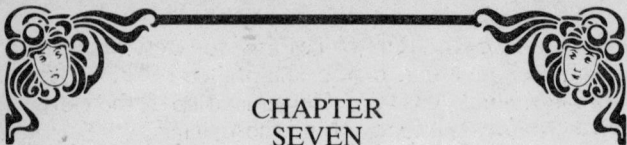

CHAPTER
SEVEN

JAN JURAWICZ, the senior filing clerk in Adam's department, stood by the desk and gazed down with avuncular concern at the stone-cold, untouched cup of coffee he had brought an hour ago. Jurawicz liked Major Dubrowski, partly because they were compatriots and partly because he was, in Jurawicz's phrase, 'quick on the uptake', which made the clerk's life a lot easier.

'Shall I bring you some more coffee, sir?' he asked in Polish. When he and Adam were alone, they always spoke Polish. When anyone else was there, they spoke German. People didn't trust you if they couldn't understand what you said.

Adam, a smouldering cigarette clenched between his teeth and a ferocious frown on his brow, grunted. It was obvious that the question had passed over him unheard. 'Jan,' he said abruptly. 'If I told you I couldn't find a particular file, you'd be able to suggest some places I might look for it, wouldn't you?'

'Which file?' demanded Jurawicz instantly. 'Who says a file is lost? Not one of my files!'

Adam waved his cigarette irritably at him. 'No, no, man! I said *if*. Just answer the question.'

Jurawicz reconsidered the question, brightened, and replied smartly, 'Yes, sir.'

'Right.' Adam jabbed the glowing cigarette-end towards him. 'Now, suppose I turn the question round. If I give you a list of places to look, can you suggest what I might be looking for?'

'Are we still talking about files, sir?' Jurawicz enquired cautiously.

'No, we are not. The places are, for example, let's see—a race meeting, or the Hauptallee of the Prater on a busy, sunny day . . .' He glanced up at the clerk. 'What would you expect to find there, Jan?'

'Folk with a lot of money,' he replied promptly, 'and nothing to do.' He scratched his bullet-shaped, cropped head. 'Lot of fast young devils with rich papas.' The Major seemed to be waiting for more. 'Good-looking women, I suppose. Some of them not too fussy, if you know what I mean, sir.'

'So,' Adam said softly to himself, 'I am looking for a young, wealthy man, of some well-known and important family, perhaps a bit of a womaniser. Damnation!' He stubbed out the cigarette angrily. 'It's a description that could apply to a hundred young idiots. It could apply to *me*!'

Jurawicz raised his eyebrows and forbore to comment on this. 'I'll take your cup, sir, and bring some hot coffee.' He went out, but a moment later he was back, holding a letter in his hand. 'This just came for you, sir. A lady left it.' His expression was quite blank.

Adam took the envelope, and dismissed Jurawicz with a nod. When the man had gone, he sat for a moment turning it in his hand. It was written on delicately perfumed, expensive notepaper, and he recognised the handwriting. 'Christiane,' he murmured. 'What does she want, I wonder?' He broke the seal and scanned the contents.

I must see you and talk to you. Can you come tonight, after dinner? I shall be at home alone then. You and I both loved Max. For that reason, do not fail me.

Adam studied the note, trying to read more into the few written lines than appeared on the page. It made him uneasy. For all Christiane's assured public manner, he suspected the woman was somewhat deranged. The arrangement with Max had existed largely in her mind,

but it had taken Adam a little while to realise this. At
first he had assumed that Max's interest in Christiane
had equalled her interest in him. It was for this reason
that he had been so surprised, indeed shocked, at Max's
unexpected marriage to an unknown Hungarian. At the
time, Christiane had borne herself like a wronged queen
in a Grand Tragedy. She had been totally convincing.
'She certainly convinced *me*, anyway!' Adam muttered
now. He had not fully realised his error until the other
day, when she had called at the Clemenz house. In the
course of a long, and at times embarrassing, conversation with her he had become only too aware of the
chaotic mind behind the well-ordered façade. That was
why he had attempted his ill-received and disastrous
apology to Gabriela—a mistake he would never repeat!

Adam crumpled Christiane's note into a ball, dropped
it into his ashtray, and put a match to it. He watched
the blackened ashes turn grey and then white. He had
burned the note—but he would have to keep the
rendezvous.

'It's a Secrets Ball,' explained Mischa. 'Everyone is
masked. No one is allowed to unmask, and no one gives
a name or gives his right name. It's bound to be fun,
and, what is more, Gaby, not a soul would know if you
went, because—' he grinned '—it's a secret!'

'It wouldn't be a secret from Adam!' she told him
sharply. 'I'm sorry, Mischa, but after Adam's despicable
behaviour in the Prater, and his inexcusable and cow-
ardly attack on you, I wouldn't even consider doing
anything which would provoke him again. He's such a
madman when he's in a rage that there's no telling what
he could do!'

'To hell with Adam!' Mischa said so savagely that she
stared at him in surprise. 'I won't be thrashed in public
and dismissed—and, by God, certainly not by Dubrowski!' He leaned forward, his face quite pale. 'Come with
me to the Secrets Ball. Gaby, please? If you don't,

then Dubrowski has won. It will look as though he's frightened me off, and frightened you, too, into obeying his wishes.'

'I understand that, Mischa,' she said earnestly. 'But how can I get out of the house without his knowledge, so late in the evening—and in a ball-gown, for goodness' sake!'

'He won't be at home this evening after dinner,' Muscha said unexpectedly. 'He's going out, to the Vonnecks'. I know it for a fact.'

'To the Vonnecks'?' Gabriela turned aside so that he should not see her face. Christiane was not allowing the grass to grow under her feet. She meant to make sure of Adam. This aspect of Mischa's information so took hold of Gabriela's mind that it did not occur to her to ask him how he knew Adam's plans.

'You get ready,' Mischa urged her. 'But stay in your room quietly until Dubrowski has left the house. I'll have a *Fiaker* waiting round the corner. As soon as I see him leave, I'll bring it to the front of the house, and you can slip out.'

'Major Count Dubrowski, *Fräulein*,' the servant said.

Christiane, seated on a little sofa upholstered in yellow silk, rose and came to greet her guest, hands outstretched in welcome. 'Dear Adam! I was so worried you wouldn't get my note. I didn't dare to leave it at the house, and took it to the War Office. How kind of you to come—and so punctual.'

He bowed politely and raised her outstretched hands briefly to his lips. 'I am at your disposal, Baroness. But you could have left the note at the house.'

'No,' Christiane's grey eyes gleamed and her voice sank conspiratorially. 'No, Adam, I couldn't. You would not have received it. She would have intercepted it.'

'I don't think,' he said gently, 'that Gaby is in the habit of censoring my letters.'

'Adam, you don't know her. Believe me! Do come and sit down here, beside me.' She led him to the sofa and seated herself, looking up at him invitingly.

Adam sat down and surveyed her. She was a fine-looking woman with handsome, rather than pretty, features, a little flushed now. She wore a dark blue satin evening gown, tightly laced—perhaps the cause of her high colour—and cut very low to reveal a splendid bosom on which sparkled an expensive parure of diamonds. He wondered why she hadn't married. She was attractive, and worth a fortune.

'She's a great beauty, Adam,' Christiane said, her tone brittle. She seemed excited. 'I don't deny it. I can well understand why poor Max . . . well, that's all in the past now.' She covered his hand with hers confidingly. 'She hasn't a penny to her name, Adam,' she went on in a beguiling tone, 'and she's an adventuress of the most skilled kind. Sometimes I think that Max was spared. He would have found out, you know, in the end.'

'Found out what?' Adam asked evenly, but there was a touch of ice in his voice. He removed his hand from beneath hers, and the flush on her cheeks darkened. With her heightened colour and glittering eyes, she almost seemed to be in the throes of a fever. He wondered whether she was ill.

'She's so pretty, and has that way of turning those great blue eyes on people. Men like her, of course. She likes to be admired. Or, should I say, she has always liked to be surrounded by admirers?'

Adam expelled his breath in a faint hiss. 'Have a care, Christiane. It would be a mistake to say something now you might regret later.'

'My only regret,' she burst out vehemently, 'would be if I failed to speak out and you, Adam, fell into the same trap that snared poor Max!'

The sudden rise in her voice and an increased agitation in her manner triggered an alarm signal in Adam's brain. She really did look strange now, breathing heavily, and quite wild-eyed. He patted her arm, and beneath his touch she sank back and seemed to relax, stretching and arching like a cat, and smiling up at him.

'It's warm in here,' he said soothingly. 'Let me ring for some water.' He did not wait for a reply but got up and went to the bell-pull. When he sat down again, it was not on the sofa, but on a chair a little way from her.

They said nothing until the servant had brought the water and left again. Then Christiane stood and walked to the table where the tray with the water carafe had been set, and began to pour out a glass. 'Do you like me, Adam?' She gave him a little sidelong glance.

'I've always had the greatest respect for you, Christiane.'

Discontentment crossed her face briefly. 'I'm not asking for respect, Adam. I said *like*.'

'Of course I like you,' he said.

She came over to him, the glass of water in her hand, and standing over him, put her free hand on his shoulder. 'I've always liked you, Adam. You were such a tower of strength when Max married—her. You've never married. Why not?'

'No one will have me,' he said lightly.

'Don't joke. I know a dozen women whose hearts you've broken.' She took her hand from his shoulder and traced one finger lightly along the curve of his jaw. 'You're a very fascinating man,' she whispered. 'Everyone has gone out, you know. Wouldn't you like to come upstairs with me?' She ran the tip of her tongue across her full upper lip, and fixed him with her bright gaze.

'Christiane,' he said evenly. He reached up to take hold of her hand and remove it from his face. 'If I want a woman, I tell her so myself. I said that I respected you, and I should like to continue to do so. I think I did not hear your suggestion, and that, if you've nothing else to tell me, it's time I went.'

She drew a deep breath and swayed slightly—and then she dashed the contents of the glass into his face. Adam leapt up with an oath and thrust her aside, wiping the water from his skin. She fell back, crumpling like a puppet of which the strings have been suddenly released, and sprawled on to the floor in an expanse of blue satin. The clasp of the diamond necklace had become detached, and the rope of precious stones fell on the parquet.

'Adam, please . . .' she gasped, and caught at his boot, scrabbling to gain a hold and restrain him. He jerked his foot roughly away from her clutching fingers, and started back so quickly that he almost trod on the spilled diamonds.

'Let go of me, damn it!' He saw her mouth open, the hysterical scream forming, and stooped to grasp her chin. 'Stop that! One shriek, and I'll slap your face. I mean it, Christiane! I won't put up with melodrama.'

She gave a little moan, and huddled on the floor, looking up at him piteously. 'Don't go away, Adam. Please don't go away . . .' she pleaded.

'You're not well, my dear,' he said soothingly. 'I'm going to fetch your maid, or someone to help you. Tomorrow you'll feel better.'

He went quickly out of the room and ordered the footman in the hall to send the maid down. Then he let himself out of the house and ran quickly down the steps. He was a fool to have come—he should have known. He stood in the street, undecided, then muttered, 'Damn all so-called respectable women!' He flung up his arm to hail a passing *Fiaker*, and ordered, 'To the Golden Fleece!'

Gabriela put her fingers to the black velvet mask which covered the upper half of her face, and asked nervously, 'You're sure no one will recognise me, Mischa?'

'Why should they? Even if they do, it will still be a secret. I told you, this is a Secrets Ball.' He took her elbow and guided her up the steps of a large, well-kept mansion. The strains of the orchestra floated out from open windows, intermingled with chattering voices and the tinkle of glass. 'Everyone is masked, and no names are exchanged under any circumstances!' he went on cheerfully. 'I know for a fact that at least one highly respected judge's wife will be here, also her lover—and at least one Russian prince, if he's sober enough!' He smiled at her in his happy, ingenuous way.

'But whose house is this?' They were into the vestibule now, and a footman was taking her cloak.

'It belongs to a Czech nobleman, well known for his parties.' Mischa was having to raise his voice, because they had entered the ballroom.

Her eyes were dazzled by a blaze of light and a kaleidoscope of colour. She had not expected to see so many people, but the room was full, leaving little space to dance. One wall was lined with mirrors, doubling the numbers of the assembly in their reflection, so that there seemed to be an endless throng of people. The women were garbed like parakeets in mauves, emeralds and indigos, all the hues of the new chemical dyes, as though they were jostling, laughing and chattering beneath the canopy of some Amazonian jungle.

Someone, a perfect stranger, was welcoming them. Was this the Czech aristocrat? And how many of these people *were* strangers, and how many familiar faces would be revealed if the masks were torn away? It was impossible to tell. Mischa was continuing to talk in her ear, but she was unable to catch more than a third of what he was saying. He had steered her to a corner, beneath a painting, and was trying to tell her something, pointing at the same time across the room. He was saying he was leaving her for a moment, and would be back shortly. She nodded vigorously to show she understood, and he smiled and disappeared into the crush.

Gabriela stood alone for a few moments, hoping he would not be long. All the guests seemed to be enjoying themselves tremendously. Some of the women were laughing immoderately and teasing their escorts with robust banter. She suspected them of being actresses from one or more of the Vienna theatres. It certainly seemed a very mixed company, and slightly rakish. The air was stiflingly hot and the noise well nigh unbearable. Perspiration was breaking out on her body, and she put a hand to the black mask and fiddled with it. It was uncomfortable, and stuck to her damp skin.

'You're alone, dear lady?' a pleasant, cultured voice asked by her ear.

She started. A slim young man stood by her, who bowed, and added courteously, 'Don't be alarmed. I'm sorry I startled you.' He smiled. 'No names here—so I can't introduce myself, only ask if you would do me the honour of being my partner.' He gestured towards the open area of the room, where dancers were slowly taking their places.

'I'm afraid I'm waiting . . .' she began.

But he interrupted her. 'Oh, he'll be a little while. I think he's marooned on the other side of the room.' He held out his hand. 'Come . . .'

He seemed quite young. Gabriela peered up into his face and wondered if, were the mask removed, this was one of the faces she would recognise. She had an odd feeling that she ought to know him, yet she could not say the voice was familiar. Rather, it was the eyes visible through the mask, a very bright gaze, just a little disturbing. He had a high forehead, and wavy dark hair. The chin and mouth were sensitive, but weak, and from time to time a muscle at the corner of his mouth twitched slightly. She wondered if he were nervous, though his assured manner belied this. There was a kind of suppressed energy about this man, which communicated itself to her and made her feel uneasy.

The orchestra had struck up a waltz by the popular master, Herr Strauss. Her partner was a very good dancer, who must have been excellently taught. He held her lightly but firmly, and guided her dextrously between the many other swirling couples. Gabriela loved to dance and, despite her reservations, felt the lilting music catch her up and bear her away on its seductive rhythm.

'You're enjoying yourself, Countess?' her partner asked, smiling down at her.

She gave a gasp, and almost missed a step. 'You know who I am!'

'Ah, but don't take fright!' he said immediately. 'And don't be angry if I make a confession to you. I recognised Brenner, and I knew he meant to bring you. Besides, I've seen you before.'

'Where?' she demanded bluntly. This was a Secrets Ball. Mischa had promised that no identities would be revealed. Where was he? She glanced quickly round her, but a sea of swirling figures made it impossible to look for any person in particular.

'I was driving in the Prater the other day, along the Hauptallee, and I passed you driving with Brenner. I have a gig with a grey mare. Perhaps you didn't notice it.'

'Yes, I did notice . . .' Gabriela said slowly.

The music had finished, but her new acquaintance was not disposed to leave her.

'It's very warm in here,' he said. 'Why don't you come out on to the terrace for a moment?' Seeing her hesitate, he added, 'Just for a breath of fresh air, and then I'll tell someone to hunt out Brenner for you.'

As she allowed him to lead her to the terrace, something about his last sentence struck her. It was the way he had said, 'I'll tell someone . . .' He was used to giving orders. She noticed, too, that they were not quite alone on the terrace. A burly man with a pointed black beard had followed and stood a little way away by the french doors through which they had come, tactfully out of earshot, but not out of sight. She remembered now that when her new companion had first approached her to ask her to dance, this same man had been near by. He wore evening dress, but, unlike the others, had no mask and something about him suggested that he was not a guest. He spoke to no one and stood watching the throng in a detached and professional manner. It occurred to Gabriela that he was some kind of superior personal servant—a bodyguard, even. He was certainly built for it. This thought was confirmed when her partner made a signal to him which was immediately understood, for the fellow stepped back into the room and reappeared almost at once, followed by a footman carrying a silver tray with glasses of champagne.

Her companion handed a glass to her, and took one for himself. The burly man then ushered the footman away and resumed his post by the french doors. She wondered whether her partner was possibly the owner of the house, the Czech nobleman, or even the Russian prince. She had the most extraordinary sensation of participating in some game or pre-arranged play in which all the players knew their parts and what was going to happen next, but she alone did not, and moved blindly. Mischa's continued absence, hitherto a nuisance, now began to assume an almost frightening aspect.

Raising his glass in a salute to her, the young man said gravely, 'You are alarmed, and, I expect, angry. But I'll tell you everything. You see, I want to be frank, and truly, there's nothing to fear. After I saw you with Brenner, I made some enquiries about you.'

'Really?' Gabriela answered coldly, 'And what did you find out?'

'Well, for one thing, you're Hungarian. *Tudok magyarul*,' he added unexpectedly. 'I speak Hungarian. I'm a great lover of your country and have many good Hungarian friends.'

She turned the words over in her mind, sipping the champagne to gain time. Far from reassuring her, this new information made her more uneasy. Everything seemed to fit together too well. Coincidences happen in life—but not in the well-ordered way they seemed to be occurring now. The bubbles tickled her nose, and she was obliged to put the glass down.

'Then you will also know,' she said carefully, 'that I was widowed earlier this year.'

'Yes, I'm very sorry.' He sounded as though he meant it.

Gabriela looked up at him. 'You don't find it odd that I should be in a company like this, so soon after—after my loss?'

'If you were not,' the young man said, 'I should not be able to talk to you now, and the loss would be mine.' Before she had time to respond to this accomplished piece of flattery, he added more briskly, 'The laws of Society are tedious and misleading. Black weeds don't always mean a broken heart, nor silk dresses a happy one. Besides, I do know what loneliness is, Countess. And I know that, although surrounding oneself with people may be a poor substitute, sometimes it is the only one at our disposal.'

'That's true,' she said cautiously, 'But strange observations from one so young—too young to be consoling lonely widows, I think?'

She had intended to put him gently in his place, but his assurance was proof against reproaches.

'But permitted to offer consolation to a wayward widow, perhaps?' he countered, 'without it being misunderstood?'

'You are impudent!' Gabriela told him sharply.

He dismissed this with a wave of his hand and a charming smile. 'Faint heart never won fair lady. Come, let me send for some more champagne.'

'I'd prefer you to send for Herr Brenner!' she said quietly but firmly. This conversation had gone far enough. He held an unfair advantage in knowing her identity, but had no intention of relinquishing it by confessing his own. She did not like that. For all his unforced charm, she felt that she was being manipulated by her companion; gradually eased, with considerable skill, into a situation from which she would find it hard to escape. 'Straight away, please!' she said decisively.

He seemed a little surprised at her authoritative tone, as if he were unused to being addressed in such a way. But after the barest hesitation, he glanced towards the burly man, and ordered, 'Fetch Brenner!' The servant disappeared immediately into the crowded ballroom.

'I think,' Gabriela said, 'I should wait inside.' It was clear to her now that the women attending this ball belonged to the *demi-monde*, that shadowy world of easy morals and expensive corruption, which lived out its days and nights in a parallel to polite society, complementing it, but never crossing its path. Her very presence here was a signal to this young man that he might speak as he wished.

'No, please stay!' he said. Polite as it was, he was not asking her to stay, but ordering her to do so. She turned her back and walked resolutely towards the french doors, and he started after her and caught at her arm. Gabriela jerked furiously to free herself, there was a brief scuffle, and he stepped on the hem of her ball-gown of cream chiffon. The frail material gave way and a jagged rent appeared at the stitching of the waist.

Her companion was overcome with profuse apologies. 'Forgive me! So clumsy . . .'

'It's all right!' Gabriela snapped, really angry now, and finding him less charming by the second. 'I'll go and see if one of the maids can find a pin.'

'I have a pin!' He put his hand to his starched shirt front, and withdrew a small gold pin with a diamond head. 'Allow me . . .'

'You can't use that!' she protested. 'It's very valuable.'

'It has no value to me, except to repair the damage I've caused,' he told her with easy gallantry. He pinned the two sides of torn material deftly together before she could prevent his taking this liberty.

'Where shall I return it?' Gabriela asked unwillingly. It was the very worst of developments.

He hesitated. 'You will keep it,' he said in a firm voice which it was difficult to refuse; almost an order again. 'You will keep it as a token of my esteem. If I wish to—borrow it back again, I'll send a message, and you can bring it . . .' He took her hand and kissed her fingers lightly, saying, in the Hungarian manner, '*Kezét csokolom!*' Then he released her and walked quickly back into the ballroom. He passed Brenner in the doorway, but made him not the slightest acknowledgement.

'Who *is* that?' she demanded furiously. 'You know who it is, Mischa! You told him who I was. You had no business to do that!'

'Don't be offended, Gaby,' Mischa coaxed her. 'I wouldn't give your name to just anyone. He's a very pleasant and generous young man of the most distinguished family. But I can't tell you his name, not without his permission. You see, if his family knew he was here, they wouldn't like it. He's obliged to be discreet.'

'So am I, Mischa, or perhaps you've forgotten that!' she retaliated sharply. 'You told me this was a Secrets Ball. Obviously the secrets are kept on one side only! I'd be grateful if you'd take me home.'

'All right, all right,' he agreed. 'I'll order them to call a cab.' His dark eyes fell on the diamond pin. 'You tore your dress?' He looked at her curiously.

She flushed. 'Your secretive friend trod on the hem. The pin is his. He had the effrontery to tell me to keep it.'

'Then I should keep it,' Mischa told her calmly. 'No point in hurting his feelings.'

'I can't possibly!' she exploded angrily. 'It's a very expensive item of jewellery!'

'He's a very wealthy man,' Mischa said casually. 'He won't miss it.'

'That's not the point. A lady never accepts jewellery! Besides, he said that if he wished to "borrow it back", he'd send for it. Send for *me* was what he was implying! Who is he, Mischa?'

'Don't get so agitated, Gaby. You misunderstood him. Come along, I'll send for that cab. But don't lose that pin, my dear. It wouldn't do if anyone else picked it up.'

Although Mischa did his best to coax her into a good humour on the way back to the Clemenz mansion, Gabriela was not disposed, for once, to listen to him. She was uneasy about what had happened that evening, and she was particularly annoyed with Mischa for his part in it. He had let her down, and his obstinate refusal to tell her the identity of her strange acquaintance fuelled her resentment. At the same time, she knew it was largely her own fault. She had allowed him to persuade her to attend the ball against all her better judgment. It had been a mistake, and the diamond pin signified, worryingly, that she had not heard the last of the mysterious stranger.

She parted from Mischa with unusual coldness, which seemed to upset him very much.

'You haven't forgotten that we arranged to go again to the Prater tomorrow?' he pleaded earnestly. 'To the fairground.'

'I don't know, Mischa,' she told him unkindly. 'Perhaps you have some other mystery waiting for me there!'

'I haven't, I swear! Look, you're angry with me. It's my fault, and I'm sorry.' He seemed truly contrite. 'Come to the fairground tomorrow. It will cheer you up.'

'Very well. But I don't want to meet any masked strangers.'

The old doorkeeper, obliged to wait up for her, was grumpy and disapproving as he let her in. But in the family's first-floor apartments someone else was still up and about. Lamplight gleamed dully through the half-open drawing-room door, and the aroma of cigarette smoke drifted out and filled her nostrils. Adam was in there, returned from the Vonnecks. Was he waiting up for her? Gabriela really had no wish to see him. For one thing, she was beginning to wonder if he hadn't been right about Mischa. But he must have heard her come in. She pushed open the drawing-room door and entered.

Adam lay on his back in his shirtsleeves, sprawled out along a chaise-longue, his boots resting on the expensive brocade. He was smoking, blowing the blue haze up into the air and watching it float to meet the ceiling. Somehow the sight of him was unexpectedly reassuring. At least there was no mystery about Adam. He turned his head slightly to look at her.

'Good evening, my pretty *puszta* rose. Come in, why don't you?' His voice was faintly mocking, but not aggressively so. It was as if he mocked himself, rather than her.

Gabriela went in and across to the chaise-longue. He moved his feet an inch or two, and she sat down on the far end and surveyed him appraisingly. He hadn't got into this state at the Vonnecks; he must have gone on elsewhere.

'I won't ask you where you've been,' he said, jabbing the index and middle fingers of his right hand, between which the stub of cigarette smouldered, towards her, 'because you've been with that two-faced little pimp. Good luck to you—and bad luck to him.'

'And you've been to the Golden Fleece,' she returned evenly.

'That's right,' He patted the narrow space on the chaise-longue beside his hip. 'Come and sit here.'

'I'm already on the same seat.'

'Too far away. Come on, I don't bite.'

Gabriela, with some misgivings, got up and went to perch, fairly insecurely, beside him on the spot he had indicated. 'You're drunk!'

'Just very slightly, my angel. I've been sitting in the Golden Fleece, listening to those rascally gipsies murder Polish tunes, and drinking some vile Russian vodka. Polish vodka . . . She should lay in Polish vodka. I told Jetta so, old hag.' He drew on the cigarette and glanced up at Gabriela. 'I wasn't tumbling any of the girls there, if that's what you're thinking.' He saw the look of disapproval on her face, and added insolently, 'Come along, now—it isn't *my* behaviour which is the gossip of Vienna.'

'I'm not going to be criticised by you,' Gabriela said coldly. 'And if you are going to talk to me in that way, I shall leave.'

He knew she meant it. 'Stay, pussy-cat, stay where you are.' He moved his free hand and laid it lightly on her thigh to restrain her. 'Don't scuttle off.'

A shiver ran through her at that gentle, insistent pressure. 'I ought to go,' she muttered awkwardly.

'Beware of the wolf, Grandma said. Especially if he says he has no evil intentions! I have no evil intentions, Countess.' He handed her the smouldering stub of cigarette. 'Put that out for me? I can't reach the ashtray.'

Gabriela took it with a sigh and leaned over to a near-by table to stub it out distastefully in a porcelain dish. 'Why do you go to that place, Adam? You didn't want a woman, the gipsies play badly, and you don't like the brand of vodka. Why go?'

He patted her thigh. 'To escape, my dear, and because I am, like you, an exile in Vienna. An oddity. They don't care for us Poles here, you know. Don't trust us. Think we're always plotting something. Now, at the

Golden Fleece, everyone is an oddity in his or her way, and the air is so damn thick with plotting that you can't see across the room!'

He seemed quite relaxed, but she sensed he was slightly depressed, possibly maudlin, but he was not nearly as drunk as she had at first thought. A strange sense of possessiveness came over her as she looked at his familiar, muscular, shirtsleeved figure, and a kind of sadness. He looked like some kind of recumbent animal, a wild animal, not a domestic one, smiling amiably at her now, but not to be taken for granted. She did not want Christiane to have him, but she was powerless to prevent it. She even felt a momentary spasm of jealousy towards Jetta's bawds.

'What sort of girls are they?' she asked. 'Where do they come from?'

'Honest enough, and hard-working in their way. It's a pretty wretched life. It's not their fault. They come from all over the place. Some are native Viennese, born to the business, daughters and grand-daughters of whores.' His voice was precise and sober now. 'Some are country girls who have committed a little indiscretion, alas, and been obliged to leave their villages in disgrace.' A gleam entered his eye. 'At least one is Hungarian.'

'Are any of them Polish?' she retaliated.

'No!' His expression changed, the good humour wiped from his face, and his whole frame stiffened. 'Polish girls don't . . .' He broke off and relaxed again. 'I wouldn't go in that case.' He eyed her. 'Your friend Brenner goes there. They know him well.'

'What if he does?' she said lightly. She knew that Adam wasn't joking or lying, but somehow she found it hard to associate Mischa, who was so fastidious, with such a sordid scene.

'But then,' Adam went on, 'I found *you* there, didn't I? Or just outside, hiding in the rain.' Gabriela flushed and looked away. He had never mentioned that episode since their conversation the morning after it. But she could hardly have expected him to have forgotten it. 'A kitten,' he said lazily, speaking in the slightly slurred manner of a drunk. 'A half-drowned, miserable little kitten, with wet fur and eyes like saucers. So I put it in my pocket and took it home. Was it grateful? Not a bit of it. It scratched me.'

'What are you talking about?' she demanded uneasily. 'I didn't scratch you.'

'Yes, you did. Not with your sharp little claws—with your sharp little tongue!'

'I want to go now, Adam!' she said quickly, trying to rise, but he caught her wrist and forced her to sit down again.

'Stay and talk to me.' His voice had an obstinate, sullen note—that was the vodka taking over.

'I don't want to stay and talk to you, Adam!' She tugged against the grip he had on her wrist. 'Let go of me. It's late. I want to go to bed.'

'So do I . . .' Adam said softly.

Her heart gave an odd little lurch and seemed to miss a beat. He was watching her face. The look in his eyes was one that she recognised very well. There was a moment when men all had that look; she had seen it even in Max's eyes for a fleeting second or two, when they had made love—a desire to master, and to take . . .

Gabriela jumped to her feet. 'As for you, you've drunk too much vodka and it's very late. You need to sleep it off, Adam.' She walked resolutely to the door.

He sat up, swinging his long legs to the floor. 'You're right, I suppose,' he said, quite agreeably, to her relief. He ambled idly to a chair, picked up the blue jacket thrown across it, and slung it over his shoulder. 'After you, Countess.' He swept his hand towards the staircase.

She climbed the stairs uneasily, knowing he was just behind her. They reached his room first. She turned, intending to say 'goodnight', but it was her undoing. He took a quick step forward, and putting his arms one on either side of her to prevent her escape, trapped her against the door.

'Why don't you come in?' he whispered throatily. 'You came in the other morning. Come now.'

'Let me pass, Adam, please . . .' she faltered.

'Don't be afraid.' He stopped and pressed his mouth against the lobe of her ear. 'I'm not that damn drunk. I'm not going to maul you about. I want to make love to you. You're lonely—I'm lonely. Come and spend what's left of this night with me. Don't you want to?

Gabriela closed her eyes. 'I can't . . .' she whispered. His warm breath brushed her bare neck, and the touch of his lips on her ear caused her senses to stir urgently.

'I said, don't you *want* to?' He took her face in his hands and tipped it up gently towards his.

She gave a little moan as she felt his lips close upon hers and his powerful body push up against her. 'No, Adam, I can't, and I mean I can't!'

'Not with me?' he asked quietly.

'Not with anyone—and especially not with *you*!'

'Why not?' Rejected, a hard note born of thwarted sexual desire was entering his voice, a warning of approaching aggression. 'What do you want?' he asked insolently. 'An archduke?'

Her eyes opened, staring at him wildly. It was as if a hundred bells suddenly sounded in her head. A terrible realisation flooded over her, and at last she knew the secret Brenner had so prudently kept, and the path down which he had been leading her so carefully from the beginning. For a moment everything went hazy, and when it cleared, her eyes focused on Adam's face, creased with concern. He was shaking her shoulders, calling back her attention from the abyss into which it had momentarily plunged.

'Gabriela? What the hell is the matter? What's wrong?'

'Adam?' She gripped his arm. 'Adam, listen to me.

You must listen to me, please! You—you remember when Mischa took me driving, in the Prater? Before we met you, we passed a gig with a young man driving. I didn't see his face well, but we passed him twice, and it seemed so strange—as though . . . Mischa wanted that man to see me.' She paused, and looked urgently up at Adam to see if he was listening.

'Go on,' he ordered quietly.

'Tonight I met that young man again. We were at a masked ball. No names and everyone masked, all nonsense really—and I know I shouldn't have gone . . . But, Adam, I know now why Mischa took me driving and why he wanted so much to take me to that ball tonight. It was to meet that man!' Her voice sank to a barely audible whisper. 'And that man is the Archduke Alexander, Adam, one of the wealthiest men in the Empire—and more than a little crazy!'

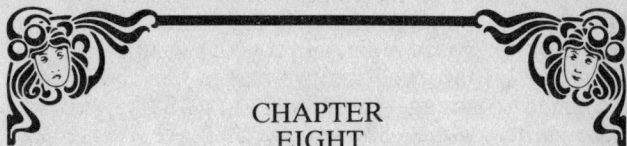

CHAPTER
EIGHT

THE TOTAL stillness in the corridor lasted only a little while, but seemed an eternity. Then Adam narrowed his eyes and said softly, 'So that's it. Not the crown jewels, by heaven, but something worth almost as much. Control over a dissolute young rake and his vast fortune. I didn't think that little rat Brenner had so much imagination—or boldness!' Completely sober now, he turned his gaze back to Gabriela, standing white-faced before him, and something in those deep-set eyes unmistakably spelled danger. 'Well, my dear, what are you going to do?' he asked her calmly.

'Adam?' She stared at him incredulously. 'Surely you can't imagine I would agree? Have you heard the stories whispered about Alexander?'

'Only whispered,' Adam said with a thin smile. 'He's one of the richest young men in Austria-Hungary, and a close friend of the Crown Prince Rudolf. No scandal would ever be allowed to touch his name openly. Brenner is clever—cleverer than I thought. I made a mistake. I assumed him to have much more modest aims, and I was looking in the wrong places.' He scowled thoughtfully. 'Well, my dear, you have made a notable capture.' The same thin smile touched his face. 'I wish you well.'

In those last few words, he offered the greatest insult of all. Adam, who had so pointedly refused to wish her joy on her marriage, now offered her his ironic congratulations! Gabriela drew a deep breath.

'Mischa is everything you ever said he was, Adam; I see that now. But he is much mistaken if he imagines I shall go along with such a despicable plan—and if you believe it, you are no better than he is!'

Adam hunched his broad shoulders slightly and seemed unperturbed, though he looked at her a little oddly. 'Perhaps friend Brenner thinks you'll accept, once you've thought it over. Alexander's behaviour may sometimes be a little erratic. You phrased it too strongly, my dear, he isn't crazy—not yet, anyway. But he is heir to one of the biggest fortunes in Europe. Besides, most women find him charming, and his reputation for prowess in the bedroom is formidable, I can tell you. As for the stories about him you mention, most women seem to find they add a *frisson* of excitement to an affair with him. Every lady I've heard mention him has said she's found him delightful and quite irresistible. Why should you be different? Especially, Gabriella, given your own circumstances. Here you are, without a penny of your own, and with Alexander at your feet . . . Why on earth should Brenner think you would refuse? You should be delighted. No, play your cards right, my dear Gabriela, and you and he will live in comfort and independence for years.'

The crack of the blow echoed through the silent house. Slowly Adam put his hand to his cheek, scored by four distinct red fingermarks where Gabriela's palm had struck him.

'Never do that again, kitten,' he said very softly. 'I don't take that from any woman—not from any of Jetta's bawds, and not from you.'

'And I am not taking any more of your insults, Major!' she riposted, struggling for control of her emotions. 'How dare you even suggest I would agree to such a sordid business? I'd rather go out and earn my living trimming bonnets for twelve hours a day like some little milliner! So don't be in any more doubt about that. And if Mischa is in any doubt, he'll learn otherwise tomorrow. He's arranged to take me to the Prater, to the fairground. There I shall tell him exactly what I think of him and of his miserable little plot!'

Adam shook his head. 'Far better to let me tackle it,' he argued. 'I've dealt with Brenner before, and . . .'

'I shan't let the wretch talk me round to his way of thinking!' Gabriela interrupted.

'I believe you, my dear,' Adam said gently, 'but you'll find it won't be so easy to extricate yourself from this affair. It isn't just a question of Brenner's hopes. Alexander has hopes, too, and doesn't like to be disappointed. If Brenner fails, he is in an extraordinarily difficult situation. The full brunt of Alexander's fury will fall on him, and people like him, who live on their wits on the fringe of decent society, can't afford powerful and vindictive enemies. He won't just let you go, Gabriela. He'll use every trick he knows to get you to agree, and our young friend Brenner is full of tricks.'

'Adam, listen to me,' She put her hand on his arm. 'I *have* to tell him myself. If you do it, he'll believe it's simply a case of you having found out and deciding yourself to interfere. He'll still try and talk to me, whatever you say or do. Besides which, if you talk to him, it will end in violence, which I don't want. Don't tell me you won't hit him, Adam, because you will.'

'Probably,' Adam said frankly. 'The little parasite turns my stomach; he always did.'

'As for Alexander's displeasure,' Gabriela continued fervently, 'Brenner has only himself to blame. Don't give him the excuse of being able to say that Major Dubrowski is the obstacle. That would only turn Alexander's wrath on you.'

'I'm not so attached to my army career,' Adam told her quietly, 'that I would bargain my family honour for it.'

'It isn't a question of your honour, Adam, it's a question of mine—and we Hungarians also feel very strongly about that!' Gabriela told him in equally as quiet a tone, but with such conviction that he acquiesced, giving a little nod.

Nevertheless, he looked unhappy, and rubbed a hand over his chin. 'All right. We'll try your way first, and if it doesn't have the desired effect, *I'll* deal with him.' He took hold of the hand she had on his arm, and added earnestly, 'A word of advice, which you would do well to follow. You say he's taking you to the fairground. Good. It's a busy place, full of people. Stay there. Don't go anywhere else with him. The more people around you, the better.'

A cold finger laid itself on Gabriela's heart. 'You think I'm in danger, Adam, don't you?' She shook her head. 'But if I refuse to agree with Brenner, there's nothing he can do. I'm a Clemenz, if only by marriage. My father-in-law had a very distinguished career before he retired. Even Alexander wouldn't want a quarrel with the Clemenz family and must realise he can't force his attentions on me—and I'm certainly not afraid of Mischa Brenner!'

Adam smiled. 'Dear Gabriela—I don't believe you're afraid of anyone! But too much courage can turn to rashness, and sometimes it's wise to have a little fear. Above all, remember that *Brenner* is afraid—and desperate men are capable of almost anything.' He hesitated and looked down, away from her gaze. 'I . . . didn't really think you would be a party to such a thing, but I had to be sure. You do understand?'

'I understand, Adam, that you doubted me,' she told him.

He flushed, but made no answer. Watched by him, she walked steadily down the corridor to her own room, and went in. Arlette was dozing in a chair, waiting up to undress her mistress on her return. She sat up with a start.

'*Mon Dieu*, madame, you're earlier than I expected!'

'Unhook me!' Gabriela ordered sharply.

As Arlette's fingers dealt with the hooks of the bodice, Gabriela stared frowning and unseeingly ahead of her, trying to marshal her thoughts and bring some order to

events which had moved with an alarming rapidity.
Adam was worried. That surprised her. Anger and
scorn she had expected, but not anxiety. As for Brenner
. . . A cold anger rose up inside her. She had not
thought anyone could behave so despicably. She had
given him her friendship, trusted him, defended him to
Adam—and the result was a particularly nasty betrayal.
If she had discovered that Brenner had wanted her for
himself, his behaviour, though devious, would at least
have been understandable. But to offer her to someone
else was a vile business which made her feel sullied and
humiliated. Tomorrow he would find out exactly how
much she despised him.

Arlette exclaimed 'Ouch!', and put her thumb to her
mouth. 'There is a pin in your gown, madame. You
have torn it?'

'Give me that pin!' Gabriela quickly snatched it from
the maid. She had forgotten Alexander's 'token of
esteem'. Or first payment, she thought in a burst of
anger, and with an exclamation of disgust, she hurled
the little trinket away from her. It fell to the ground a
few yards away by the dressing-table, and lay there with
the diamond head glowing like white fire in the dim
light. She looked at it with loathing, and then turned
her head away from it scornfully.

Arlette had been watching her young mistress closely
all this time. Her pale little eyes were suspicious and
calculating at the same time. She ran her tongue over
her lips and picked up the chiffon gown. As she carried
it across the room to the wardrobe, she contrived to
let the skirt drag on the floor, and stooped by the
dressing-table to gather up the trailing flounces. When
she passed on, the pin had vanished, but her mistress,
preoccupied with her coming encounter with Brenner,
did not notice.

The following morning dawned bright and sunny. Gabriela, who had lain awake till the early hours, turning the

latest intrigues over in her mind, fell asleep at last as the sun came up and was still slumbering soundly when Adam left for the War Office.

He chose to walk there through the early morning traffic, so sunk in thought that only a warning shout roused him in time to prevent his stepping out in front of a rumbling brewer's dray. He stood back to allow it to pass, and the sight of the barrels and the smell of the beer reminded him of the Golden Fleece, where he had been the previous evening after leaving the Vonnecks. He scowled. He had gone there to put Christiane—and other matters—out of his mind. He might have been half tempted to take Katy to bed, had she been around. But she had been nowhere to be seen, and assuming her to be occupied with another customer, he had sat in a corner of the downstairs *Weinstube*, listening with increasing dislike to the gipsies until he paid the exhorbitant bill for the vodka he had consumed, and made his way home. This morning he felt out of sorts, slightly muzzy (that was the after-effect of the vodka), and dissatisfied with events in every respect.

His mood did not improve at his office. He disliked this inactive desk job in any case, and sat in front of a blank sheet of paper on which he was supposed to be writing a report he doubted anyone would read, and glowered at the expanse of virgin paper until he became aware that Jurawicz was standing over him and repeating his name loudly.

'Sorry to disturb you, sir, but an Inspector Gruber of the Police has sent a message asking you please to go over and see him.'

Adam looked up sharply and pulled out his watch. It was a little after ten—what on earth did Gruber want so early? A feeling of unease took hold of him as he left the War Office.

Inspector Karl-Heinz Gruber was a small, stocky man with a round head, shrewd, humorous eyes and an untidy walrus moustache, the corner of which he had a habit of chewing when undecided about something. He took snuff, as the state of his waistcoat and jacket lapels bore generous witness. Otherwise he had no vices and few hobbies. He had been twenty-five years a policeman, and maintained that the life allowed a man no time for either of these indulgences if he did his job properly. Gruber liked to think he did his job properly. He spent long hours in his office, always visited the scene of the crime, and when at home, read books related to his profession. He was unmarried, and lived in domestic harmony with an elder sister and a bevy of cats, each of which bore the name of a criminal in a case which he had solved. Gruber's humour was occasionally of the black kind.

'Come in, Major, come in,' he invited affably. 'Sorry to bring you out so early. I hope it wasn't inconvenient.'

'No.' Adam answered, sinking into a chair. 'As a matter of fact, I was considering coming to see you. There has been a development in the matter I discussed with you.'

Gruber raised his eyebrows and chewed absently at his moustache for a moment. 'All right, Major,' he said briskly, 'let's have your news first.'

He sat back and eyed his companion thoughtfully, and not without curiosity. Normally he had very little to do with army officers. They were a breed apart. If they ever committed what he, Gruber, a simple policeman, called crimes, the army called them misdemeanours or breaches of discipline, and smothered all the details in their internal courts martial. The army looked after its own and, so long as it did, that suited Gruber. He had enough work. He had first met this Uhlan a little while ago when a young aristocrat, Count Maximilian Clemenz, had been killed in a street incident. The officer had forced his way into Gruber's room, raising merry hell and apparently desirous of sending a troop of Polish cavalry clattering through the streets of Vienna in search of his cousin's attacker.

Yet, despite all the unlikely circumstances, Gruber and the Uhlan had conceived a mutual respect and a kind of liking for one another. Then, recently, the Uhlan—Major Count Dubrowski—had come to see Gruber again, with a story so slight in itself, yet so curious, that after ruminating on it for twenty-four hours, and chewing one side of his moustache so thoroughly that the resulting facial embellishment had become quite lop-sided, he had reported the matter, in triplicate, to another department. As a result, he had received instructions to watch the Golden Fleece. Gruber had done so, day and night. He knew, for example, from the observer's report, the exact time Dubrowski had arrived at the brothel the previous evening, and the time he had left. He listened with interest to what the officer had to tell him now.

'Ha—hum,' he said, when Adam had briefly indicated the identity of Gabriela's admirer and the circumstances in which she had discovered it. 'This could be very tricky, Major. Whatever happens, "they" will want his name kept out of it.'

'And I want my cousin's widow kept out of it,' Adam snapped.

Gruber got to his feet and walked to his dusty window. He put his hands behind his back and rocked on his heels for a moment as he stared out into the street. 'I'll have to rely on you to keep an eye on the lady, Major. I shall be obliged to concentrate my efforts on keeping the—ah—distinguished young gentleman's name clear. The lady is at home now, I take it?'

'As a matter of fact,' Adam admitted, 'she's supposed to meet Brenner today. I tried to dissuade her, but she's very determined. Why?' He looked up sharply.

'Meeting young Brenner, eh? No fit company for a respectable woman, if you'll permit me to say so.' Gruber walked back to his desk, ignoring the colour that spread over Adam's features, and opening a drawer, took out an envelope. He opened it, and shook its contents out on the desk top. 'Recognise this, Major?'

A gold medallion and chain lay gleaming dully up at them.

Adam stretched out his hand slowly and picked it up. 'I gave this to Katy,' he said harshly. 'And she wouldn't part with it willingly. What the devil is going on, Gruber? Why did you ask me to come here?'

'You told me about this girl, Katy, before,' Gruber replied calmly. 'I've tried to keep an eye on her. But the fact is that she seems to have vanished. You, ah, were at the Golden Fleece last night, Major. You didn't see her, I suppose?'

Adam shook his head.

'The proprietress, "Aunt Jetta" as she is called by everyone, says the girl went missing early in the evening,' Gruber said. 'Jetta was very annoyed about it. Otherwise she claims to know nothing.'

'You surprise me,' Adam muttered sarcastically. 'Devil take it, I should have *asked* for Katy last night. Some harm's come to her, I know it! Idiot that I am, why didn't I ask where she was?'

'She may just have run off for some reason of her own,' Gruber pointed out.

'No!' Adam exclaimed forcibly, 'Not without coming to me first!'

'We are perplexed,' Gruber said delicately, 'because she didn't go out of the front door—or my man would have seen her. It came to light this morning when I made an excuse to call at the place, just to see what was going on there. I said there had been complaints that some of the girls were light-fingered—watches and wallets and so on, missed by customers. Old Jetta set up a hullabaloo of indignation at the idea. She fetched all the girls in, and they all denied it. That was when I noticed that the little red-haired one wasn't there. Jetta brought out the story of her having disappeared, and although the other girls obviously knew more than they were saying, they're all so frightened of "Aunt Jetta" that there was nothing to be got out of them. I had a word with the potman, Friedl, who is a thoroughly unpleasant character, employed as much to keep the girls in order as to carry beer bottles. I had him turn out his pockets—still using the pickpocketing story—and he had this gold chain on him. As soon as it appeared, one of the girls squeaked, "That's Katy's!" and then shut up like a clam and said she'd made a mistake. Friedl said it had belonged to his old mother.' Gruber snorted.

Adam sank his head into his hands. 'Poor Katy is probably floating down the Danube,' he said morosely. 'And it's my fault.'

'In the absence of a corpse,' Gruber said sentently, 'we don't presume a murder, not straight away, at least. Give it a day or two. She may turn up, in he river or elsewhere. In the meantime, we'll carry on watching the Golden Fleece, even though there's obviously a way in and out of it we don't know of, probably through the cellars. Those are old houses. It's a pity, when they cleared the rest for the new Ringstrasse, that they didn't make a proper job of it and pull those down. Nests of petty crime, they are, and worse. The Golden Fleece has a bad name, and I can tell you that people besides us would be interested to know just what goes on in that haunt of sin. "Aunt Jetta" has run foul of the law on several occasions. To see her now, you'd never believe it, but during the troubles of 1848 she was a handsome female and well known in revolutionary circles. She betrayed more than one good friend when the tide turned against the liberals! A very devious and unscrupulous woman. Where there's profit to be made by fair means or foul, there'll you'll find old Jetta. I could charge her now with attempted bribery of a police officer. She sent me a crate of champagne not so long back.' Gruber gave another snort of disgust. 'As if *I* drink the stuff! But I think we'll wait and see. What do you think?' He took a small flat tin from his waistcoat pocket and opened it with loving respect. 'Take snuff, do you, Major?'

'Gabriela!' Adam muttered, as though he had not heard. He stared at Gruber. 'What? I think, damn it, that someone else besides poor Katy is in very real danger—and I have no time to sit about taking snuff and waiting for things to happen! I must stop Gabriela going to meet Brenner!'

He leapt up, and leaving the startled Gruber staring after him, snuff-box in hand, dashed out of the police station.

'She's left, sir,' Arlette said, gaping at him, her pale eyes protruding in curiosity. 'Twenty minutes ago.'

'But it's barely mid-day!' Adam exclaimed in disbelief.

'Yes, sir, but she was going to have some luncheon with a friend, that's what she said, Major.' Arlette cast a quick, appraising glance at him. 'With Herr Brenner, she meant, sir, and afterwards they were going to the fairground, out at the Prater.'

'Damn it—I thought they were going straight to the Prater!' he muttered. 'I can't look in every confounded restaurant in Vienna.'

'I don't know, sir, or I'd tell you,' said Arlette regretfully. Inability to supply this information reduced the amount of the tip he was likely to give her. 'Very probably one of the restaurants out at the Prater,' she suggested, to show she was willing to help.

Adam sighed and gave the girl ten florins. The fairground of the Prater covered a large area and was crowded with people from early afternoon onward. The same was true of the many restaurants and cafés dotted all over it. There was little he could do but wait impatiently until the girl returned.

Going into the drawing-room, Adam flung himself on the chaise-longue. It reminded him of last night. He ran his hand over the place where Gabriela had perched beside him, and gave a wry grimace, following it with an irritated sigh. He was a confounded idiot for allowing her to persuade him to let her keep her appointment. Brenner alone might have met his match in a determined and very angry young Hungarian woman. But behind Brenner lurked the monstrous and unappetising shadow of the procuress—to whom he was linked by some bond that was difficult to guess, but which certainly existed. Adam took out his gold case, extracted a cigarette and pushed it back into his pocket. No! He crushed the unlit cigarette in his fingers and tossed it away from him. He was damned if he was going to sit here and do nothing. If Gabriela and Brenner were anywhere at the Prater, he'd find them.

He jumped up and started towards the door, but before he reached it, a woman's shriek split the air, followed by the sound of running feet. The drawing-room door burst open, and Arlette appeared, her pinched face white and stupid with panic.

'Major! *Gott sei Dank!* You're still here. You've got to come quickly!'

But Adam was already moving towards her. Subconsciously his ear registered the fact that the maid seemed to have temporarily lost her French accent and fallen into a guttural, Westphalian dialect of German. 'Where?' he snapped.

'Your uncle's study, Major. The Herr Graf isn't well, sir. I think he's very ill . . .'.

Adam thrust the girl aside and ran to Count Clemenz's study. The old gentleman had been sitting at his desk, reading. The open book and his reading glasses, which were normally kept hidden away—for the Count was not without his small vanity—lay on the desk top. But his chair had fallen to the floor and he sat, leaning against the desk, breathing with difficulty and apparently in great pain.

'I heard the fall, sir,' Arlette, following close behind,

explained. 'I came running in, and there he was! He doesn't speak, Major.'

'I can see that, you idiot girl!' Adam shouted over his shoulder to her, as he bent over his uncle. 'Go and fetch Dr Hubner in the Herrengasse! Tell him to come straight away.'

Arlette pattered off and Adam managed to lift his uncle and get the old man to a near-by chair. At least the Count seemed able to recognise his nephew, and was trying to speak, though the words came out only as unintelligible sounds.

'Wait, sir, wait!' Adam urged him. 'I'll fetch you some water.'

When he came back, the Count seemed calmer and able to drink a little of the water. 'Adam . . .' he whispered. Adam bent his head close to him, struck by the extreme agitation in his uncle's expression. 'Not the first,' his uncle muttered. 'Not the first time . . .'

'You've had these attacks before?' Adam asked incredulously. 'Does Hubner know?'

'Hubner is a good doctor,' the Count croaked hoarsely, 'but not a magician. Didn't want—to worry my wife . . .' He fell silent, and then indicated that his nephew should come closer again. 'Gabriela,' he whispered. 'When the girl first came, we were not kind to her. Our fault . . . Max loved her . . .'

'Yes, sir,' Adam said quietly.

'We must not betray my son's trust!' Count Clemenz exclaimed urgently, clutching at Adam's sleeve. 'We must look after her. Max would have wished it. Now I shall not be able . . . and my wife doesn't like her, jealous . . . *You,* Adam must take care of her . . . look after her . . . She has no one . . .'

Two thoughts competed for possession of Adam's brain. One was of Katy, vanished to an unknown fate, and the other was that of Gabriela, somewhere in the Prater in the company of Mischa Brenner.

'I'm not very good at looking after people, sir,' he said harshly.

The bitterness of his tone and his hesitation were misunderstood by the sick man. He clutched his nephew's sleeve. 'You will take care of her! Swear it!' the Count demanded vibrantly, struggling to haul himself upright. 'I want your word—your word that you will not fail me!'

'You have my word, sir,' Adam told him quietly, 'on my honour as a Polish officer.'

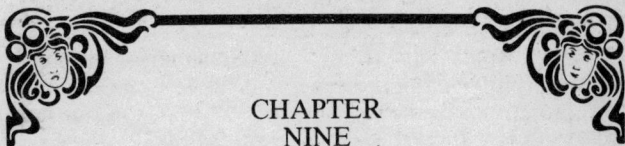

CHAPTER
NINE

GABRIELA PROPPED her chin on her hand and watched Brenner, seated across the table from her in the garden restaurant on the edge of the Prater fairground. They had finished their lunch and were drinking coffee, but so far she had said nothing of the subject uppermost in her mind, experiencing something akin to a feeling of subtle revenge while she watched his growing unease as his habitual confidence was steadily eroded. He knew that something was badly wrong, but he was not quite sure what. He probably told himself that she was still angry over the encounter of the previous evening, but he had not yet broached the subject. Either he really was nervous, or he was planning his strategy.

Mischa always planned, she thought, as she watched the movements of his slender, well-manicured fingers. He studied the advantages and disadvantages of each course of action as carefully as he played a hand of cards. She wondered what could make a man—a young man—choose to spend his life in the distasteful shadows of the *demi-monde*, with its sordid traffic in female charms disguised in a tawdry glamour. Thinking over their acquaintance, she realised now that he never spoke of himself. She knew absolutely nothing of him, other than the barest circumstances of his having been born in St Petersburg. But she was sure he would have an answer for any question, and that was why she was in no hurry now. Let *him* bring up the subject. He was fidgeting, stirring the spoon round and round unnecessarily in his coffee.

Abruptly he stopped doing so, and looked up so that

the full gaze of his lustrous dark eyes rested on her. Despite her preparedness, Gabriela was disconcerted. 'You're displeased with me,' he said soberly, with such an apparently·genuine sorrow that she felt a momentary compunction.

'Don't you think I have a reason, Mischa?' she asked him in a level voice. But despite her outward air of calm, inwardly her heart began to beat more rapidly.

He made a decision, and leaned across the table towards her. 'It's about last night, isn't it?' he asked her earnestly. 'Gaby, I'm sorry I gave that young man your name, but I didn't think for a moment you'd mind so much.'

She gave him one last chance. 'But you still don't want to give me *his* name, Mischa?'

He did not take it. Yet some note in her voice had caught his ear, increasing his unease. 'I told you,' he muttered, looking down, away from the clear blue gaze of her eyes, fixed unswervingly on his face. 'He's a member of a very distinguished family . . .'

His obstinate repetition of his previous excuse fuelled her resolve. 'You always plan everything so well, Mischa!' she interrupted him. 'But you forgot *one* thing which, really, you should have remembered!' She allowed a note of mock chiding to touch her voice.

Now he knew something had gone badly wrong with his plans, and he looked up quickly, undisguised alarm in his expression.

'You forgot,' Gabriela said in a cool, careful voice, 'that I, too, am a member of a very distinguished family, even if I only married into it. Of course I haven't met everyone, but I do know who is important, who is rich, whose conduct gives rise to whispers of scandal . . .'

Brenner half rose from his seat, in such evident consternation that she almost felt sorry for him. She watched him sink back. For once he seemed at a loss for words.

'It never occurred to you last night, did it, that I would recognise *him*?'

The faintest sigh escaped Brenner, but otherwise he continued to sit quite silent, his complexion of an alabaster whiteness.

'Oh, I admit that I didn't, at first, but something about him made me think I should know who he was. It worried at me, and after I got home, I . . . realised.' Her voice sharpened. 'I'm not wrong, am I, Mischa? Nor is it difficult for me to guess what your purpose is in all this charade! But, Herr Brenner, you are sadly out of your depth. You must be mad ever to imagine that *I* would let you use me like that!'

Brenner brushed his fingers across his perspiring forehead. 'You *are* wrong, Gaby, and you must let me explain how . . .'

'No!' she exclaimed suddenly with a vehemence he had not been expecting. 'Why should I? Why should I listen to one word you say? I lay awake last night thinking of all the things I wanted to tell you today. But now I can't even be bothered to say them. You're not worth it!' She was growing more and more heated, and her voice louder. 'I believed you to be a friend—and you're nothing but a deceitful, lying, despicable traitor!'

'For goodness' sake, Gaby,' he urged, 'half the people here are listening to us!'

'Let them listen!' she replied fiercely.

'No,' Brenner said with unexpected firmness. 'No. You don't want them to overhear, any more than I do.'

He was right, and he knew it. Gabriela fell temporarily silent, and he signalled rapidly for the bill. 'We'll take a walk through the fairground, Countess. It's always noisy and you can shout at me as much as you want. But you must let me explain! I know how it looks to you, but I swear that it isn't like that. I deserve some of what you say, but not all! I *am* your friend, believe me!'

Aware they were attracting curious glances, with an

ill-concealed reluctance she allowed him to escort her
out of the little garden shaded by overhanging lime-
trees, and they made their way towards the clamour
and gaiety of the fairground.

There was no place like the fairground of the Prater!
Not here would you see the elegant entertainments of
the fashionable areas of the great boulevards and the
racecourse. This was the People's Prater, the home of
merry-go-rounds, that were furiously powered by the
new steam mechanism, of sideshows in which jugglers,
illusionists and freaks competed to attract the attention
of the visitors, and of vendors of such robust delicacies
as hot sausages and salt-encrusted pretzels. It was always
crowded and, during the afternoon, as now, it was the
particular domain of the children. Little girls with flying
tresses clung to the painted horses of the carousels, their
black-stockinged legs and shiny button boots kicking
wildly. Their brothers, in sailor suits, rode their wooden
steeds with dash and bravado, each one, in his own
mind, leading a cavalry charge—or pleaded with the
accompanying adult for sausages and sweets. Gipsies
moved among the throng, selling flowers and telling
fortunes, and pickpockets plied a deft trade. The noise
was tremendous. The shrieks of the children, the music
of the steam organs, festooned with brightly-painted
animated figures, and the shouts of the barkers were
mingled in a single hubbub. Above one sideshow, three
huge mechanical figures of witches, eight feet high,
bowed and stooped with hideous grins and slowly
groping arms above the throng.

Yet all this was a pale shadow of the evening to come,
when daylight faded and the gas-lights were lit. Then
hundreds of pale-faced, pert and pretty girls, released
from the airless workshops of the city and clad in their
best dresses and hats, clinging to the arms of their
beaux, would descend, squeaking and giggling, on to
the fairground, all determined to enjoy a wonderful
time.

Gabriel and Brenner plunged into the midst of the afternoon family outings, passing by a screaming youngster, now being borne away by his nursemaid, thrown over her shoulder and beating on her back with his clenched fists.

'Poor child,' she thought, glancing up at the grimacing witches above them which were the cause of his terror. The grotesquely painted wooden heads leered down at her menacingly and she was reminded of the procuress, Jetta, and of Adam's claim that Brenner was well known at the Golden Fleece. What took Brenner there? Not the girls. She glanced quickly at her companion. He seemed to have little or no amorous interest in women for his own entertainment or pleasure. He had never tried to make love to her. But he intended her for someone else.

Setting her mouth tightly, Gabriela began to walk on quickly, pushing her way through the crowds. Brenner hastened along beside her, trying to catch her attention.

'Gaby! For pity's sake, listen to me! At least be fair . . .' he pleaded.

'Fair?' She swung round on him furiously. 'Is that how you describe your behaviour towards *me*?'

He had caught her attention at last and he seized his opportunity, the words spilling out of him, shouted above the screaming crowd and raucous music.

'Gaby, you're *wrong*. I didn't know *he* would see you at the Prater! And I didn't know he would be there last night. He recognised you and sent to ask me who you were. When I was told who *he* was, I couldn't refuse to tell him. Be reasonable, Gaby? You know I couldn't!'

It was the fact that he could still lie to her, when he knew she was aware of the truth, which finally hardened her heart and killed any pity she might have felt for him. This persistent, obstinate clinging to a discredited falsehood gave her an insight into his character which nothing else could have done.

She stopped so suddenly that he cannoned into her,

and she exclaimed incredulously, 'You don't know the *difference* between the truth and falsehood! You really think I'll believe such a stupid story—now, when I know the truth! Honesty, decency, fairness—these things mean nothing to you. You just don't know what they are.'

His face as white and his features as starkly drawn as one of the gargoyle figures above them, Brenner hissed, 'Oh yes, I do! I know what those things are, Gaby. And I know they are for people who can afford them—like the other luxuries of our time. I can't! And neither, my dear, can you!' There was a vicious note to his voice and a bitter sincerity which could not but impress her forcefully.

She was so taken aback that she could not find an answer for the moment. Then she tossed her head and walked on, looking neither to left nor right. Brenner dodged among the crowds, trying to stay at her elbow and speaking in urgent, broken phrases as children ran laughing beneath his feet and bursts of music interrupted his speech.

'Gaby—you *must* listen to me. You must see it my way!'

'No!' she flung over her shoulder at him without slowing her step. '*You* will have to understand my view of it. It's a miserable, sordid little plot, and I'll play no part in it. Tell Al— . . . tell your master that I'm not for hire!'

'Gaby, you can't let me down! He expects . . . Gaby!' His voice echoed above the crowd as a single, desperate cry.

She pushed on, trying to escape from him, but her way was blocked by a gipsy, an unshaven fellow with yellow teeth, who was tugging along on a chain a dancing bear, a scruffy, malodorous beast, securely muzzled, its tiny evil eyes surveying the throng with a kind of malicious bewilderment. The gipsy stopped before her, and his animal companion reared up on its hind legs and waved its paws, tipped with wickedly long, sharp claws.

'See the bear, pretty lady? He'll dance for you. Hé, Bruno! Dance!'

The bear waved its huge head and lurched to the sound of the organ music in a cumbersome and melancholy way.

'Get rid of that wretch!' Gabriela ordered Brenner, who had caught up.

The bear smelled appalling, with the raw staleness of the caged wild beast, and its gipsy master little better. She found the creature loathsome and terrifying, as the great claws swept through the air and the pig-like little eyes gleamed dully, while its pointed snout snuffled at the breeze.

Brenner thrust forward, and going up to the gipsy, began to talk to him in a low, emphatic voice. Gabriela, who had moved away a little, saw him give the man some money. The gipsy was nodding and laughing, baring his teeth, and the bear had come down from its hind legs and stood, shifting uneasily from paw to paw, shaking its muzzled snout, perhaps in painful memory of the heated tin tray on which it had been taught to dance.

Leaving the gipsy, Brenner came to join her. 'You gave him a lot of money,' she said sharply.

'So? I like the bear,' he returned curtly. 'When I was a child, in Russia, those performing bears were commonplace. I always liked the beasts. They are never tame, only cowed. A gipsy can spend half a lifetime with the beast, and never trust him. Inside the bear there is something . . .' he tapped his own chest, '. . . always free.'

Gabriela stared at him curiously, and when she walked on, she allowed him to fall into step beside her.

'Gaby,' he urged, seeking to take advantage of the slight softening of her mood. 'I know you're angry, and if it makes you any happier, I'll confess everything. Yes,

I wanted Al— . . . I wanted *him* to see you, and yes, I knew he would be there last night. But if you'll let me explain it, I know you'll see . . .'

'I won't change my mind, Mischa!'

'You would, if you'd only listen!' he cried out in real despair.

She was unmoved. 'I won't listen, Mischa. I don't want to hear a word—not one word. It's finished! It's over! For goodness' sake, let's get away from here and find a cab. I want to go home.'

She glanced over her shoulder. The gipsy and bear followed a few yards behind them. The man was calling out to passers-by, but his bright, cunning eyes, as wild as those of his ursine companion, seemed to be fixed on her mockingly. 'You should not have given him so much money,' she exclaimed angrily. 'Now the wretched fellow is following us!'

'He's not. Look, Gaby, I'm not letting you go until you've listened to me. It's not a sordid plot. It's a marvellous plan, an opportunity for us both!'

'Be quiet, Mischa. I will not listen. If you won't find me a cab, I'll find one myself! And don't call at the house again, or try and see me or write. I'm finished with you for ever!' she shouted angrily at him.

Brenner stiffened and paled as the force of her words struck him, but there was an obstinate set to his mouth which Gabriela would have noticed had she not been so agitated, and a strangely hard glitter in his dark eyes. For a moment, he almost resembled the procuress. He looked back at the gipsy, who was still following them, and the man's yellow grin broadened.

'You refuse to listen?' Brenner asked, quite calmly, as if making sure.

'Absolutely! There is nothing I want to hear from you!'

He nodded decisively. They began to walk towards the edge of the fairground. The crowd was a little thinner here, yet the gipsy and the bear still followed.

A line of cabs waited at a rank in the distance, and at the sight of them Gabriela's heart lightened in relief. Now she could not escape from the noisy, laughing fairground fast enough, and began to walk as quickly as possible. But suddenly there was a terrified shriek to the rear of them, and a woman screamed, 'The bear is loose!'

Automatically Gabriela spun round at the cry, and she saw that pandemonium reigned behind them. The bear had somehow slipped its chain and trotted alone across the ground, the gipsy after it. Children burst into tears, and people began to run wildly in all directions.

'Come on!' Brenner shouted, seizing Gabriela's elbow.

'No, let go of me!' she protested, but at the same time she was running too, borne along in the frightened crowd. He had caught hold of her hand tightly and was tugging her along at breakneck speed towards the line of cabs. Unreasoning panic clouded her mind for a few vital minutes, and she allowed him to thrust her into the first of the *Fiakers*. She could hear Brenner shouting some quite lengthy instructions at the driver, then he jumped in beside her, slamming the door, and the cab leapt forward, rocking dangerously.

'Mischa, tell the cab-man to slow down!' she cried, as soon as she had regained both her breath and her presence of mind. The cab lurched, and she grabbed at the straps to steady herself.

But the cab clattered on, and Brenner, his face white and set, seemed unwilling or unable to do anything. They had already left the Prater behind them and were heading back into the city. Glimpses of the narrow streets hurtled past the window.

'For goodness' sake!' She caught at Brenner's arm. 'The driver must be drunk. Tell him to stop.'

But he still ignored her, as if oblivious both of the hectic pace of the cab and of her pleading. That same odd, hard glitter showed in his eyes, and now she began to be really afraid—not the blind panic of her flight from the bear, but a cold, gnawing fear. She had forgotten and ignored Adam's instruction to stay in a crowded place and not to let Brenner take her anywhere alone. She had allowed herself to become trapped in the cab, alone with him, and driven apparently by a lunatic, rocking madly through the Vienna streets.

'You *paid* that gipsy to turn the bear loose!' she gasped accusingly.

Brenner still made no reply. The cab rounded a corner so dangerously that Gabriela was flung against him. He grasped at her arm to steady her, but still kept his strange silence.

Then they stopped. Brenner flung open the door and jumped to the pavement. Gabriela, anxious to escape from what had become a nightmare prison, scrambled out after him, and the driver—obviously paid by Brenner in advance—whipped up his horses and clattered away.

She looked around her and had barely time to take stock of her surroundings and gasp, 'Why, this is not . . . !' before Brenner had seized her arm tightly and pushed her unceremoniously through a near-by doorway.

Although she struggled to free herself, he was extraordinarily strong. The delicate facial features and dandyish mode of dress effectively disguised the fact that he was a well-muscled young man, and extremely fit. He thrust her ahead of him down a long, dark, corridor smelling of boiled cabbage, and then down a flight of stone steps into a dank cellar.

'This way!' Brenner ordered, speaking for the first time.

He grasped her hand again and hurried her across the cellar between firewood stacks and barrels of sauerkraut, and through a little door into yet another cellar, lit only by tiny apertures at pavement level above. This procedure was repeated, and Gabriela, despite her terror, realised that they were passing in this manner from house to house across an entire block, through adjoining cellars. Eventually he headed for a short stair which they climbed, stumbling in the darkness, and, almost falling through a narrow door at the top, came out suddenly into a gas-lit corridor.

Brenner shut the door hurriedly behind them, and Gabriela noticed that it masqueraded as a full-length mirror on the inner side, so that a casual observer would not have noticed the hinges and catch. She had a brief glimpse of a series of badly painted oils of erotic subjects which lined the walls of the corridor, before he dragged her to a door at the bottom of it and pushed her ahead of him into a small room.

It was some kind of office, airless and windowless, lit by a hissing gas-jet even in mid-afternoon. A large desk was stacked with business ledgers, and the remains of a cigar lay crushed in a glass ashtray in the centre of it. There was a distinctive smell—of cigar smoke, wine and a sweet, flowery odour of perfume. Gabriela had smelled that strange mixture before, and knew with cold certainty where she had been brought.

'I know this place—this is the Golden Fleece!' she gasped.

Brenner darted forward. 'How do you know that?'

A moment of pure horror prevented her answer. She was standing facing a large spotted mirror in a tarnished frame whose tawdriness had perhaps proved too obvious even for the seedy décor of the main rooms, so that it hung here amid the paraphernalia of a business. Now she saw, reflected in the glass, distorted and monstrous, a huge shape clad in violet, advancing—or so it seemed in a moment's optical illusion—from out of the mirror towards her.

Gabriela drew in her breath sharply and whirled round. The door had opened, unheard by either of them, and entering through it, moving with uncanny lightness and stealth for one so vast, came the grotesque frame of the procuress, filling the little office.

'Such a pity you allowed us to hear that, my dear,' she said gently.

A draught through the open door caused her violet taffeta skirts to rustle softly, and the gilt mirror on the wall rocked on its nail with an answering creak.

Dr Hubner fastened his black bag with methodical care. Adam, pacing restlessly up and down the room with his hands clasped behind his back, scowled at him impatiently, but the doctor ignored him. He buttoned his frock coat, carefully pulled on his gloves, checking each finger as he did so, flicked an invisible speck of dust from his lapels and only then turned to face the tall figure of the Uhlan.

'Well?' Adam demanded urgently. 'What have you to say?'

The doctor cleared his throat. 'You are His Excellency's nearest relative in Vienna at the moment, I believe, Major? The honourable lady is away, I understand, taking the waters—in Bohemia?'

The expression on Adam's face indicated that if the doctor did not come to the point soon, he would have a case of apoplexy on his hands as well as the sick Count Clemenz. Adam nodded curtly, not trusting himself to speak.

'Then I should tell you,' Dr Hubner said placidly, 'that the situation of the patient is very serious.'

'How serious?'

'Let us say that the Countess Clemenz should be informed,' Dr Hubner said in a careful voice. For all that, he looked and sounded his frustration. It was difficult for him to admit that there was little he could do to help a patient he knew so well and respected so highly.

'Do you mean to tell me he is dying?' Adam demanded sharply. 'Speak out, man, don't beat about the bush.'

'My dear Major,' Dr Hubner exclaimed angrily. 'I do not "beat about the bush". Neither do I make rash statements which may be misunderstood.' He tugged at his goatee beard and then added crossly, 'Well, since you are his nephew and the honourable lady is not here, I shall give you my frank opinion. I do not say that he will die. But one must bear in mind that His Excellency has suffered previous attacks, though none so severe, and naturally each successive attack has left him less able to overcome the next. I fear we cannot hope for a full recovery in the sense that he will be as he was before. He will be an invalid, obliged to take life very easy, and above all, to avoid any strain or stress. Business matters will be, of course, beyond him. I do not know—nor is it my place to enquire—to what extent Countess Clemenz can manage the family affairs alone. I take it that she will be heavily dependent on you.' This last sentence was not a question, but a final note. Hubner picked up his bag, and having made Adam a formal bow, stalked out.

'Pedantic old fogy!' Adam muttered unkindly when the doctor's rigid figure in its black frock coat had disappeared. 'If you think my uncle likely to give up so easily, you don't know him at all!'

He went to the Count's study and hunted through the desk for the telegram forms he knew were kept there. It was difficult to compose a message which was both adequate and the least dramatic possible in such circumstances, but he managed it somehow and sent it off with a footman to the nearest post office.

Gabriela had slipped his mind during all this, but he recalled her now and took out his watch. If nothing had gone wrong, she should be home soon. He glowered. It was getting late. Where the devil could she be?

Even as he asked himself this, the rustle of a woman's skirts at the door caught his ear, and he turned quickly, exclaiming in relief, 'Gabriela?'

'It's I, Adam,' Christiane said. She came a little further into the room and paused, looking at him hesitantly. 'I met the maid in the street, running for the doctor,' she went on. 'I came to see if I could help. I am so sorry to hear that Count Clemenz has been taken ill.'

'That's kind of you, Christiane,' Adam said in a clipped voice. 'I'm afraid he is very ill. I've sent for my aunt.'

'So serious?' Despite her expression of sympathy, Christiane's voice and figure had regained something of her usual assurance. She had been uncertain of her reception, but Adam clearly had other things on his mind than her ill-fated attempt at seduction of the previous evening.

'You expected Gabriela,' she said now with an assumed casualness. 'When you turned just now, you spoke her name. Where is she?' Curiosity entered her voice.

'I don't know,' Adam replied evenly. 'Out lunching with—with a friend.'

'With Brenner?' Christiane suggested mockingly. 'A very good friend!' She raised her delicately arched eyebrows. 'They're taking a long time over it.'

'What are you hinting at, Christiane?' he asked her sharply.

'My dear Adam, all Vienna knows of her *affaire* with Brenner. Such a pitiful, sordid business, but only to be expected. The girl is of very—shady—origins herself. Her father was a notorious wastrel and rake. With Brenner she has found her level, and the kind of company to which she was accustomed before Max married her.' Christiane shrugged.

'Rubbish!' Adam said curtly, and a tide of scarlet flooded over Christiane's pale cheeks. He glanced at his watch again impatiently.

'So,' she said in a dulcet voice. 'I'm wrong, am I? She's late, though, isn't she? Perhaps she won't come at all?' A sudden vicious note echoed in the sweetness, like the echo of a cracked bell.

'What do you mean?' He looked up, a dangerous glint in his eyes. 'If you know something, speak out!'

'I don't know anything in particular, Adam, I swear!' she said quickly, warned by that coldly aggressive gleam. 'But if you don't know how the girl has been behaving since Max's death, you're the only one who doesn't. It's the subject of half the gossip in Vienna.'

'I don't listen to gossip,' he said harshly, 'only facts. If and when you have evidence, I'll listen, but not before!'

Christiane came swiftly towards him. 'But I have evidence, Adam!' The excited note was again in her voice, mixed with something very like triumph, and her grey eyes burned with that feverish light. 'Look, Adam . . .' She fumbled at her glove and withdrew something which had been tucked inside it on her palm. 'The maid gave me this!' She held out her hand, which trembled with excitement.

A gold pin lay there, its diamond head glinting in a ray of light from the window. Christiane peered up into his face eagerly.

'It's a man's article of jewellery, Adam. No woman wears a pin like this. It's from a dress shirt front, and you know as well as I do that Mischa Brenner couldn't afford an expensive trinket like this. This diamond is of the first water, and the gold of the highest quality. Whoever owned this was a rich man! Rich enough and enamoured enough to give it to our *sorrowing* widow to pin together a rent in a ball-gown. Don't you understand?' She was almost stammering now in her agitation. 'We have only to find out to whom this pin belongs, and we have her trapped! She won't be able to deny it. How many jewellers in Vienna sell items like this? A select handful. Any one of them will be able to tell us at once by whom and for whom it was made!'

In a single lightning movement Adam picked the pin

off her palm and slipped it into his pocket. 'I'm obliged to you, Christiane. I'll see it's returned to its owner!' he said crisply.

Outmanoeuvred, she gaped at him in a mixture of surprise and disappointment. 'But Adam . . .'

'Listen to me, Christiane. My uncle is a very sick man, and this is not the time to go spreading tales of scandal involving this family all over Vienna. Do you understand me? You'll say nothing of this to anyone; *nothing*, do you hear, to a living soul!' His voice rose threateningly.

'In order to protect *her*!' Christiane cried out wildly. 'That Hungarian trollop has bewitched you just as she did poor Max! But I won't let it happen again, I won't! I lost Max to her, but I won't lose *you*!'

She saw his expression harden, but caught up in her own emotional frenzy she could not stop herself, and as he tried to walk past her, she caught hold of his sleeve. She clung to it so tightly that he was unable to shake her free and, unwilling to use brute force against her, was obliged to stand still, visibly losing the precarious grip he had on his temper.

'Let go, Christiane!' he snarled at her. 'Pull yourself together, for goodness' sake. We're not going to have another stupid scene like last night's, I hope. You can play it out alone. I've no time for this nonsense!'

'It wasn't a stupid scene. I love you, Adam!' she gasped, trying to embrace him. 'You know I do—and you'd love me, if only she weren't here!'

'I don't love you, Christiane,' he said curtly. 'And, as it happens, Gabriela isn't here, and should be! I'm going out to look for her.'

'No!' She clung to him even more desperately and began to cry, or rather to sob, dry-eyed, in a hysterical way, her face flushed and her hair becoming loosened and falling about her face. 'If she's not here, it's because she's with Brenner. In his bed, most likely! She ran off before, Adam, on the night of the funeral. She's done it again, that's all—this time with her lover. Don't go looking for her. She isn't worth it! Adam, please, don't go . . .'

He swore, and taking her wrists, pushed her forcibly away from him, but she sprang back like a tigress and barred his way.

'I won't let you do it!' she panted. 'Adam, let her go! Let her go with Brenner, or her other lover whoever he is. Oh, my darling Adam, don't you see? Your uncle is sick and could even be dying. She's been waiting for this—waiting for the only obstacle—Count Clemenz—between her and you to join her husband in the grave!'

'Get out of my way, Christiane!' Adam said in a low, hard voice, and she broke off her tirade and stared at him fearfully, cowed by his expression and tone. 'I never struck a woman in my life, but I swear, if you don't stand aside, I'll remove you forcibly by whatever means are necessary!'

Christiane swallowed nervously and licked her dry lips. Her grey eyes still glittered wildly and her bosom heaved with laboured breathing, but she moved aside a little to allow him to pass.

'Adam . . .' she moaned.

'I'm going to look for my cousin's widow,' he shouted at her. 'And I don't want to find you here when I get back!'

Christiane's pale face changed, contorting in rage and spite. 'You treacherous Pole!' she hissed at him. 'You dare to cast me aside—for her!'

She leapt towards him, her hands outstretched as if she would have clawed at his eyes. Adam grasped her arms and thrust her out of his path. She fell back, still railing at him, yet still pleading with him between the curses.

He ignored it all, and ran down the staircase to the main door. As the old doorkeeper hastened forward to open it for him, they heard the first of the screams piercing the air shrilly between the first floor and where they stood. It gathered power and momentum as it was repeated, again and again, in a shattering crescendo.

The doorkeeper, struck motionless, turned horrified and enquiring eyes on Adam for an explanation.

'It's nothing!' Adam told him curtly. 'Baroness Von-neck is having a screaming fit.' He signalled to the man to open the door, and as he stepped through it, ordered, 'Have her thrown out!'

CHAPTER
TEN

'LET ME deal with this, Jetta!' Brenner exclaimed sharply.

He urged the fat woman back into the dim corridor and followed her, shutting the door after them. Through it, their voices rose and fell, audible to Gabriela at first only as an exchange of murmurs, but then growing louder and clearer. She crossed quietly to the door and put her ear to it.

'You should not have brought the widow here!' Jetta was saying hoarsely.

'How should I know she'd recognise the place?' Brenner replied sullenly, adding passionately, 'Just let me talk to her, Jetta, and it will be all right!'

'And if it isn't, my dear? We cannot let her go, you know that!' The woman's voice, ostensibly so mild, filled the listening girl with a frozen dread.

'I won't allow you to harm her!' Brenner's tone was aggressive.

'Now, now, my pigeon. You're a young man, and the widow is pretty. It's natural you should take a fancy to the girl. But you mustn't allow it to cloud your business judgment. Remember—you forced her here against her will, and for a purpose no one must learn, involving a name no one must hear! Only think what she'll do, if we let her leave. She'll sing like a canary, and bring us endless trouble. She knows where she is . . .'

'The devil knows how!' he interrupted fiercely.

'She knows, it is enough! I warned you, my pretty fellow, that you played a dangerous game. Let the girl leave here and she'll run straight to the Uhlan. Let me tell you, my dear, the Pole may spend his evenings here with my girls, but when it comes to the honour of his own women, aha! A different matter, eh? If he gets his hands on you, he will kill you, my pigeon, and I don't exaggerate! If he once hears what she'll have to tell him, he won't rest till he's found you.'

'I'll talk her round; just give me a chance!' Brenner maintained obstinately.

'Try it, my dear, try it. Let us hope you are successful. If you are not—well, you brought her here through the cellars, and no one can swear she was ever here, eh? She won't be the first to have gone out of here that way, and no one the wiser!'

Gabriela stifled a cry and jumped away from the door as it re-opened to admit Brenner. He shut it behind him carefully and put a finger to his lips in a conspiratorial manner, to motion her to silence. They stood for a moment, both listening, and then Jetta could be heard in the corridor outside, moving away. He breathed a sigh of relief, and dragging out his handkerchief, mopped his freely perspiring forehead. 'Sit down, Gaby, and don't worry,' he muttered.

She was only too glad to sit down, because her legs felt like jelly, but she managed to maintain a calm front. 'You are the one who should worry, I think, Mischa.'

'None of this would have been necessary if you had only listened to me out there at the Prater!' he said accusingly, as if all this were her fault and he, not she, were the victim. 'I had to bring you here. Though I wouldn't have done so, had I known you'd recognise the place! I don't know how you did, but you are here now, and you've got to listen!'

'There's nothing you can say which will change my mind, Mischa,' Gabriela said quietly. 'I won't be Alexander's mistress—neither for you, nor for any threats you may make.'

'I'm not going to threaten you, for pity's sake!' he exploded. He came to prop himself on the edge of the desk and lean over her entreatingly. He was an attractive young man, and she had to admit it, even now. There was a beguiling innocence in those delicate features and glowing dark eyes which made it the more incredible that what he was suggesting should be so vile. 'Gaby, it isn't a foul plot!' he whispered eagerly. 'Before you start refusing, think! You and I, my dear, are, whether you like it or not, two of a kind. We exist in the best society, but have no true place there. You have no husband any more, Gaby. He was your link with that glittering world, and he's gone. All you have now is beauty, intelligence, and *me* to advise you. No!' He raised his voice slightly, seeing her mouth open. 'Let me finish. How long do you think the Clemenz family will continue to support you? Countess Clemenz hates you, and her husband must be influenced by his wife eventually. What happens when they throw you out? I see you're silent now. You've no answer. And Dubrowski? How long will he tolerate you? And how long before he invites you into his bed? He will, Gaby, he will! I know the man!'

'It is still none of your concern!' she managed to say.

His dark eyes flickered over her shrewdly. 'He has asked already, hasn't he? Don't answer—I can see it in your face. He won't take refusal for ever, Gaby. If you want to stay in that family, you'll have to stay on Dubrowski's terms!' Brenner relaxed, more at ease now, sure of himself. 'You know, my dear,' he said, 'I shall tell you the truth, just to show you that I can. I admit that at first I saw you only as the ideal woman for my purpose. But later, as I got to know you, I wanted my plan to succeed even more, for *your* sake, as well as for mine! I am your friend, Gaby. I do care what happens to you. We are kindred beings, and I want your happiness as I want my own.'

'Yet you'd sell me to Alexander, just as Jetta sells those wretched girls who work here!' she burst out vigorously, disgusted by his apparent sincerity.

'No!' Brenner's handsome face darkened with anger.

'That isn't what I'm proposing. I'm offering you one of the richest men in Austria, and a liaison which could be permanent—why, as good as respectable—if you only play your cards well. And, Gaby, you hold *all* the cards. You're beautiful and charming and free—no enraged husband and no furious papa or brothers to buy off. Alexander is head over heels in love with you and can't wait to meet you again.'

'I cannot imagine,' Gabriela said slowly, 'whatever made you think I would ever consider such a proposition, even for one moment.'

'But why won't you?' he insisted, exasperated and frustrated by her indifference to his arguments. 'The man is young, he's good-looking, charming—half the women in Vienna would give their eye-teeth to be in your shoes.'

'Then find one of them to carry out your plan!' she burst out. 'If you can't understand my reasons for refusing, Mischa, I certainly can't explain them to you. You're not capable of understanding. But my answer is No, and always shall be. If you like, I'll tell Alexander so myself.'

'That would be very foolish,' Brenner said gently. 'He does not like to be refused. I'm sorry, my dearest' —there was a real note of sadness in his voice—'but you cannot refuse. His anger will fall on us all. Nor will the old woman allow you to leave here if you don't agree.'

'I don't think that she's going to allow me out of here in any case,' Gabriela said, meeting his dark eyes with a level look of her wide blue ones.

He flushed. 'She will, if you agree, believe me! Look, Gaby, I—I have some influence with the old witch. I'll get us both out of this mess, but you *must* agree!'

'I don't agree. And remember, if I suddenly disappear, Major Dubrowski will turn Vienna inside out, there will be a real enquiry and a hunt, and the whole horrible scheme will be known to everyone. I'm sure

Alexander doesn't want an open scandal, Mischa!'

He gave a bitter little laugh. 'Believe me, Gabriela, there will be no scandal. Your admirer is a bosom friend of the Crown Prince. No, if you attempt to tell your story, Alexander will declare he has never heard of either of us. He wasn't driving in the Prater, and he wasn't at the Secrets Ball . . . and a dozen impeccable witnesses will swear to it.'

'And if I disappear?' she demanded.

Brenner shrugged. 'Those about him, whose business it is to take care of his problems, are not concerned with you, only with him and his reputation. His friends will rush him away, spirit him off to some place in Bohemia or Transylvania to hunt. He won't return until it's all over and forgotten. Vienna forgets very quickly, Gaby. A thing is only of interest as long as it is a novelty.' He smiled at her in his boyish way, just as if nothing were wrong, and all their old, easy friendship still existed untarnished. 'As for the Pole, he is an army officer, bound by his oath to support the Empire and defend its interest and its good name. That means that he will obey orders, however unhappily. He will be told to keep his mouth shut and not to embarrass such a close friend of the heir to the throne—or he'll risk disappearing himself into some military gaol.'

Gabriela tried not to let her fear show in her face. He could be right. What he said was certainly plausible. But Adam had called him plausible. It sounded like the truth, but was it? She let her eyes travel slowly round the little office. There was no way of escape, not even a window. Brenner was placed between her and the one door, and in the corridor beyond lurked Jetta, and who knew who else? She would never be allowed to reach the stairs leading to the pavement outside. Her gaze fell on Brenner, propped elegantly against the desk, dapper and debonair as ever; only his ruffled hair and skin glistening with beads of perspiration betrayed his agitation. It was so hot in here . . . perhaps as befitted the kind of hell it was. She had to gain time. Adam would know, if she failed to return, that something was wrong.

'Mischa,' she asked. 'What gave you the idea in the first place?'

He avoided her eye. 'Well, I do favours for people,' he admitted reluctantly. 'I got to know of Alexander's taste in women, and I realised there were possibilities to be had out of it.'

'What sorts of favours?' she persisted, genuinely curious.

He looked up, his dark eyes mocking her. 'Girls.' Seeing that she did not understand him at once, he went on, 'There are plenty of men, oh, most respectable fellows, who like to relax sometimes in pleasant company . . . or young fellows with plenty of money who give parties for their friends, and ask me . . .'

'To supply the girls,' she finished for him.

He smiled slightly and hunched his shoulders by way of an answer. He did not look embarrassed at such an admission, only rueful and a trifle amused.

'But surely there's a girl, among all those, who would please him?' she asked. 'Why did you need me?'

'Any of them could please him for an hour or two,' Brenner said frankly. 'But none of them could keep him. He's a cultured and intelligent man, and a lonely one. Rich men often are, my dear, very lonely.' A note of passion entered his voice. 'You have intelligence, charm and breeding. You could keep him. Only think what it could mean to us both!'

'I think,' Gabriela said, 'you are the lowest form of life I ever encountered.' She held his gaze unswervingly. 'You seek not only to use me, but to make use of that poor young man—poor, even though he is so rich, because he will always be surrounded by unscrupulous people like you. How dare you associate your interests and mine?'

He flinched as though she had struck him, and colour flooded his pale cheeks. 'You're wrong to despise me,' he said sullenly. 'You need me. You think you don't, but you'll see that you do!'

He pushed himself away from the desk and went out of the office. A click indicated that he had locked her in. Gabriela could hear him talking outside to Jetta, but although she pressed her ear against the door panels again, the only entire sentence she could catch was, 'It's worth the risk, it's my only chance!' from Brenner. After that, she heard footsteps retreating, and then there was silence.

Gabriela did not know how long she sat in the airless little office. It must have been well over an hour. Once or twice she heard footsteps outside and the shrill voices of Jetta's girls, but no one came near her. What on earth did they plan now? And Brenner—where had he gone, and what was his 'only chance'?

Then, quite unexpectedly, there was a muffled noise outside, the click of a key turning, and the office door opened. Gabriela, her heart beating painfully, rose to face the man who entered. 'Well, Mischa . . .' she began, but her voice trailed away in disbelief as she saw who entered.

The handsome, pale-faced young man shut the door quietly. 'Dear Countess,' he said with gentle courtesy. 'I can only apologise. Brenner is a fool. Believe me, none of this was at my instigation. I had not the slightest notion, until Brenner came to me just now, that things had come to such a pass!' He leaned forward with an earnest anxiousness.

Gabriela swallowed, and made a determined effort. 'This is a strange place and odd company for someone such as yourself, I think, sir.' Her voice sounded strained and choked, even to her own ears.

The newcomer smiled ruefully, glancing at the tawdry surroundings. He twitched his shoulders. 'The mountain will not go to Mahomet, so Mahomet must go to the mountain,' he said. He crossed towards her and taking her hand, which she was too dismayed to refuse him, bowed over it. 'I hadn't thought Brenner could make such a confounded mess of things!' he exclaimed suddenly, a pettish note in his voice.

Gabriela became aware of how bright and agitated his eyes were, belying the calm façade of his manner, and she knew she must not lose her nerve. As before, there was that air of suppressed restlessness about him, and now he was at a disadvantage. This was not how he had envisaged events, and he was displeased, and nervous—a volatile combination.

'Brenner has done us both a disservice,' she said loudly. 'He was wrong from the beginning in assuming I would agree. I do not agree, and I would be acting unfairly by you, sir, if I pretended otherwise.'

'But you don't understand,' the young man broke in eagerly, clasping her hand more tightly, though she tried to free it. 'I have the greatest respect for you, Countess!'

'Then tell them to let me go!' Gabriela almost shouted at him. Suddenly she thought, They must let me go, eventually, now that Alexander has been here. They would not dare to involve him so directly in crime. At the same time, the oddest notion struck her, that Brenner had deliberately brought the Archduke here not only because he believed Gabriela would not refuse such an illustrious admirer to his face, but also to protect her from Jetta. Alexander's presence rendered Jetta powerless. 'Please,' she repeated aloud to him, 'ask them, tell them, to let me go.'

Her visitor ignored her plea, although he must have heard it, anxious to pursue his own speech, speaking quickly and urgently. 'Since the moment I first set eyes on you, Countess, driving in the Prater with Brenner, you have filled my thoughts completely. I beg you will not reject me. I offer you my heart in all honour.'

'Honour?' she cried. 'You ask me to surrender mine!'

The young man seized her arms and whispered passionately, 'But I am in love with you, Countess, don't you understand?' He pulled her towards him and attempted to kiss her roughly.

Gabriela cried 'No!' For a moment he stared at her uncomprehendingly, and then, taking advantage of his momentary hesitation, she twisted herself free and pushed him away from her with all her strength.

He was caught off balance and stumbled back against the desk. He was deathly pale, breathing heavily and apparently in the throes of some uncontrollable emotion. Gabriela held her breath. At that moment there was a burst of commotion in the corridor. Her would-be admirer whirled round as the door burst open and Brenner appeared, flushed and panic-stricken. Without preamble, he gasped, 'It is the Uhlan . . .'

'I mustn't be found *here!*' Alexander shouted furiously. 'Damn you, Brenner, can you do nothing right?'

A babble of voices filled the air, and the clatter of stamping feet. One of the girls was shouting and screaming abuse, and a man's voice, the most welcome voice in the world to Gabriela's ear, yelled furiously, 'Get out of my way!' followed by something expressed with bloodcurdling vehemence in Polish.

'Adam!' Gabriela shrieked, 'I'm here!'

The door flew open again, and Adam's tall figure burst through it. 'Thank God!' he exclaimed.

She ran across the room, past Alexander, who stood as if stupefied, and threw her arms round Adam, clinging to him. She pressed her forehead against his chest, almost sobbing in her relief.

'It's all right, kitten,' he said softly. His hand stroked her dishevelled hair. 'It's all right now.' Then he disengaged her arms from about him and moved her aside, so that she no longer stood between him and the Archduke.

A silence had fallen on the room, crowded now with people. Besides the three of them, Jetta, her wig askew, and Brenner stood by the door, and now Gabriela saw that someone else had come in and was listening intently

—a stocky man with an untidy walrus moustache and a snuff-stained waistcoat. She wondered who on earth he could be.

Then Alexander moved, breaking the spell. He straightened his cuffs and assumed a manner of authority. Adam put his hand to his tunic pocket, and as the two men exchanged silent, hostile glances, he withdrew his hand and held it out towards the Archduke.

'I believe, sir, you were so kind as to lend a pin to a lady in distress,' he said with cold formality. 'Perhaps you would permit me the honour of returning it?'

The muscle at the corner of Alexander's mouth twitched, but he made no reply. Abruptly he snatched the gold pin from Adam's hand, and thrusting his way past them all, strode out.

Brenner saw his chance, and slipped out of the door quickly in his wake. Seeing his quarry escape him, Adam darted forward, but the stocky man put a restraining hand on his sleeve, and murmured, 'Don't worry. Brenner can't leave. My men won't let him. They'll let only the important gentleman leave the building.'

They had all forgotten Jetta. The woman had been standing in the corner, near the door, watching and listening, her boot-button eyes flickering from one to the other of them. Now, as the little man spoke, Gabriela saw a mocking smile flit across her bloated countenance . . . and she understood it.

'Brenner *can* get out!' she exclaimed. 'There's another exit—out in that corridor, through a door which looks like a mirror. It leads out through all the cellars, under all the houses in the block!'

'Damnation!' Adam exclaimed, starting towards the door. 'The little monster has a head start, but I'll catch him!'

Jetta moved with astonishing speed. She flung herself forward and subsided to the ground in a billowing mass of rustling violet taffeta, like the sails of a great ship heeling over in a storm, blocking the door completely.

She wrapped both pudgy white arms round Adam's legs, and although he struggled furiously, swearing at her, and the man with the walrus moustache tried to drag her away, they were unable to loosen her grip. Her sheer weight and bulk anchored Adam effectively to the spot, and eventually he and the other man were obliged to admit defeat, Adam exclaiming bitterly, 'It's too late now. The young hound must be a mile away!'

Jetta released her grip on him and sat back on the floor, panting and still blocking the door. Her bronze wig had fallen off and her hair beneath was scanty and white, but the grotesquely rouged face peered up at Adam with an expression of triumph.

'Yes, he's gone!' she crowed. 'You won't catch my pretty boy, Pole. You won't get your hands on him!' She chuckled, and it tailed away into a spluttering, hoarse cough.

'Katy told me you doted on the young devil,' Adam said viciously. 'Though I doubted it, because I didn't believe you capable of affection, even for him!'

Who was Katy? Gabriela wondered.

Jetta's little black eyes shone up at Adam, and she drew in her breath with a wheeze. 'He is my daughter's child, my grandson!' she said. Seeing the amazement on their faces, she smiled sadly, and went on, 'I bought my daughter a respectable marriage. I gave her the dowry of a princess—and she deserved such a dowry, because her father was . . .' she broke off and shook her head. 'It doesn't matter now. All are dead. I married my daughter to a fur merchant in St Petersburg. An Austrian he was, exporting the furs to Vienna and doing well. I wanted her to have a good life. But the wretch of a fur dealer turned out a drunkard and a gambler. He broke my daughter's heart and spent every last florin of her dowry. The boy—that boy . . .' She waved one pudgy hand towards the corridor, 'He is all I have of her . . .' The woman's voice echoed softly in the silence. 'No good,' she said sorrowfully. 'The boy is like his smooth-tongued, wastrel father, but he is *her* child, flesh of my flesh and blood of my blood . . .' She looked up at them again, and added in a stronger, brisker voice, 'Well, give me your hand and help me up, Uhlan! For I'm older than any of you think!' She gave a gurgling laugh. 'I always saw you were well looked after when you came here as a customer, Uhlan. Don't refuse me your help now, to get to my feet!'

Adam and the stocky man took hold of one arm each and hauled the procuress upright.

'My wig!' she ordered, and the man retrieved it and gave it to her. Jetta dusted it off and set it on her head, peering into the stained gilt mirror on the wall and nodding in satisfaction to her raddled reflection when the wig was safely back in place.

'What happened to Katy, Jetta?' Adam asked in a cold voice.

'What do I know, Uhlan?' she jeered at him, her eyes mocking him from the mirror. 'I can tell you nothing. That police inspector there'—she turned and pointed at the little man—'was already here asking foolish questions. Do with me what you like, I'll tell you no more —nor will you get your hands on my boy!' she added, a sudden note of hate entering her voice, and her little eyes glared at them, filled with spite and cunning.

'You loathsome old witch!' Adam said in disgust. He looked towards the inspector. 'Whatever fate befell poor Katy, Gruber, happened in this hell-hole. There must be some evidence!'

Jetta chuckled, a curious inhuman sound, and Gabriela shivered. Whoever Katy had been, the girl pitied anyone who had fallen foul of this evil old woman. She moved towards Adam instinctively, and he put out his arm in an automatic gesture to encircle her shoulders. But he was watching Gruber, and seemed almost to have forgotten that she was present.

Gruber had been poking about among the papers on the desk, and was now examining the latest page of the

accounts ledger, disfigured by a large inkstain. 'Careless
. . .' he murmured, and began to rock on his heels and
chew at one straggling end of his drooping moustache.
'Not like you, Aunt Jetta!'

'You should go home!' Adam said suddenly to
Gabriela, as if her presence was now a hindrance.

'I'll never do anything so stupid again, Adam, I
swear!'

'No,' he said curtly. 'You won't get the chance. From
now on, Countess, you'll take your orders from *me*!'

Brenner was far away, goodness knew where, running
hatless and panting through the back streets of Vienna
in panic. But his voice echoed in Gaby's ear. 'If you
want to stay in that family, you'll have to stay on
Dubrowski's terms!'

She knew then, with inexplicable but unshakable
certainty, that she had not seen the last of Brenner, and
that the final reckoning was yet to come.

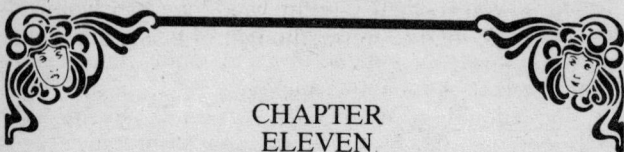

CHAPTER ELEVEN

FROM SOMEWHERE a *Fiaker* was summoned. Adam handed Gabriela in.

'You're not coming?' she asked.

'Later,' he said briefly. He paused, his hand on the door. 'Gabriela, when you arrive home, you will find that my uncle has been taken ill. That's why I was so long in coming to look for you. He's not dying, but it's serious enough for me to have sent for my aunt. He's to know nothing of what's happened today.' Before she could answer, he slammed the door on her pale-faced figure and called out loudly to the cab-man, 'Drive on!'

The news that her father-in-law was so ill struck Gabriela as a final blow on a horrendous day. Not since that grim morning, when they had brought the news of Max which had plunged them into grief and set in motion the present train of events, had she felt so utterly numbed by misfortune. That evening she made a pretence at dining, alone at the table, as Adam had still not returned, and then went upstairs to sit by Count Clemenz's bedside for a little, watching him as he slept.

During these last few weeks, especially since the departure of her mother-in-law for Marienbad, Gabriela had felt herself drawn closer to Max's father than she had ever thought possible. Now he lay before her, propped on the pillows, his breathing so shallow that she several times caught her own breath and bent over him anxiously, fearing that he might have slipped away from them all in his slumber, despite Adam's assurances. The old gentleman was more than a friend; he was an ally in a hostile world, and one discovered late and in an unexpected quarter when she had believed herself alone, and even the thought of losing him filled her with despair.

'Please get better,' she whispered. 'You must . . .'

Although she spoke the words barely audibly, the Count stirred and opened his eyes.

Gabriela leaned forward again and whispered, 'It's Gabriela, Papa. Do you know me?' She waited anxiously for his response. She had never called him 'Papa' before at any time during her stay in this house, either as Max's wife or Max's widow. But it came naturally to her lips now.

He smiled faintly up at her. 'Dear child . . .' He made a movement with his thin, blue-veined hand, as if he would have stretched it out towards her but lacked the strength. Gabriela put her own hand over his, and he nodded, pleased that she had interpreted his wish aright.

'I am glad you have come, Gabriela.' His voice, though weak, was quite clear and firm. 'Don't look so fearful, my dear. I am as weak as a baby, as you see, but don't worry. We shall sit over our games of Bezique again.'

'Soon, Papa,' she whispered, her voice sticking in her throat, unable to pass by some lump which seemed to be lodged there.

'Now, now, no tears!' he commanded fretfully. 'You must pay attention, Gabriela. I have something important to say to you . . .' He paused to draw breath, and seemed to be struggling to find the words to express whatever vexed his peace of mind.

'You're tired, Papa,' she said gently. 'It can surely wait.'

She made to take her hand from his and rise, but his fingers curled round hers with a surprising energy, that she had not expected and that his frail appearance belied.

'No, child! Later will be too late. I must talk to you now, before my wife . . .' The old man broke off and then resumed, 'Before the reins are taken from my hands by others and I no longer control the coach, eh?' He smiled faintly at her. 'You have not been as happy here as you should have been, when my son brought you to us as a bride, Gabriela. I admit it freely—we were at fault. My poor son was sadly scatterbrained, and we feared the worst of a marriage of which we knew so little. We did not judge you fairly. Well, nothing can be done about that now. But I have made arrangements so that whatever happens to me, *you* will never again be alone and friendless.'

He fell silent again, and Gabriela, puzzled, asked, 'In what way?'

'I have asked Adam,' he said clearly and carefully, 'to take care of you.'

'Adam!' she exclaimed loudly, her shock and alarm reflected in her voice and expression.

A wry smile flitted across the sick man's face. 'You and Adam are both endowed with fine tempers. I beg you will not lose yours with me now! Listen closely. It is the prerogative of the sick and old to insist that others listen to them! Adam is a fine man—a little quick-tempered, I agree, but seldom to the extent of harming anyone, except those who have seriously wronged him. In such cases he is likely to take matters into his own hands and not hesitate.'

'I know . . .' Gabriela muttered.

'But he is an honest fellow and completely trustworthy, a man of his word,' Count Clemenz insisted. 'He has a good, clear brain, too. That is why I want you to promise me, Gabriela, that now I am unable to advise or protect you, you will be advised by Adam and do as he thinks fit.'

'Papa, I know you mean well,' she protested, keeping her voice as calm as she could. 'But I hardly think Adam wishes to be burdened with *me*. Besides . . .' she hesitated.

'When he was younger,' the Count went on, as though

he had not heard her, 'Adam was something of a wild fellow, and a ladies' man. Perhaps that reputation makes you hesitate, and I admit that I should not have sought to entrust you to him then. But now he is over thirty and those years are behind him . . .'

'Perhaps not!' she interrupted impulsively.

He turned his gaze, still surprisingly sharp, towards her. 'Adam is a lonely man, Gabriela. He seeks company and distraction where it may be found. I think, my dear, *you* will understand that! Outwardly he is assured, but inwardly he is bitter and confused. He is a Polish patriot and an Austrian officer. There are many like him, in our Empire, torn in two by conflicting loyalties. He needs someone of his own, and a relationship of which he can feel sure, in which there are no doubts. Now I am very tired. So don't argue, child. Promise me that you will do as Adam says.'

'I'll do my best,' Gabriela told him quietly. 'I'll try to take his advice. I know he is—he is better informed about some matters than I am. But I can't promise you more, Papa.'

'It will do,' the old man said. 'Run along, child.' He patted her hand and closed his eyes.

Gabriela went out of the room and leaned back against the closed door as though her senses reeled, as it seemed they did, prey as they were to a turbulent host of emotions. Her father-in-law's meaning had been quite plain. He wanted her to marry Adam. As if in echo of this shattering thought, Adam's voice reverberated at that moment in the hall. He had returned at last.

She met him on his way up the stairs, as she came down. 'I was going to see how my uncle does.' He paused with his hand on the banister.

'I've been with him,' she said quietly. 'He's sleeping. Go later.'

Adam nodded, and they went down again together into the drawing-room.

'Have you eaten?' Gabriela asked, noticing how tired and drawn he looked.

'What?' He glanced at her. 'No, it doesn't matter. I'm not hungry.' He was pulling irritably at the buttons of his tunic, shrugged it off, and threw himself on the sofa. 'I could do with a drink,' he said abruptly. 'Tell someone to bring the brandy, there's a good girl.'

'I'll fetch it,' she said, glad of something to do.

When she came back with the brandy, he had lit the inevitable cigarette and was leaning back, his long legs stretched out in the familiar way, his head resting on the back of the sofa and one forearm across his eyes, as if the light troubled him. She turned the gas-jets down and went to sit by him.

Without moving, he asked, 'You don't mind if I smoke?'

'No.' Realising that he probably did not feel like answering questions, she hesitated to ask what had happened after she had left the Golden Fleece, but unable to control her desire to know, tentatively put the question to him.

He took his arm away from his face and sat upright. 'To put it briefly, Gabriela, all hell is breaking loose. However, the wheels of state are in motion, and everything is being taken care of.' He leaned forward and poured himself a glass of brandy.

'What do you mean?' There was something in his face she did not understand, but which made her uneasy.

'Well, Gruber and I, and a couple of Gruber's men, turned that place upside down. We found the exit through the cellars, but needless to say, no Brenner—or any sign of what might have happened to Katy.' He stared moodily into the liquid swilling round in the glass.

'Who was Katy?' she asked him, remembering he had mentioned this girl's name in Jetta's office.

He looked surprised, then exclaimed, 'Of course, you wouldn't know. She—she was one of the girls who worked there. I persuaded her to spy for me. She'd overheard Jetta and Brenner plotting, and she told me about it.' He drew a deep breath. 'I should not have done it. It was unforgiveable of me. I knowingly put her in danger. The worst of it is that I may even have killed her.'

'*Killed* her?' Gabriela gasped in horror.

'You see,' Adam said gently, 'even the criminal world has its code. That code never forgives an informer —and never allows an informer, once caught, to go unpunished. Katy betrayed old Jetta to me. Now the poor child has vanished, no one knows where. Nothing will ever be proved, of course, in the unlikely event that the truth does come out. But I shall carry her on my conscience until my death,' he finished bitterly.

'Did you—were you fond of her?'

'She was a good-natured girl, and willing. I liked her. I couldn't have done her a worse turn if I'd disliked her! However . . .' He made a visible effort to speak in a brisk, dispassionate voice. 'The result of our search was nil. So we went to Gruber's office, and then, my little Hungarian rose, things really started to happen! He had already been in touch with Another Department. There arrived a pair of very polite and distinguished-looking gentlemen in frock coats, resembling a couple of wise and cunning old ravens. They said they were sure that no one wished to embarrass the Archduke. Any hint of scandal would be sure to spill over on to his close friend, the Crown Prince. They were sure that I, as an army officer, could be relied upon to keep silent. Gruber is a policeman, and they were already sure of him.' Adam turned his eyes on Gabriela and added soberly, 'I had to vouch for you, Gabriela, and assure them of *your* silence.'

'I understand,' she said. 'Well, I'm certainly not going to tell people how stupid I was!'

'Good. But don't blame yourself for any of it. I've known Brenner quite a while, on and off—I should have thrown him down the steps the first time I found him here!' Adam consoled her.

Gabriela shook her head. 'You don't have to be kind to me, Adam. Everything I did was wrong. I thought I could defy convention and do as I wished, and that it couldn't hurt anyone. Now I know that whoever we are or whatever we do, it touches other people. I was selfish and inconsiderate. I've made trouble for you, and possibly for that girl you told me of. I—I am very sorry.'

There was what seemed a long silence. Then he took her hand gently in his. 'Look, Gabriela'—his voice was as gentle as his touch—'don't be so hard on yourself. You couldn't have known. So, cheer up, mmn?' He released her hand, and smiling, reached out and pinched her cheek. 'Come along, let's see some of that Hungarian spirit!'

Gabriela smiled back at him wanly, and there was a curious moment when their eyes met and time and movement around them seemed suspended.

Then he said briskly, 'That's better. There will be no charges out of this, anyway. Jetta and Brenner are as free as birds. Katy isn't worth officialdom's valuable time. Brenner did not kidnap you and take you to the Golden Fleece. You never met a certain gentleman— and as for that certain person himself, I am informed that everyone will be told that he is in Bohemia, where he has gone to hunt. Between you and me, he has gone for a rest cure to a discreet private clinic in Switzerland, suffering from a "nervous collapse". So, you see, it's all been nicely smoothed over.'

Despite everything, Gabriela almost laughed. 'Mischa was right,' she said ironically. 'He said that's how it would be.'

'Ah, Mischa . . .' Adam said softly, and in a way which boded ill for Brenner, if ever he fell into his hands. 'I'm afraid he's escaped me—for the time being, at least. I can wait.' He took a long pull at his cigarette, and watched the smoke circle ceilingwards.

'I'm not sorry he's escaped you, Adam,' she said impulsively. 'Though he behaved so badly, he was kind to me when I needed someone to be kind—when no one else was.'

How often in the coming months was she to rue those words! Even as she spoke them, she realised how imprudent they were and likely to be misunderstood. Adam's features seemed to freeze, as if carved in stone.

'I see,' he said slowly and in a voice drenched in sarcasm. 'If that is how you feel, it's as well he got away. I should not like to harm any friend of yours!' The words hung in the air like icicles.

Gabriela wanted to cry out at once that he had misinterpreted her meaning, but one glance at his face told her that any protest on her part would only make matters worse. She fell unhappily silent, hoping that he would forget, dismissing her words from his mind as the passing thought, spoken aloud, which they were in reality.

But Adam was a man who forgot nothing. Her sinking heart told her that.

Countess Clemenz returned twenty-four hours later. She had travelled in the greatest haste from Marienbad, without even having packed, leaving her maid and luggage to follow. She went at once to her husband's bedside and remained there until nightfall.

But the following day, Count Clemenz's condition proving stable though frail, his wife shut herself in the drawing-room with Adam and held a family conference, to which Gabriela was not invited. One person who was present, however, was Dr Rimmer the lawyer. He bustled into the house, as much of a little pink and white mouse as ever, twitching at his pince-nez, and rustling an armful of papers in a nervous gesture as if he contemplated making himself a nest of them.

From the safety of the landing above, Gabriela watched him pass through the hall, and then she went back to her own room and sat down to take stock of her situation. For it was quite clear what was happening. She did not need to be present at that drawing-room meeting to know that. Count Clemenz, in his invalid state, could no longer control his affairs. His wife could manage family and household matters. Control of his business, and matters arising from the estates in the country, would now fall into the hands of Adam, who must make decisions on his uncle's behalf.

Unfortunately Gabriela herself undoubtedly came under the heading of 'family and household'—which meant that she fell into the hands of her mother-in-law. She had no more inveterate enemy. Her days in this house were numbered. Adam might intercede for her —and he might not. She had not forgotten that he had once suggested packing her off to Budapest. But even if Adam wished to help her, there was probably little he could do.

Voices drifting up from below indicated that Rimmer was making his departure. Gabriela was not surprised when, a few minutes later, a servant came up with a message that the honourable lady would like to see her straight away.

She went down to the drawing-room, calmly aware that sentence was about to be passed on her. Adam was not there, for which she was profoundly grateful. At least her humiliation was not to take place before him.

There was a look of cold triumph in Countess Clemenz's eyes, which she made no attempt to disguise. She gestured with a beringed hand at an uncomfortable straight-backed chair. 'Sit down, Gabriela. I have things to say to you, and they might as well be said now.'

She sank down on her seat and waited. Countess Clemenz, however, jumped to her feet in barely repressed glee, and began to turn up and down the room, pacing like a restless female panther. She stopped abruptly, and fixed eyes on the girl that held no hint of any understanding, only a deep and relentless enmity.

No stalking great cat ever eyed its trapped prey with a crueller triumph.

'So, Gabriela, now your future in this house lies with me,' she said tersely. 'Rest assured that I shall not share this roof with you one moment longer than is necessary. I must ask you to pack your things and leave as soon as possible. You may have a week to make arrangements. You see,' a cold smile crossed her face, 'I give you a week's grace, seven whole days longer than you mourned my son! It was formerly my husband's wish that you should be given a home here, but you have continually and wilfully abused his kindness and dishonoured our name, my son's memory and yourself.'

Gabriela felt a tide of red suffuse her cheeks, not from shame but from anger. With the greatest difficulty she managed to control herself and reply, 'I understand. I shall go as soon as possible.'

The Countess did not ask where her son's widow would go, or how she would fare. She nodded, satisfied, yet took a seat facing the girl, apparently having more to say.

Unexpectedly, she exclaimed, 'I have always known there were women like you—and never understood how it could be.'

'Like me?' Gabriela demanded, her temper breaking through the restraints she had put on it.

'Yes.' The Countess ran a critical eye over her daughter-in-law. 'You're a beauty, I do not deny it. But that is not sufficient explanation. I have known women as plain as ever a woman could be, and yet, like you, they held some fascination for men which is beyond my comprehension. Men pardon women such as you anything, Gabriela, any sin, of commission or omission, any failing. They are prepared to defend you, to sacrifice their careers and their other relationships for you, as if some madness possessed them.' Her voice grew quieter but not less venomous. 'My poor son, who always knew his duty to his parents and his family name, ignored all that, and his obligations to the unfortunate Baroness Vonneck, to marry *you*!' She spat out the last word as if it had tasted sour.

'Max never intended to marry Christiane Vonneck!' Gabriela retaliated fiercely. 'If Christiane says otherwise, she lies! Max loved me, and I loved him. You say you don't understand me, but what you don't understand is *love*!'

'And my husband?' the Countess returned coldly. 'How do you account for him? He was as distraught as I was when Max first brought you here. I watched him change. I watched you weave your spell, even over him. I was mistaken in going to Marienbad at Adam's suggestion. I see that, while I was away, you lost no opportunity to extend your influence over my husband. Well, girl, it will have gained you nothing!'

'I thought,' Gabriela said quietly, 'that I had already met the wickedest woman I could ever know. I was wrong. You are worse than she is. What you are saying is utterly loathsome, and without the smallest element of truth.'

Countess Clemenz smiled thinly. 'Is it?' She placed the tips of her white, beringed fingers together. 'I am glad you are leaving, Gabriela. Because now I see that even my husband's nephew is not safe from you. I would have expected Adam to show a harder head and heart. Goodness knows, he was always addicted to female company—usually of the lower kind—and ought to have enough experience to withstand your charm, whatever that may be! But not so. He, too, is beginning to show towards you that fatal indulgence so marked in my poor husband . . . and more, I have seen how Major Dubrowski's eyes follow you. I am not a fool, or an innocent. I know that look in a man's eyes which means that the message signalled by his loins is overruling the reasoning of his brain. And I know what attracts him to you.' She put her hands on the arms of her chair, gripping so tightly that the bones strained against the skin. 'Adam is attracted to you because, like those cheap wantons of his, you are a slut!'

'You are a terrible woman,' Gabriela told her quietly. She made a supreme effort to control her voice, shaking in her emotion. 'I'll say no more, out of respect and affection for Count Clemenz, but you always hated me, and were jealous of me, and there is nothing I could ever have done which could have changed your mind. When I came to this house I was a stranger, a girl of nineteen. I was in a country which was not my own, among people who spoke a different language. You made not the slightest effort to welcome me. Oh, you were polite! I was Max's wife, and you feared that, obliged to choose, Max would have stood by me! But I have always known what was in your mind. Can you be surprised that I looked for friendship outside this house, after Max died? There was no comfort to be had here.'

'How dare you speak to me like that, you wretched little nobody?' Countess Clemenz leapt up out of her chair, her eyes blazing. 'Get out of my house! There is no place for you either here, or in my nephew's bed! You are right in believing me your enemy. I shall be your enemy until the day I die.' She sank back. 'One week . . . !' she repeated. 'You have one week.'

CHAPTER TWELVE

GABRIELA LEFT the room and walked slowly towards the staircase. This, then, was the ultimate result of her wayward behaviour. She now faced the future without a penny of independent fortune, a shadow over her reputation, and more enemies than she cared to think about. She would have to leave Vienna, that much was certain. If she sold her jewellery, she would have enough to travel to Budapest and take a room in a cheap hotel or pension, there to take stock of an unpromising situation. But she would not regret leaving Vienna, and as for this dreadful house, she could not get out of it fast enough. A week was almost too long.

As she put her foot on the bottom stair, a movement behind her interrupted her thoughts. Adam had come out of the study. He walked quietly over and put one hand on the supporting pillar of the banister.

'Rimmer has left,' he said, 'and I fancy my aunt has had her say. I should like to talk to you, Gabriela, if you have a moment. Won't you come into the study— please?' He gestured towards the open door.

She followed him unwillingly, and he pulled out a chair for her in an unusual gesture of courtesy.

'What do you want, Adam?' she asked him uneasily.

Outside it had begun to rain, a light, autumnal rain, trickling down the panes and carrying on it scraps of fallen leaves, washed down from the gutters and roof-tops. Adam seated himself on the other side of the desk and swept a hand over the papers the lawyer had left behind. 'It's my uncle's wish that I take care of his business affairs, but Rimmer will have to sort all this

out. I don't understand the half of it.' He looked up. 'I
want to talk to you about your future.' His tone brooked
no argument; one way or another, things were going
to be settled now.

Gabriela drew a deep breath. 'I've already been
turned out of the house, Adam. I think from now on,
my future, such as it may be, need concern no one here.'

'You're wrong,' he cut in. 'My uncle . . .'

'I know what your uncle asked of you, Adam, but *I*
don't ask it of you!' she exclaimed. So that he should
not see the humiliation written on her face, she jumped
up from her chair and went to the nearest window,
where she stood, her back turned to him, staring out at
the distorted view of the empty street through the wet
panes. A solitary figure, a sturdy Viennese housewife,
was hurrying down the road, her skirts pinned up above
her ankles and her head buried in a large black umbrella.
Gabriela leaned her burning forehead against the cold,
wet glass, and closed her eyes. She heard Adam stand
up from behind the desk and come slowly over to her.

'Gaby . . .' She felt his hands rest lightly on her
shoulders and shivered beneath his touch. 'Gaby, turn
round, look at me.' His use of the familiar form of her
name surprised and disturbed her, as she had expected
a formal speech. He turned her gently to face him as he
spoke. She opened her eyes, but not wanting to look
up into his face, fixed her gaze on his tunic. 'I know, or
can guess, what my aunt has said to you,' he said in a
practical voice. 'Now I want you to listen to me. Of
course you cannot stay here. But I have a home in
Cracow, and I'm offering you a place in that.'

She thought she must have misheard. It seemed so
incredible, and truly, quite impossible. 'You can't!' she
whispered. 'You're an unmarried man . . .'

'Don't play games!' he interrupted impatiently. 'I
know an unmarried man can't take a young unmarried
woman into his household. But if we were married to
each other . . .'

'You're offering me marriage, Adam?' Gabriela lifted her head sharply. 'Just like that?' she added drily. 'When my reputation is in tatters, and I've done nothing but demonstrate to you a total lack of good sense?'

Adam flushed. 'I don't find the idea as preposterous as you seem to do,' he replied stiffly. 'There seem to me to be very good reasons.'

'I know your uncle asked you to take care of me,' she said with a rueful smile. 'But he would not expect you . . .'

'Of course he would!' Adam sounded angry. 'He knew exactly what he was asking of me. How else can I look after you, other than by marrying you?'

Gabriela felt an insane desire to laugh, but he was so serious that she dared not. He would have been mortally offended, and genuinely hurt. He saw where his duty lay, and he would do it, no matter what his personal feelings were. But he was doing something more—he was offering her back her self-respect.

'You are a truly honourable man,' she told him soberly, 'my dear, gallant, Polish Uhlan.' She smiled, and taking his hand, laid his palm gently against her own cheek, as a Hungarian peasant woman would. 'But no, Adam, I can't accept your offer. I do thank you, and I do appreciate your generosity. But I don't ask such a sacrifice of you. I shall make my own way.'

He turned the hand she held against her cheek so that he gripped her fingers tightly. 'It's not a sacrifice, Gaby. Look . . .' He seemed embarrassed and awkward. 'I'll try and explain it, but if I don't say it well, then forgive me and bear with me. I never proposed to anyone before!' He smiled at her briefly, and her heart gave a painful little lurch. 'I'm thirty-one years old, Gaby, and it's high time I married. I need a wife. It's as simple as that. I'm able to support one. Of course I should have to ask you to set up house in Cracow. I don't think anyone wants to see me around Vienna for a while. Certainly the army doesn't, or certain illustrious personages! Nor would it be wise for us to remain so near to my aunt if—if you agree to marry me. I'll be frank. There's someone else I'd prefer to be well away from —Christiane Vonneck, who is, I am convinced, more than half out of her mind, and will never cease to make mischief while either of us remains here.'

He hesitated, and looked grave. 'Gabriela, there's another reason, one which I had hoped to spare you, but I think it perhaps better you should know. The imperial court has let it be known that it would also like to have *you* out of the way. Highly placed persons want you out of Vienna. Alexander cannot be kept in Switzerland indefinitely and sooner or later must return. They want you placed beyond his reach, safely married. Although that is not a reason to accept *me*, you should realise that, not to put too fine a point upon it, if you cannot see your way to marrying me, they will put pressure on you to accept a husband of their choice.'

He saw the alarm on her face, and added soothingly, 'It's not so bad. I told you once before that I should like to take you to Cracow, and so I should. It's my home, and why should I make excuses for it? I believe you'd like it there. I'd trade Vienna for it any day! It's an old and beautiful city. My house is quite large and central. It's a little run down, perhaps, but that is because it has been a bachelor establishment for so long! You could make any changes you fancied, and have it redecorated to suit your taste.' His voice was gaining in enthusiasm. 'It's perhaps not such a bad proposition as you seem to think, Gaby. As for myself, I promise you that I'll look after you to the best of my ability.' He paused. 'What do you say? Do you agree?'

He was telling her that, in effect, she had no choice, but that things could be worse. But not even to secure the peace of mind of the imperial entourage, anxious to prevent an open scandal at so high a level, would she rush into a marriage with Adam without certain questions resolved.

'You say,' she replied, choosing her words carefully, 'that you need a wife. That implies that you would like children, certainly an heir. You do realise I was never pregnant at any time during my previous marriage, and that there is a distinct possibility I should not bring you any children.'

'Well,' Adam said evenly, 'that is in the lap of the gods. One can never guarantee these things.' A smile touched his lean features again, softening their severity. 'We shall just have to keep trying.'

She looked away, knowing that he was waiting for her answer. There were so many other things she would have liked to ask him. Chief among them was the simple question, 'Do you love me, Adam?' But it would be a foolish question in these circumstances. Neither of them had talked of love, and she lacked the courage to introduce the subject now. Adam was indeed an honest man, and he would not lie about so important a matter. He would reply 'No', and she did not want to hear him say it.

'You hesitate,' he said, when she remained silent. 'Perhaps you don't think much of the idea of me as a husband?'

Gabriela, shocked, exclaimed, 'I didn't say that!'

'Perhaps you should,' he returned unexpectedly. 'I don't have any illusions about myself, Gaby, and I shouldn't want you to have any. Oh, I'm not trying to put you off, to wriggle out of it!' He grinned at her broadly, but then grew serious again. 'I'm impatient, and quick-tempered, and dislike having to explain myself. I dare say I'm self-centred, too. Anyone who has been thirty-one years a bachelor, pleasing no one but himself, must be.'

'I understand.'

'I can't change, Gaby,' Adam told her softly. 'As I am, so you'll have to put up with me.'

'Yes,' Gabriela said. 'I know that, too.'

He was offering her a marriage of expediency, and

spelling out its terms with a painful honesty, clumsy and
sincere. If she made this marriage, she made it on his
terms, and he wanted her to know that. If she agreed,
he would probably ask Rimmer to draw up a marriage
contract. Max had proposed in a garden by moonlight,
where they had hidden from the other guests behind a
trellis of climbing roses. The scent of the flowers had
pervaded the air as he had stumbled over his ardent
declaration of devotion.

Now she sat in this room, with the rain trickling down
the windows, to receive a carefully worded proposal
from a man who had talked of everything except love
—a man she respected, and to whom she was beholden,
but whom in her heart of hearts she knew she feared.

A little tremulously she said, 'I agree.'

Quite how Adam obliged his aunt to accept the news
of the proposed marriage, Gabriela never knew. The
entire household heard Countess Clemenz's initial reaction. Her screamed words, 'No, no, never!' lanced
through the air of the whole house. The rest of what
must have been a fierce battle of bitter accusations,
recriminations and naked passions was a secret Adam
always kept to himself. Perhaps he had invoked imperial
will and the threat of imperial displeasure were the
marriage to be hindered. Perhaps he had just dug in his
heels and stood firm. He was an obstinate man, more
than a match for his aunt. Count Clemenz, weak and
frail, gave his blessing from his sick-bed, and it was
likely that, unable to call upon her husband to oppose
the match, Countess Clemenz saw herself deprived of
the support she needed. Whatever had happened, the
resulting decision was that they would marry at once,
and very quietly.

It was not yet a full year since Max's death, although
it seemed to Gabriela that she had lived a whole lifetime
since then, but any kind of celebration was obviously
quite out of the question. Countess Clemenz made it

clear that she would not attend the ceremony, and took herself off to stay with a friend, declaring she would never publicly acknowledge the marriage. Adam and Gabriela would be married, and return to the Vienna house for one night. The next day they would leave for Cracow. Only when the bridal couple had departed would Countess Clemenz return to the house from which their tainted presence had been removed.

With the lack of time, and so many arrangements to be made and affairs to be set in order, it was the strangest wedding day anyone ever had, Gabriela thought. The service was crammed in during the morning between organising the packing and signing papers for, and giving instructions to, Dr Rimmer. The general air of haste and urgency seemed to affect even the priest, who gabbled through the formalities and dropped the rings. It was hardly a good omen.

'Not much of a Polish wedding!' Adam observed drily as they walked out of the church, and he handed her up into the waiting carriage. 'We usually celebrate for days.'

A small group of curious bystanders had gathered to watch, as always, before any church where a wedding was in progress. The handsome Uhlan and the pale but beautiful woman on his arm made a striking couple, but even to these strangers, an unusual bride and groom. When the carriage had left, they fell to exchanging possible explanations.

'Perhaps they've eloped,' offered one rosy-cheeked little maidservant with a basket on her arm, sentimentally.

'More like he got her into trouble!' was the more robust suggestion of a young workman, who had stopped less to watch the bride than the maidservant.

'Oh, yes?' snapped the girl. 'Well, perhaps *he's* a gentleman!'

'Gentlemen do it, too! Here . . .' He eyed her hopefully, 'Carry your basket for you?'

She tossed her head. 'I ain't broken my arm!'

'I was being a gentleman!' said her aggrieved admirer, and was further disappointed to see this was not well received.

As time wore on, it seemed to Gabriela to be even less of a wedding day. First, Arlette gave way to minor hysterics and announced that she wouldn't go to Galicia with madame, not if wild horses tried to drag her there. It was the back of beyond, Galicia was, no one understood a word of any civilised language, and it snowed for months on end.

More than satisfied to be rid of the girl, Gabriela told her sharply that it was as well they part company, and she trusted that Arlette would find new and suitable employment quickly. The maid replied snappishly that she had had a very good offer already, and left the house there and then, without even finishing the packing. Her parting shot was that all Slav men beat their women— it was well known.

So Gabriela struggled to complete her own packing, as it happened uninterrupted, for later that day Dr Rimmer scuttled in, bowed beneath a bulging leather case of documents, all of which Count Dubrowski, as administrator of his uncle's affairs, must read and sign before he left for Cracow. She managed to finish and found herself, on her wedding night, surrounded by trunks and boxes, preparing to go to bed alone, as her new husband was still closeted with the lawyer downstairs. The steady drone of their voices through the study door did not suggest that Adam was likely to arrive soon.

Gabriela undressed slowly and took her time brushing out her hair. Someone had turned back the bed, and the twin lace-trimmed pillows were plumped up, pristine and untouched. She felt inexplicably nervous, almost afraid, of those crisp white sheets. Not even the first time, on her first wedding night, had she felt like this. Then, both she and Max had been nervous and a little fearful. This time only she was afraid. Of Adam? She turned the thought over in her mind, seeking an explanation. He was a man who expected a great deal of people. Perhaps he would expect a great deal of her, in that bed. After all, she had been married before, and he had a right to assume that she was a woman of some experience and not a timorous virgin. But Max had asked so little of her in the terms of their physical relationship, and now, thinking of Adam, she knew it was his love-making she feared. She had a premonition of failure on her part to be able to give what he would ask of her. It would have been different if she had known that Adam would come to her as a lover, seeking only to prove his love and ask a token of hers, in a union as emotional as it was physical. But Adam did not love her. Perhaps, in his heart of hearts, he even despised her. Had he not offered her marriage as much because of his promise to a sick man, or orders from his imperial overlord, as out of any interest of his own? He would come to her bed and take her in an act of male lust and nothing more. It would even be judged, perhaps, by comparison with experiences he had had with other women. Her blood ran cold at the thought. She extinguished the gas-light to blot out the mocking sight of those smooth white sheets, and scrambling quickly into the bed, pulled the covers over her.

The last thing she expected was that she would fall asleep. But the hectic day and the onerous packing had taken its toll, and she fell into a restless slumber almost at once, tossing on the pillows and muttering to herself.

Gabriela awoke with a suddenness that disorientated her. She knew instinctively that it must be very late, and also that she was not alone in the room. A pale moonlight filtered through the shutters, and silhouetted against them was the dark figure of a naked man. Her heart gave a tremendous leap of panic. 'Adam?' she whispered tremulously.

'I thought you might be asleep.' His voice came back

quietly. The dark figure moved closer to her. 'Did I wake you?'

'No . . . I don't know. I was asleep, I think . . .' she mumbled, confused.

'Rimmer was prepared to go on for ever until I reminded him that it was my wedding night. Then the poor old fellow dropped all his papers and took himself off, apologising like fury!' Adam chuckled, and she felt that strange tremor run along her spine. The sheets were pulled back, and the side of the bed sank beneath his weight. 'Move over . . .' he said impatiently.

She obediently wriggled out from the warm spot she had occupied in the middle of the bed and retreated to the colder outer edge. The touch of the chilly sheets cleared her brain. How used I must be to sleeping alone, she thought ruefully. When one sleeps alone, one automatically settles in the middle of the bed. You forget that, when you share it with someone, you have to stay over on one side . . .

Adam slid into the bed, and his foot brushed against her leg. That feeling of panic returned and she felt her body freeze. He slipped his arm across her breast and rolled over towards her, pulling her towards him possessively, seeking her lips urgently with his mouth. Try as she might, she could not respond, and he sensed it from the rigidity of her body beneath the gentle, exploring touch of his hand.

He propped himself up on one elbow. 'Gaby?' She could see the shape of his head and shoulders bent over her. 'What's the matter?'

What on earth could she say? Be patient, Adam, give me time . . . He wouldn't wait. Rimmer had already delayed him downstairs for hours and now he was out of patience. The ancient animal instincts lurking within man had awoken and roused him, and were demanding the completion of the physical act they existed to perpetuate. That much she had already seen in the brief glimpse of him against the moonlit shutter. She said nothing.

'For pity's sake!' he exclaimed angrily, 'You're not sulking because I was late? It's not my fault that Rimmer came over with his confounded papers, and I got rid of him as soon as I could!' He was angry and disappointed, teetering on the edge of losing control.

'No,' Gabriela whispered. 'It's nothing to do with that. It's . . .' She fell silent, knowing she could not explain. 'I'm sorry . . .' she said miserably.

For a while Adam did not move or speak. The long silence increased her alarm. She plucked up courage to stretch out her hand, and her fingers touched the bare flesh of his arm. 'Adam . . .'

But her attempt at conciliation was lost as he suddenly threw aside the bedclothes and jumped out of the bed. 'It's all right!' he said harshly. 'You don't have to sacrifice yourself—I'm not interested in rape!'

Gabriela scrambled upright and exclaimed, 'What are you doing?' as she saw him walking towards the door.

He paused. 'It's very late, Gabriela, and I'm sorry. I forgot that you would be tired and probably asleep already. I shouldn't have come. I'll . . . go back to my own room. I'll see you in the morning.'

'But Adam . . .' she began, aghast at the result of her lack of enthusiasm, and how it had been interpreted by her bridegroom.

He interrupted her. 'We have to make an early start, Gaby. Try and get some sleep. Good night.'

The door clicked behind him, and she lay back on the rumpled pillows and stared into the darkness. Adam had given her his name and a chance to redeem her mistakes. But, as if bent on her own downfall, she had only compounded them by making an even greater error. Her unwillingness had been a rejection of both him and the hand he had reached out to her in her need. She had insulted him in his pride and in his manhood, and too scrupulous to force himself on a bride who so obviously recoiled from his approach, he had gone to sleep alone. Wherever Mischa Brenner was now, if he could know this, what satisfaction and revenge he would gain from the knowledge! In the darkness, Gabriela could almost imagine his mocking laughter.

Gabriela slept fitfully, and awoke with a heavy head and heart. Yet, to her surprise, Adam was singing. She could hear his voice floating down the corridor, warbling loudly but tunefully—he had a good voice—some folk-song in Polish. Getting out of bed, she opened the door, listening incredulously. From his dressing-room, the sound of splashing water indicated that he was in his bath.

She closed the door and frowned, puzzled. She had been expecting that after the unfortunate experiences of the previous night, he would be out of temper and morose, but apparently not so. She shrugged, vaguely annoyed. Could she really be of so little importance to him? Still, it would make it easier to face him over the breakfast table.

When she did come downstairs a little later, Adam had finished his breakfast and was sitting at the table alone, drinking the last of his coffee.

'There you are!' he greeted her briskly. 'Come along —we've a train to catch.'

Gabriela wondered whether she ought to go and bestow a wifely good morning kiss on him. Would he expect it? Her courage failed her, and she took the seat opposite him.

'I heard you singing,' she said brightly. 'You—you sounded very cheerful.'

He looked very cheerful, she thought. Younger, more at ease, as if some weight had been lifted from his shoulders. The sun shone on his chestnut hair, making the red lights gleam in the dark brown, and his face retained its vivacity and intelligence, without the sharpness.

He looked up and met her puzzled blue eyes, studying him. 'Of course,' he said. 'We're going to Poland today. We're going home!'

Only then did she realise just how much he had disliked being in Vienna, and how unhappy he must have been here. He jumped to his feet and with a final good-humoured, if slightly impatient, command to her to 'hurry along, for goodness' sake', disappeared through the door.

He, also, had made no attempt to kiss her. He was happy because he was going home. His cheerfulness served another purpose, too. It pushed aside any problem with his new marriage. There was a horrible familiarity about it all. Max had always been cheerful. Max, after the first few heady weeks together, had not really wanted her, either. It was this glittering, brittle, worldly and corrupting Viennese life which poisoned relationships. The provincial charms of Cracow suddenly seemed to Gabriela to hold out a promise of hope.

They travelled by rail, and because Adam was anxious not to lose time, they took the express service which carried them as far as Oderberg, near the Prussian frontier. A tedious journey, but it lasted a mere six and a half hours. At Oderberg they changed to the slower train, which would take all of another three and a quarter hours, stopping along the way at stations with unknown and unpronounceable names. Adam, who had been visibly bored until they changed trains, began to fidget after they crossed the little river that marked the frontier between Silesia and Galicia. Once they had crossed the Vistula, winding its way into the heart of the country, towards Cracow itself, he was like a schoolboy, peering out of the window and calling Gabriela's attention to everything of the slightest interest they passed. She was almost as eager as he was to see this new and, for her, adopted country which was to be her home.

Though she knew Adam loved his homeland, she had not realised until then just how much it meant to him to be among his own people again. He got out of the train at every stop, ostensibly to smoke a cigarette on the busy platform, but in reality to chat to the kerchiefed peasant women sitting by their bundles and baskets, waiting for the slow country trains which would take them to and from the markets in the towns. Sometimes, by way of an excuse to talk, he bought some produce from them, apples or flowers, and a pile of goods gradually began to fill the compartment. But frequently he came back with much odder things . . . eggs, home-churned butter wrapped in greasy and none too clean paper, even gaudy religious pictures connected with the various Polish shrines.

'It's not my doing,' he explained with unanswerable charm, when she protested. 'They ask where I'm going. Peasants always want to know your business. They already know each other's! I tell them that I'm coming home, from Vienna. Then, because I'm a Polish soldier on his way home from so far away, they give me these things, welcoming presents. I can't refuse.'

So they progressed, their compartment gradually starting to resemble a cross between a florist's shop and a grocery.

'Bronia will use all these things up,' he said optimistically, emptying the butter, fruit and vegetables into one bag, but fortunately not the eggs, which he donated to a startled old lady who got off the train at Trzebinia.

Soon after that, he touched Gabriela's arm and pointed. The railway was running alongside a country road, and on it was a long, colourful and noisy peasant wedding procession. The orchestra led the way, fiddling merrily, and behind them came what must have been the entire village, bearing in their midst the bride, as stiff as a wooden doll in her layers of embroidered petticoats, her head weighed down by a massive crown of interwoven flowers and ribbons. Now she understood

Adam's wry comment on their own sparse wedding, hardly a wedding at all in his eyes. She wondered, a little sadly, if, had they married for love, as had his father and mother, he would have insisted on more festivity. Perhaps, for a marriage such as theirs, the gabbled service had been enough.

'It costs a peasant family a fortune to marry off its daughters,' Adam said to her, breaking into her thoughts. 'But it's a matter of pride and self-respect, so even if it puts him into debt for years, the farmer entertains the whole village and no expense is spared.'

'But what happens if he's too poor?'

'Then the poor girl doesn't get married. There's no such thing as a penny-pinching wedding in this part of the world. I had a young fellow who worked for me once, who was in despair because he'd been engaged to a girl for three years and bad harvests had meant the family couldn't afford the wedding, and it was put off indefinitely. It can happen, you know, that the couple are obliged to wait so long that they give up altogether. But this boy was set on the girl, and was an honest lad, so that in the end I lent her father the money for the wedding. He undertook to pay me back in kind, over a period of years. This has meant, in effect, that every so often he appears at my back door with a piglet or a couple of chickens, or an offer to do odd jobs about the place. Everybody is happy.' He smiled at her.

Adam was an odd mixture of a man, Gabriela thought: touchy, intransigent and aggressive, but extraordinarily kind when one least expected it. He never took advantage of another person's weakness. Behaviour like that was beneath him.

However, she was especially curious to see the countryside through which they passed, because she remembered Brenner's disparaging description of it. It was true that many of the villages did look wretchedly poor. The wooden cottages had tiny windows and must be dark and airless within, especially housing such large families. There was no shortage of children, running along beside the train tracks and waving. But they seemed lively and healthy enough, and some of the peasant girls with long braids and coloured aprons who waited at the rural halts were extremely pretty. She remarked on this to Adam.

'They're pretty,' he agreed, 'but life is hard in the country, and the bloom soon fades from them. But they are good girls, very religious.' He grinned. 'And virtuous!'

'Is that the voice of sad experience?' she was bold enough to ask him.

He hunched his shoulders. 'Not since I grew old enough to know better! But when I was about eighteen or nineteen, and had no sense, I was chased out of more than one barn by an enraged farmer with a pitchfork! In the end, my father, who was a practical man, took me aside and said that since *that* appeared to be all I had on my mind, he advised me not to run myself and respectable girls into trouble and to confine my activities to the establishments which existed for that purpose.'

'That is when you began your habit of visiting places like the Golden Fleece?'

'Yes,' Adam replied briefly.

The mention of the Golden Fleece had been a mistake, as she quickly realised. A sour note had been struck, and their light-hearted conversation came to an abrupt end. Adam grew morose, in marked contrast to his previous happy mood. At last they rocked slowly past a wooden sign bearing the legend in three languages:

KRAKÓW—KRAKAU—CRACOVIE

'Well,' he said to her in a stilted voice. 'You are here.'

They managed with some difficulty to load themselves and their luggage, including the assortment of flowers and comestibles they had collected *en route*, into two

open cabs and rattled through the streets of the lovely
old city.

On the steps of Adam's house they were greeted
effusively by a plump, voluble woman with a perspiring
face, who first hugged Adam, then Gabriela, and finally
burst into tears.

'It's Bronia, my housekeeper.'

'Why is she crying?' Gabriela asked, bewildered.

'She's pleased to see us,' he said simply. He held
out his hand towards Gabriela. 'You are Countess
Dubrowska,' he said soberly. 'You are mistress of this
house now.' He took her hand in his, and led her over
the threshold to her new life.

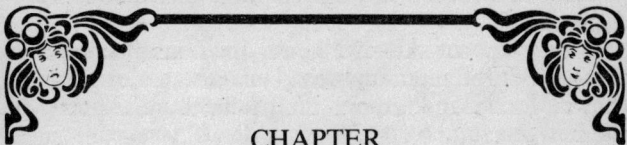

CHAPTER
THIRTEEN

THE HOUSE was old. Its woodwork creaked, and the stairs were crooked and worn smooth from countless footsteps. From the narrow windows could be seen Wawel Hill, topped by its ancient castle, and the descending pitched roofs of the houses lining the winding streets.

It was very much Bronia's domain. With the help of two sturdy, country-born maids, she had run this house for many years, including during Adam's frequent absences. Gabriela wondered just how the housekeeper would accept a new mistress, who would want to make changes and who, unused to running a home, would certainly make mistakes.

In fact, Bronia showed surprisingly little resentment, and seemed delighted that the house had a mistress at last. 'It's as it should be,' she said, as she conducted Gabriela proudly into every nook and cranny, filling her ears with information spoken in a broken, voluble German, helped out by many gestures. There was not a single stick of furniture, it seemed, that had not its own history or some individual characteristic.

'This cupboard now,' said Bronia, pausing for breath before a large, patriarchal clothes press which looked very much as though it might have stood there since since the days of King Jan Sobieski, 'You've to put your foot against the bottom of the door, press and pull, and then it opens sweetly. If you don't, it won't open and that's that. It's a family piece, and it's grown to be like one of the family in its ways.'

'How do you mean, Bronia?' Gabriela asked, puzzled.

'Every Dubrowski is the same,' the housekeeper said firmly. 'All the men, anyway. Handle them aright and they're good, kind fellows, no trouble at all. Approach them wrong, and oh my! They're devils. Everything has to be done as they want it done, even if you know a better way. If you try to change them, they get obstinate and awkward, turn their backs on you and sulk. They've tempers, you see, and pride. Every Pole has pride but a Dubrowski has enough pride for twenty!' Bronia turned to the cupboard and eyed it ferociously. 'And you, you wooden brute, you're a Dubrowski at his worst.'

'I see,' Gabriela said thoughtfully.

Perhaps pride was the key to Adam, but even so, she was finding that unlocking the doorway to a true understanding with him was far more difficult than getting to grips with a house and a few pieces of awkward furniture. So cheerful and optimistic on their journey to Cracow, now that they were here he seemed, in total contrast, to have been overtaken by some kind of monosyllabic and gloomy humour which she could not understand.

Pressed by her to say what troubled him, he grew evasive. 'We have troubles here in Galicia—you wouldn't understand them.'

'I might, if you'd explain!' she objected in exasperation.

Adam heaved a sigh. 'You wouldn't be interested. Look, we sit here on Russia's doorstep, and the Tsar has an eye on our territory; not all of it, but Eastern Galicia. It's easy for the Tsar to send in his agents and stir up trouble. They're at work now, but winkling them out isn't easy. Nor do their activities stop there. There are certain Polish elements, even here in Cracow, who are restive under Austrian rule—they don't like to see those Austrian uniforms up there on the hill, guarding

Wawel Castle.' He waved towards the window. 'Well, we none of us like . . .' He broke off and corrected himself. 'It's not a perfect situation, but it allows us to keep what we have . . .'

But it was not only politics that bothered Adam. Gabriela began to fear it was the sudden change from carefree bachelorhood to domesticity. When he was at home, he wandered about the house, as if inspecting it critically, stamping on its uneven wooden floors and muttering over stiff catches and hinges, glaring morosely at furniture and fittings. She was eager to tell him that she had quite fallen in love with the house, despite— or even, perhaps, because of—its oddities, but he just grunted, and muttered about getting the decorators in.

When the painters did arrive, they worked quite a transformation. The dark rooms, under a new coat of lighter paint and pastel wallpapers, seemed more spacious and airy. Gabriela hoped Adam would be pleased with the results. But the presence of the workmen did cause a great deal of inconvenience and fuss. The smell of paint haunted the house for weeks, and moving from room to room was fraught with difficulties for a time. Objects disappeared beneath dust-sheets and could not be found again until the men had moved out. On one particularly trying occasion, they put a fresh coat of paint in the vestibule and failed to tell anyone, so that Adam, hanging up his military greatcoat on coming home, found it securely stuck to the wall when he wanted to leave again. There was an increase in the messages sent home to say that he would be dining out.

Despite all this domestic upheaval and discomfort, Gabriela comforted herself, and Adam, that when the workmen had gone, everything would be better.

It wasn't. Adam's mood did not improve, and it seemed to Gabriela that the newly painted house mocked her. '*He* liked me the way I was before,' it seemed to say to her. '*You* have made changes.'

But she persevered. She bought herself a Polish grammar and set herself to learn this language which seemed, from the printed word, to consist of far too many consonants without enough vowels to go round. She practised her Polish assiduously on Bronia and the maids, and occasionally on Adam. But he—quite contrary to what she had expected—seemed, if anything, irritated by her attempts to learn his language. He listened impatiently and was apt to say, 'No, that's wrong!' and then walk off without bothering to explain the mistake, which was annoying and hurtful.

Winter was drawing near, and Bronia began to store away the stacks of jams and pickles, and strings of sausages. Gabriela rolled up her sleeves, tied on an apron, and went down to the kitchen to learn how it was done.

'Bronia, there's enough here to feed an army!' she protested.

'Our winters are very long, dear lady,' puffed Bronia, her face redder than ever, as she teetered insecurely on the topmost rung of a stepladder, piling jars of pickled cucumber into a high cupboard.

Adam came unexpectedly into the kitchen in the middle of it all. 'What are you doing?' He picked up her hands and turned them over. 'Your hands are getting red,' he observed disparagingly, 'and you're breaking your nails.'

'That was yesterday,' Gabriela explained ruefully, 'when we moved the jams.'

'Why the devil were you moving pots of jam?' he snapped. 'If we haven't enough servants, I'll hire some more!'

He turned and strode out, leaving Gabriela angry. A tear rolled down her cheek, and she scrubbed it furiously away.

Bronia had climbed down from the stepladder and put an arm round her shoulders in comfort. 'Don't cry, my dear. He didn't mean to be sharp with you. It's his way. Very likely he doesn't care to see you down here in my kitchen. You're his wife. You're a lady. He thinks you ought to be doing something different.'

'I haven't got anything else to do!' she said vehemently, and then stopped, struck by her own words.

It was true. She hadn't anything else to do. It was a small city, socially a backwater. Cracow might have been a million miles from Vienna, not some two hundred and sixty. She had grown to love it dearly, but it offered few entertainments. Adam was away a great deal about his garrison duties, and frequently he went out in the evenings and did not return until after she had gone to bed. She had to admit that she was lonely. She washed her hands, took off her apron, and went to find Adam. He was sitting and smoking, staring moodily out of the window. He looked distinctly unapproachable, but she had to make the effort. Her first marriage had been marked by a diverging of interests and a slow drifting apart which, had Max not died, would have continued to become a chasm. There was a chasm in her second marriage, and it must be bridged.

'I didn't think you'd mind,' she began defensively. 'I thought I ought to know how it's done, or how can I direct other people?'

'I have a housekeeper,' he said in a clipped voice, without looking up. 'Bronia is quite capable.'

'Then what am *I* supposed to do?' Gabriela exclaimed, suddenly losing her temper, because his attitude seemed so unfair and her well-meant efforts unappreciated. 'I don't know anybody here. I can't walk round the town all day. There's nothing else to do!'

He drew a deep breath but did not answer. After a cold silence, he indicated some papers on the table before him, and said, 'I've had letters from Vienna. My uncle has made some small improvement . . . and Christiane Vonneck has returned to Silesia and married some square-headed Prussian landowner.'

'They are probably well suited,' she replied unkindly.
'But she would much rather have married you. And
perhaps you should have married her, Adam, and not
me!'

'And what is that supposed to mean?' The deep-set
eyes rested on her in an unfriendly fashion.

'You would not have been burdened with me!' Gabriela cried out angrily. 'You should have left me in
Vienna!'

'You may regret you married me, Gabriela,' he said
quietly, 'you may not like it here, and you may even
not like *me* very much. But you are married to me, and
we must *both* make the best of it, my dear.'

'But I didn't mean . . .' she began hastily, but Adam
jumped to his feet and ground out his cigarette in a
rapid gesture. 'Where are you going?' she asked, as he
made towards the door.

'Out!'

When he had gone, she threw herself disconsolately
on to the chair he had vacated, and sighed.

Adam's cheerfulness on leaving Vienna had led her
to hope that, once they reached Cracow, it might be
easier for them both to make a new start. Alas, these
sanguine hopes had remained unfulfilled.

The unescapable fact was, that since their disastrous
wedding night in Vienna, he had made no further
attempt to visit her bed, though they had adjoining
rooms, both giving on to the same corridor and also
linked internally by a connecting door. Gabriela found
herself in a kind of limbo. She remained Max's widow,
and was not yet truly Adam's wife. Their marriage was
a shell of outward convention without any physical
reality.

Little wonder Adam's mood remained sombre. She
bemoaned her unwelcoming reception of him in her bed
in Vienna. Other obstacles stood between them, but all
might have been overcome, she told herself, had she
been able to show herself more willing then. Putting

matters right now was by no means easy. Her attempts to build a relationship with him fell on stony ground. As for any attempt on her part to make the first approaches in love-making, that was something no respectable married lady was supposed even to contemplate, and no husband expected. Convention's heavy hand lay even on the marriage bed—no more so than in marriages of convenience, such as theirs.

So, whenever Adam stayed out late—as he frequently did—she would lie awake until she heard his returning footsteps on the stair and in the corridor outside her room. Sometimes he paused there, as if he debated whether or not to come in. Her heart would begin to beat more rapidly, and she would hold her breath, wondering if, this time, the door handle would turn, and he would enter. But then he would pass by. She would hear him moving about in his own room, getting ready for bed, and then there would be silence throughout the house, broken only by the creak of the aged wood moving in the changing temperatures of night.

Gabriela was left alone with her disappointment and despair, lying awake in the darkness, seeking a solution and an explanation, and wondering how much longer this situation could go on. She herself could not bear the pretence much longer. Her desperation was compounded by a half-recognised jealousy. Adam was a man to whom women were a necessity, she understood that well enough. So if he was not coming to her bed, she very much feared he was going to someone else's. She wondered whether he had a mistress, in whose arms he could find a warm and ready welcome, and forced herself to consider this possibility as dispassionately as possible. Eventually she came to the conclusion that it was more likely that he had simply slipped back into his old habits of frequenting the colourful, disreputable cabarets and the cheerful, outspoken company of their painted hostesses, whose conversation amused him and who asked nothing of him but his money. Adam had told her he had wanted a wife. But a wife asks of her husband a part of his life. Adam had never given any woman that. In her heart, Gabriela began to fear she had become a nuisance to him.

The day after their quarrel over her activities in the kitchen, Gabriela awoke to a curious, muffled atmosphere all round and a luminous light filtering through the shutters. When she threw them open, a wonderful sight greeted her eyes. Overnight it had snowed. Everything glistened fresh and white. Children were throwing snowballs, and the air was as clear as crystal.

'Now it starts!' said Bronia. 'Now we'll need our pickles and jams.'

Gabriela pinned up her skirts and went out to walk in the snow. As a child she had always loved to do this, to tread through the crisp, glittering crust of the first snowfall. Everywhere looked so pretty, the snow veiling the steep-gabled roof-tops and the church towers and spires, and the air was so crisp and dry that it did not seem to be cold at all. The cab-horses wore blankets, and sacking tied over their hoofs to prevent them slipping. The drivers were wrapped up like Egyptian mummies, only their eyes peering out through layers of scarf. There was a rank before the city's fine ancient Cloth Hall, and as she passed by it, a young man stepped out from under an arcade to engage one of the cabs. They stopped, face to face, and stared at one another.

'Mischa . . .' she said, in a resigned voice. 'I always knew you'd turn up again.'

Brenner looked at her silently for a moment, then asked quietly, 'Do you want me to walk away? I will, if you prefer.'

It seemed as if he always turned up when she felt especially lonely or friendless. She knew she ought to say 'Get out of my sight!', but to see a familiar face was so precious to her that she could not bring herself to drive him away at once.

She shook her head. 'No.'

He brightened. 'It's cold out here,' he said briskly. 'Come and sit in one of the cafés for ten minutes.'

'Someone might see us.'

'Not if we go to a small café. I don't mean us to sit in the middle of Cracow's most fashionable coffee-house —supposing that Cracow *has* a fashionable haunt of any kind!'

Gabriela laughed, for the first time in several days. 'How rude you are, Mischa. It's a lovely old city.'

'It's as dead as the moon. Come on!' He led her firmly into a little café just round the corner from the cab-rank. It was undistinguished enough. Some of the cab-men were drinking their coffee there. But it looked bright and friendly and it was warm, and she relaxed. It was highly unlikely that they would be recognised in here.

Brenner ordered *herbata*, the Polish tea, and then sat back and studied her with open appraisal. 'You look lovely, my dear, but peaky. You looked better when *I* took care of you. You are Countess Dubrowska now, I suppose?' When she nodded, he said moodily, 'I always suspected you might marry him. Well, and how *is* the Polish stallion these days?'

That was so far from the truth, at least as far as *she* was concerned, that she exclaimed, almost in pain, 'Don't call him that!'

Brenner's dark eyes ran over her shrewdly. 'You're not happy. I warned you. This is the most boring place on earth.'

'Then what brings *you* here, Mischa?' she asked sharply.

He smiled in his boyish way, and held up an admonishing finger. 'Ah!' he said playfully.

'You're up to no good, I suppose,' she said accusingly.

'Call it that if you like. I call it earning a living,' he replied sullenly.

'Tell me what you're doing. And tell me the truth if you can!'

He looked hurt. 'Of course I can.' A mocking
expression entered his dark eyes and he leaned back in
his chair. 'I'll tell you exactly what I'm doing here,
Gaby, because I know you won't give me away to
Dubrowski. You won't give me away because you'd
never dare to tell him you've seen me again!'

He was quite right. In a sense he had her trapped.
Once again he had set his snare, and she had stepped
neatly into it. 'You think yourself clever, Mischa,'
Gabriela told him evenly. 'But you weren't clever
enough before. Don't try any tricks now.'

But as she spoke she wondered whether he might not
be tempted to get his revenge, now that she had fallen
into his hands again. Mischa Brenner never forgot a
grudge, or a slight.

At the moment he radiated confidence as he grinned
impudently at her across the table. He lowered his
voice. 'After our little *contretemps* in Vienna, I had to
get away. You see, Countess, unlike some other men,
who inherit fortunes, *I* have to earn my crust of bread!
The Tsar's government are very interested in Eastern
Galicia. That is to say that they have certain territorial
ambitions there, and in the Bukovina.' He shrugged. 'I
don't care who rules it,' he continued frankly. 'It only
puzzles me that anyone should want it, but there! Well,
I know Galicia. I speak not only Russian and German,
but Polish, and Ukrainian. So . . .'

'So the Tsar's agents have sent you here to stir up
what trouble you can for Austria,' Gabriela concluded
sweetly. 'I should think you're very good at that,
Mischa.'

'I am,' he replied confidently. 'The Russians appreciate my good work, and they pay me very well.'

So he was a traitor to Austria, too. She was not
surprised to learn it—he had no loyalties. An idea
struck her. 'Jetta isn't here with you, is she?' she
demanded in a cold little voice.

'No, she damn well isn't!' Brenner snarled. 'As far as

I know, the old witch is in Prague. She had to go there to get out of the way of that confounded snooping policeman, Gruber.'

The news that honest, phlegmatic Gruber, despite all official pressures, had not given up his investigations but clung doggedly to his task pleased Gabriela immensely. But Brenner's words recalled a very unpleasant subject indeed. It occurred to her, belatedly, that quite possibly she was sitting here, drinking tea, with a man who had contributed to a despicable crime.

'What happened to the girl called Katy?' she asked coolly.

His eyes flickered over her. 'Dubrowski's girl, you mean?' He phrased it that way deliberately because he knew it would hurt her, and when he saw her cheeks colour, he smiled. It was a cruel little smile, as if she had put into his hands a weapon with which he could be revenged on her. 'She's here,' he said casually. He relaxed in his chair and watched her face closely. Innocently, he added, 'Didn't the gallant Pole tell you? No, I don't suppose a faithful—or not so faithful— husband would.'

'You're lying to me, Mischa,' she whispered, her face as white as the freshly fallen snow outside the windows.

'No, I'm not.' Perhaps he was sorry for having hurt her so deliberately, because he added quickly, 'Perhaps Dubrowski doesn't know of it, but he certainly will sooner or later. She is here, I swear . . . and it would surprise me if he didn't know. After all, she could have come here only because of him. She's plying her old profession, frequenting a place on Wawel Hill, near the castle, convenient for the officers of the garrison! You could send someone up there to ask for her, if you don't believe me. She's a pert-looking girl with red hair. I never cared for her myself. She doesn't know *I* am here, or she'd probably run away again.' Brenner grinned, then added seriously, 'I'm not particularly anxious that

she should see me, as it happens. She can't be trusted
to keep her mouth shut.'

Gabriela grasped at a straw. 'But she vanished, in
Vienna, and no one could find her.'

'She was afraid of old Jetta,' he said, adding savagely,
'oh, I know Dubrowski thinks I probably murdered
her, but Dubrowski makes up his mind about all sorts
of things, and isn't always right. Look Gaby . . .' his
tone gained a note of entreaty, 'I'm not ashamed of
anything I've done, because I do it to live. No one ever
helped *me*—and I owe no one anything. But I'm not a
common criminal. I can't answer for Jetta, or that
creature Friedl she employs, of course.' He seemed to
think this sufficient explanation and excuse, and added
stubbornly, 'Where else would the girl come, but here?
She was always sweet on Dubrowski. Perhaps she had
visions of his rescuing her from a life of sin and making
an honest woman of her! But he wouldn't do that. That
would offend his noble ancestors and his drunken fellow
officers. Dubrowski thinks himself better than the rest
of us. I think that's why I dislike him.'

'No, it isn't.' Gabriela was regaining her composure
at last. 'He did something to you. I don't know what it
was, but it's something you don't forgive.' Brenner gave
her a bitter little smile, and said nothing. But Gabriela
was remembering things now, and piecing them
together. 'You were in Galicia before. You have some
grudge against the whole place—not just Adam, but
every Pole, and especially every Polish officer.'

'I don't have to like the place,' Brenner parried.
'Dubrowski likes it because he's in his element here.
He can get together with his Uhlan brothers and they
can get drunk and fight among themselves, and beat up
the occasional Austrian if they find him alone . . .' He
had not meant to let that slip, and bit off his last word,
half uttered.

'Is that what happened to you when you were here
before?' she asked him soberly. When he flushed and

did not reply, she added with a heavy heart, 'Did Adam do it?'

He avoided her eye, looking away across the stuffy little café to where the cab-men sat, partially unswaddled, to drink their coffee. They sat in a huddle in one corner, ignoring everyone else in the café, a race apart.

'They were of the opinion,' he said quietly, 'that I failed to show proper respect to the Polish nation, and decided to teach me some.'

'I'm sorry,' Gabriela said awkwardly, 'and I apologise.'

He looked surprised. 'Why should you apologise?'

'Because he is my husband.'

For the barest second, an extraordinary expression showed itself on Brenner's face, anger and bitterness and obstinacy. Then he began to drink his tea. Gabriela studied him. Perhaps he had told her the truth. With Brenner, one never knew. He had such a hazy conception of truth and falsehood that probably he was constitutionally unable to give an entirely truthful account of anything, even if he wanted to. He had a trick of rearranging any event to justify his own part in it. He did not do this consciously; it was an automatic process operated by his brain.

Gabriela gathered up her belongings. 'I'll have to go, Mischa. I didn't mean to stay out so long. I told Bronia, our housekeeper, that I'd only be an hour.'

He nodded and smiled at her. 'Meet me again,' he said. 'You don't have anyone here, and neither do I. I told you before that we were two of a kind: We need each other, Gabriela.'

She told him it wasn't true, and she told herself it wasn't true, but gradually she fell into the habit of meeting him regularly. They sat in quiet little back street cafés, much like the first one, changing the venue like any pair of furtive lovers. Except that they were not lovers, and all they did was talk.

The greatest change was that this time, unlike their previous acquaintance, Brenner began to talk to her of himself. He did this at first like a person who is learning to do something new, at first hesitantly and reluctantly, and then in fits and starts, one day loquacious, the next reticent. Some of the things he told her shocked her profoundly, some made her angry, and some even moved her to a kind of pity. She found herself reasoning with him, arguing with all the fervour of an early missionary with a particularly obstinate pagan. She tried every way she knew to get him to see that his way of using people and battening on their weaknesses was wrong. That he was not justified in acting in defiance of any natural or moral law just because it suited his purpose.

But he seemed quite unable to understand. He listened patiently, but it was quite useless. At the end of her most impassioned arguments he remained completely unconvinced, even untouched by what she had said. She realised, in growing frustration, that she might as well be speaking in Sanskrit for all the effect she was having. Gradually she became aware that behind the attractive, delicate features with their crown of glossy curls and the ingenuous, boyish smile lay a mind which seemed somehow to have grown deformed.

Perhaps it was not surprising, considering his background. He had an appalling childhood, of which he told her just enough to allow her a glimpse into its horrors. He had lived with a drunken, brutal father and an ailing and terrified mother in a house in which no ray of human love had ever shed its kindly light. After the death of his parents, he had existed at first on erratic remittances from his unspeakable grandmother, who had taken a fancy to the pretty boy, and later, clever and ambitious, on his wits. His plan to establish Gabriela as the Archduke's mistress was to have been the climax of his career, and he still regretted its failure, which he blamed on the fact that, as he saw it, she had 'fallen for Dubrowski'. He was twenty-four years old, and seemed to have lived a hundred existences, all filled with the dregs of human behaviour.

Slowly and disturbingly, yet unmistakably, one other fact emerged from their conversation. Gabriela became aware that Brenner, in so far as he was capable of any such feeling for another, was fond of her. Sometimes he behaved almost possessively towards her and was jealous of Adam. He hated her to mention her marriage. He didn't love her, because the passion given that name by most human beings was quite beyond his comprehension. He had never experienced it, didn't know what it was, and never would. But he appeared to take great pleasure in sitting with her in these small and nondescript cafés. He seemed to like to hear her voice speaking to him, even if it was only to tell him how wrong he was. He sat and watched her drink her tea, and button her gloves, and a host of other silly little actions which seemed to hold for him an endless charm and delight. Perhaps it was the novelty of an innocent pleasure which appealed to him. But, with her, Brenner seemed happy and at ease, whereas she noticed that at the first approach of others, a wary look appeared on his face. He was like a dog that has been mistreated and become vicious. Now it trusts no one, and is always alert to discover whence will come the next blow, so that it may bite the attacker first.

With a dread sense of the approaching inevitable, Gabriela knew what must be the result of this intimacy, what must surely happen. One day, it did.

Brenner leaned across the café table and whispered urgently, 'I'm going to St Petersburg on the Friday train. Come with me. I've Russian travel documents for two people. Meet me on the platform for the morning train.'

'So that you can set me up with a Russian grand duke,

I suppose?' Gabriela challenged sarcastically. But the sarcasm was a shield to hide her alarm.

'No!' he retorted vehemently. 'I wouldn't do that!'

'Oh yes, you would, Mischa, if the opportunity presented itself,' she told him. 'I know you too well. Don't lie to me.'

'We all tell lies,' Brenner said, unmoved. 'Sometimes to others, and sometimes to ourselves. But I'm not lying to you now, Gaby. Why should I? The Russians pay me enough for both of us to live well on it. You're not happy with Dubrowski. Don't pretend you are. Come with me.'

'I would be mad,' she gasped, 'to run away with you!'

Brenner smiled at her. 'No,' he said softly, 'not mad, my dear, only desperate enough . . .'

Gabriela pushed her chair away jerkily, so that it scraped across the tiled floor. 'I'd never go with you!'

'Why not?' His voice was quite harsh now, unlike his usual tone. 'One day soon, if he hasn't done so already, Dubrowski is going to climb Wawel Hill and go through the doors of the place up there, and waiting for him will be Katy. I want you. He doesn't. Don't pretend otherwise, Gaby. If you do, *you* lie. You lie to yourself!'

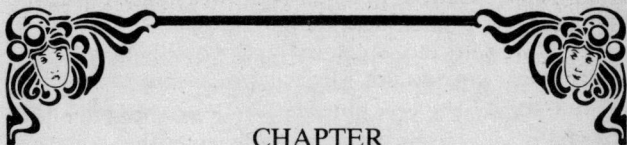

CHAPTER
FOURTEEN

BRONIA REMOVED the overflowing ashtray with a disapproving look, and when Adam took no notice of this, continuing to read his newspaper, the housekeeper heaved a loud sigh and put her hand on the small of her back. She waited.

Adam glanced up. 'What's the matter?'

'This cold weather I feel my years,' she said comfortably. 'But mustn't complain.'

He put the newspaper down. 'Send out to the farm and ask Tadeusz if he can spare one of his girls to come in and lend a hand in the kitchen.'

'I can do without those girls of his, day-dreaming in my kitchen and making eyes at the butcher's boy!'

A hint of amusement gleamed in Adam's eye and did not pass unremarked.

'Oh, it makes you laugh, does it, to know I've a bad back? Over twenty years it must be, since I first came here to work in this house, and that's my thanks!'

'You were my nurse, Bronia, and you know to the day how long you've been here. You also know that you are a member of this family,' he said firmly.

Bronia chose to take this as an invitation to sit down, folding her hands on her spotless apron. 'How time flies! It seems like yesterday—and only imagine, this time you've brought a wife home with you.'

Adam picked up his newspaper again and began to read.

'You were a bonny baby,' said Bronia sentimentally, adding sternly, 'but what a temper you had, even when you were still in petticoats. And if you didn't get your own way, my, the tantrums!'

'You're making it all up, Bronia. I was a model child,' he said from behind his newspaper.

'I remember.' She was undeterred, and used that tone of voice adopted by elderly people when they intend to reminisce whether the listener wishes to hear it or not. 'I remember you had a little carved wooden horse and cart. Tadeusz out at the farm carved it for you one Christmas.' She stared fixedly at the newspaper. 'And one day you flew into one of your tempers, fancying something amiss which wasn't, and threw the toy away and broke it. Then you were upset! The tears we had. You wouldn't be comforted. You loved it, you see,' she said slowly, 'but you broke it, and for no good reason —and it couldn't be mended.'

He put down the newspaper. 'I do understand what you're trying to tell me.'

'Oh, do you, now?' Bronia stood up and smoothed her apron. 'Then you'd best do something about it. You haven't much time.' She gathered up the full ashtray and set off for the door. 'If you don't,' she called over her shoulder, 'she'll go—with *him*!' She whisked round the corner and out of sight.

Adam glowered at the empty space for a moment, and then crushed the newspaper into a ball and hurled it into the corner of the room. He sat for a while after that, until the afternoon light began to fade, then went out into the hall. From the kitchen came the sound of Bronia berating one of the maids. The other maid came into the hall and he asked her for his coat. As she was helping him into it, he asked her, 'Where is your mistress?'

'She went out, sir. She didn't say where.' The girl fixed him with round, curious eyes.

Even this girl knows . . ., Adam thought.

He turned up his coat collar against the chill wind and walked quickly down the street. Winter now reigned.

It was in the air, and it grew dark early. He felt ill-tempered and out of sorts, striding along, looking neither to right nor left, and obliging people to scurry out of his way as, heads bent against the cold wind, they hurried homeward. He had no particular objective in view, but an instinct to seek warm shelter and congenial company, not to say—as he had to admit wryly—old habit, took him up the steep street that climbed Wawel Hill and brought him to the door of an establishment which, though it bore a different name, was not unlike the Golden Fleece in appearance. He pushed open the doors and went in. He had not been there since his return, but once he had been a recognised patron. It was not very busy so early in the evening. Adam seated himself in a secluded corner and ordered coffee. Then he leaned back, relaxing as the stuffy warm air entered his chilled muscles, and fixed his eyes unseeingly on the frosted glass candelabra and velvet hangings.

Sunk in his thoughts, Adam was not aware of the approach of a woman until a rustle of skirts by his ear, and a scent of cheap perfume, drew his attention to her arrival. Even then he did not take much notice. In a place like this, any man sitting alone could expect to be accosted by a personable young female in tawdry finery. He waved his hand in dismissal, and murmured, 'No, my dear, not now. Run along.'

'Major?' the girl replied, a little nervously.

At the sound of her voice, his senses awoke instantly, and he looked up in astonishment. 'Dear God—Katy . . .' he whispered.

The red-haired girl pulled a face, half embarrassed and half amused at his amazement.

'Where on earth have you been?' Adam demanded energetically. 'I looked all over Vienna for you. So did Gruber. We feared the worst!'

'We can't talk here, Major,' Katy said quickly in a low voice. 'The waiters have ears like foxes, and pick up every word. We can go upstairs. It's private, and no one will ask *why*.' She smiled ruefully at him.

He followed her up the narrow stairs. In a tiny room on the floor above, Katy carefully shut the door and turned to face him. Adam stared down at her for a minute in silent scrutiny, and then crossed to the bed and threw himself down on it, his back propped against the headboard and his boots resting on the coverlet.

'Well?' he asked curtly, his relief expressing itself in a momentary anger. 'You've led us all a merry dance. Perhaps you'd like to explain why? I thought old Jetta had dumped your body in the Danube . . . and it was my fault!'

'I fancy she had the idea to do it, Major.' Katy came to sit on the end of the bed and rested her well-rounded arm on the brass railing. 'She was on to me, Major— knew I'd been talking to you. It was that Brenner, I reckon, who gave her the idea. He never did like me. Well, she called me into her office. Friedl, the potman, was there.' Katy shivered at the memory. 'I thought my last hour had come, Major, and that's the truth. I decided to try and run for it, but Friedl caught hold of me, and as I was trying to get away, I knocked over the inkpot on old Jetta's desk. That saved my life, I reckon. She let out a great screech and tried to save her money ledger, and it took Friedl's eye off me for just long enough. I was out of there like an arrow from the bow. I ran down into the cellars; there's a way through into the next house down there. I hid till Friedl was out of the way, and then ran through all the cellars till I came up into the street on the other side of the block. I begged a ride on a cart going out of the city, and just kept going. They would have killed me if they'd caught me.' A despondent expression crossed her face. 'I lost the gold chain you gave me, Major. Friedl broke it in our struggle.'

'For pity's sake, girl, why didn't you contact me?' Adam asked in exasperation.

'I came here to Cracow,' she said simply. 'I knew it

was your home, and that sooner or later you'd turn up
—and I'd see you again . . .' Her voice faltered slightly.

'Well, I am glad to see you, Katushka,' he said at
length, after a silence. 'What are you doing now?'

'Same as ever.' Her tone was matter-of-fact. 'Only
job I know.' She looked up at him. 'You're married,
Major, now. I'd have looked you out, but when I found
you'd brought a wife home with you, I thought I'd better
stay away. Wives, and girls like me, they don't get along
together generally.' She pulled a face.

'I married my cousin's widow,' Adam said without
expression.

'Thought you might.' Katy looked down, away from
him. 'I've seen your lady.' Her voice was elaborately
casual. 'A real beauty, she is. You must make a handsome couple.'

'A handsome couple,' he said bitterly, 'that's about
all.' Suddenly he leaned forward and enthusiasm
entered his tone. 'I am glad I found you, Katy. I was
worried . . . and just now I'm in need of a friend to talk
to. I've missed you . . .' He stretched out his hand and
touched her rouged cheek. 'We had some good times,
Katy,' he whispered. 'Come on, now, for old times'
sake . . .' He patted the mattress beside him invitingly.

'No, Major!' Katy caught at his hand and pushed it
away. She looked straight into his eyes, her own brassily
pretty little face with its snub nose and untidy mop of
henna curls pale and fixed in a determined expression.
'You were always something special to me, Major.
Something a bit more than a customer. That's why you
mustn't—and I mustn't. Not now, not any more. Those
days are gone. You're married, and you belong to
someone else. She's young and she's beautiful.' Katy
drew a deep breath. 'Go home to your wife, Adam
Dubrowski. This is no place for you.'

Adam swung his legs to the floor and slowly stood
up. He stared down at Katy in her plum-purple plush
gown with its garish sequinned trimmings, the rouge

staining her full lips. Her skirts were bunched up as she sat on the bed, and from beneath the flounces of her cotton petticoats her black-stockinged legs swung free of the floor, like a schoolgirl's. She had a hole in the toe of one stocking.

'This is no place for you, either, Katushka,' Adam said gently. 'No life for you. Let me help you. I'll give you a good dowry, and you should be able to get a husband. Settle down and make a good, respectable housewife, eh?'

Katy wrinkled her snub nose as she considered his suggestion. 'There's old Marek, the butcher,' she said in a practical tone. 'He's no beauty, but he's a kind man, and his business is doing well. I'd have a silk dress for Sundays, that's for sure. He keeps telling me that he wants to take me away from all this!' She swept a hand at the bed, and suddenly collapsed with a fit of giggles.

It was contagious. Adam began to laugh, too. It had been some time since he had laughed so much over so little, and he wiped his eyes in mirth.

'Here,' Katy said, sobering, 'it's not funny, you know. Old Marek would probably marry me, if I had a dowry. I'd sit there in the shop, counting the cash while he cut up the schnitzels.'

'I'll insist that all our household meat is bought from you,' Adam promised. 'Leave Marek to me. You can start putting your trousseau together—you have my word on it.'

She put her hands on the brass bedknob and propped her chin on them, looking up at him through a tangle of red curls. 'You're a good man, Major,' she said softly.

'I make mistakes,' Adam told her ruefully. 'Sometimes I get the chance to put them right—as I will do for you, Katy. Sometimes I don't.'

Gabriela lay sleepless, staring into the darkness, and wondering when Adam would return home, and where

he was. It was very late. In the stillness of the night
the woodwork creaked, and a faint scattering of claws
suggested that Bronia should set a mousetrap in the
morning. She tried to concentrate on this domestic
detail, to prevent herself thinking of Adam, but it was
in vain. Perhaps he sat drinking with brother officers,
and playing cards. Perhaps he was with pretty, cheerful,
uncomplicated Katy. That thought hurt—but perhaps
it was true, as Brenner had jibed, that Adam simply
didn't want her. Mischa Brenner. Tomorrow was
Friday, and he'd be on the station platform looking for
her and wondering whether, after all, she would come.

'If you are desperate enough . . .' Gaby knew she
couldn't go on like this, so constantly and obviously
rejected. She had either to face Adam openly, or she
had to leave this house for ever.

A sudden, louder creak echoed in the silent house.
Although Gabriela had not heard the front door, Adam
must be back. She sat up in bed and listened intently.
He was moving about, very quietly, downstairs. She
imagined him taking off his army greatcoat and *czapska*,
probably stopping at the foot of the staircase to light a
cigarette. She had frequently wondered whether he ever
smoked in bed, and if they would be awoken one early
morning to find the house in flames. She heard his
footstep on the stair, louder now, coming closer. He
was coming along the corridor, walking slowly, and
then, outside her door, the footsteps stopped. Was it
possible that tonight, at last, he would come in?

The polished brass handle of the door was faintly
discernible in the dim light, and Gabriela watched it as
if mesmerised. Adam stood for such a long time outside
that she wondered what could be going through his
mind, and then, unbelievably, the door handle moved,
very slightly, downwards. Her heart leapt into her
mouth, with a wild hope, only for it to be dashed.
The handle was abruptly released and sprang back into
place. Adam walked on, and she heard the door of his

own room next door shut with a decisive click.

'No,' she whispered to herself, 'it's too much. This is the last time . . .' She threw back the covers, scrambled out of bed and ran barefoot to the connecting door between her room and his. She pulled it open and went through.

Adam was standing by the bed, lighting a candle. The Cracow house had no gas. He whirled round at the noise and stared at her, standing by the door in her nightgown, her blond hair loose on her shoulders.

For a moment neither of them spoke, and then he said brusquely, 'You'll catch cold. Go back to bed.' He turned away and put the candlestick on the washstand.

Gabriela came further into the room. 'You stopped outside the door for so long,' she said, a quiver in her voice, 'that I thought you would come in . . .'

Adam began to undress, pulling his shirt over his head. The candlelight jumped and flickered, sending his shadow leaping wildly about the wall behind him.

'I—decided you might be asleep,' he said, tossing aside the shirt. He was avoiding looking at her directly, and sat down on a chair to pull off his boots.

'I'm not asleep, Adam,' Gabriela said in a loud, clear voice. She came across and sat down on the edge of the bed.

He looked up now, one boot held in his hand, his features distorted and enigmatic in the candlelight. 'I said, go back to bed, Gaby!' he ordered in a low voice.

'No,' Gabriela said, determined but tense, and he stared at her in some surprise. 'I want to be your wife, Adam. I'm sorry if, in Vienna, I was cold towards you. Everything seemed so . . . so hurried there, and there was so much discord in the air. Besides, I thought you hadn't really wanted to marry me . . .' Suddenly she burst out passionately, 'And I was right, wasn't I, Adam? You've always despised me! You never wanted to bring me here as your wife!'

'Stop that!' he said savagely, and at his tone she fell
silent. 'I am proud of my family name—' Adam's words
cracked in the air like a whiplash '—and I should not
have offered it to you if I had thought you unworthy of
it.'

'Then, why won't you . . . ?' she faltered.

He drew a deep breath. He walked across to her, and
stooping, took hold of her arms and pulled her to her
feet. 'It's late, Gaby, and it's cold. Go on back to bed.'
His voice was not unkind, but it was quite firm and
decided. 'Tomorrow we'll talk about it.'

Trembling at his touch, she whispered, 'Talk?
Haven't I tried to talk to you? I've even tried to learn
your language! We don't talk, Adam, we don't do
anything! You don't want my body any more than you
want my company or my conversation. I am your wife
—but if I disappeared completely, I doubt you'd even
notice!'

'I notice a lot of things!' Adam retorted harshly, and
his grip on her arms tightened. 'I notice that my wife
spends her days out of this house, and for all her
professed desire to "talk" to me, she is strangely secretive about where she goes or what she does!'

Gabriela flushed. Could he know about Mischa? Her
heart began to beat painfully in alarm. 'I have never
betrayed you, Adam,' she said evenly.

'It's as well,' Adam replied curtly. 'I told you—I am
proud of my family name and not prepared to see it
dishonoured.'

Anger swept over her. 'How dare you talk to me of
honour?' she gasped. 'Where were *you* this evening—
and in what company?'

'I met an old friend,' he said coolly.

'Indeed? And does she have red hair, by any chance?'

He gave her a suspicious look. 'How do you know
that? Yes, I came across Katy, if you want to know.
She escaped Jetta in Vienna, and now she's here. But
I wasn't . . .'

Gabriela did not wait to hear the rest. She tore herself free of his grasp and turning, ran blindly back into her own room. She heard him call 'Gaby, wait!' But she no longer wanted to hear. She slammed the door and locked it, panting and crying, oblivious of her frozen feet, and wishing she could run away that very minute, outside—outside into the snow if need be—and run, run, as she had done before on the night of Max's funeral.

Adam came and tapped on the door once, and called softly, 'Gaby?' But she put her hands over her ears, and scrambling back into bed, buried herself under the sheets. She could still hear him moving about in the next room. Perhaps he had stubbed his toe, or the candle had gone out, because he was cursing quietly to himself. But, after a while, all was silent.

Gabriela lay back on the pillow. She no longer had a decision to make. It had been made for her.

Mischa was standing on the platform, rubbing his hands and stamping his feet to keep warm. Station staff had brushed away the snow, but the wind blew icily along the platform, bearing on it the little specks of frozen snow it had carried all the way from Siberia. The tiny particles stung Gabriela's face painfully, as the blast of the wind struck her. The train was in and waiting. Every so often the engine heaved a sigh, like an old lady loosening her corsets, and sent up a puff of steam which hung in the icy air.

He watched Gabriela approach. As she came up to him, he smiled, satisfaction in his dark eyes. 'I knew you'd come.'

'I could only bring this small bag,' Gabriela answered in an expressionless little voice. 'Bronia would have asked questions, otherwise.'

'It doesn't matter,' he told her cheerfully. 'I've plenty of money waiting for me in St Petersburg. I'll buy you new outfits and we'll stroll along the Nevsky Prospekt, turning every head!' He leaned forward and kissed her cheek warmly, something he had never done before.

Gabriela shivered. Last night it had seemed that she had no alternative, no other way forward than this. To go with Mischa had seemed to her a means of escape. Now it appeared in its true light, here, on this cold, windswept railway platform. She was leaving her husband for another man. She was going with Mischa, putting her future in his hands. Adam didn't want to come to her bed, so she was taking herself to Mischa Brenner's. Yet even the thought of being subject to Mischa's caresses appalled her.

'You're cold,' Mischa was saying, in concern. 'You're shivering. The train is warm. Jump in; it's due out shortly. We'll put this place finally behind us!'

'In a minute,' she said awkwardly. He had put out his hand to take her elbow and she moved away automatically, not wanting him to touch her.

'I shall be glad to get out of here.' Mischa pursued his theme fervently. 'Dubrowski is welcome to it. He wasn't at home when you left?' He raised his eyebrows questioningly.

She shook her head. An old woman was hobbling along the platform, carrying a basket out of which she sold bread rolls and little cakes to the passengers. The basket was heavy and she was muffled up against the cold. When she saw them, she called out, 'Bless you, gracious lady and gentleman! Are you hungry?'

Mischa laughed and shook his head. 'Not now, mother, later maybe!' He gave the old woman a coin, and she raised her withered hand and made the sign of the cross in the air over him and said, 'The saints will grant you safe journey, my handsome fellow!'

'You see?' he said comfortably to Gabriela. 'Nothing can go wrong! So don't look so nervous.' He smiled broadly at her. His teeth were very white, small and sharp, like an animal's.

The conductor was walking down the platform

towards them, and called out now in a loud voice, 'All aboard, please!'

She drew in her breath and stepped back. 'No—I'm sorry, Mischa, I can't! I can't go with you. I'm not coming . . .'

'Don't be stupid!' he said sharply. He darted forward and grasped her wrist. 'You've nothing to stay here for.'

'It doesn't matter!' She twisted her wrist in his grip, but he wouldn't let go, and she remembered how he had dragged her through the cellars to Jetta's office. 'It was a mistake coming here. I'm sorry, Mischa, but I can't do it. Let go of me, please!'

'Of course you can,' he said in that soft, coaxing voice he knew so well how to adopt. 'You can, Gabriela, it's easy. All you need to do is step up into the train. Come on.' He released her wrist and held out his hand, 'Give me your hand.'

He jumped lightly up into the carriage doorway and smiled down at her, his hand outstretched. She looked at him, handsome, boyish and debonair, with a smile as ingenuous as a child's. The medieval artists were wrong, she thought, to depict the devil and his minions as ugly creatures. Of all the angels, Lucifer, the Fallen Angel, had been the most beautiful. Beautiful and evil. Corrupted and corrupting.

'I am Adam's wife,' she said clearly and calmly. 'I am Adam's wife, whether Adam wishes it or not and whether you wish it or not. My place is here, with him.'

'No!' he snarled. He leapt down to the platform, with something truly animal in his movements and expression now. 'I won't leave you here for Dubrowski. He won't beat me—he won't win—he shan't have you!' His voice rose in wild passionate tones.

'Why,' Gabriela gasped, 'you don't want *me*, you want to hurt Adam! You've always hated him, and that hate has festered in you like a sore. You have been storing up vengeance all this time, until the other day you saw the chance to use me to strike at him! You know what it would do to Adam, to have everyone know that I had run off with you. But I wouldn't play your little game for you before, Mischa, and I won't play it now!'

'Everybody on board, please!' yelled the conductor. He raised his flag.

She backed away, and turning, began to run back down the platform towards the barrier.

Behind her, she heard Mischa shout, 'Wait one minute, man!' to the conductor, and then, 'Gaby, you're wrong. Gabriela, come back!'

She ran on, pushing through the barrier at the entry to the platform, and cannoning into a tall figure in a military greatcoat who had been standing in the shadows and watching them.

'Adam . . .' she whispered in dismay.

The figure stirred. 'Are you going with him?' he asked very quietly.

Gabriela shook her head. 'How do you come to be here, Adam?'

He shrugged, and a tired, mirthless smile crossed his face. 'I knew you'd been meeting him. This is a small city, and I'm well known in it. If my wife is meeting another man in back street cafés, all Cracow knows it —and so do I!'

'It wasn't like that,' she murmured. 'I was lonely . . .' She swallowed. 'You were watching us on the platform all the time, and you didn't try to stop me.'

'Go with him, if it's what you want,' Adam said. 'It's better than dragging my name through the gutters of my own town. I won't force you to stay here with me. I've never forced you to do anything you didn't wish.'

'But I don't want to go with him!' Gabriela cried out wildly. 'I want to stay here with you. But you don't want *me*! If you did, do you think I would have come here today?'

Adam paled. Then he reached out his hand slowly, so slowly that it was almost as if the muscles were impaired and would not obey his brain. He touched her face, but before he could speak, running footsteps approached them and Mischa appeared, breathless, at the barrier.

'Gaby, for pity's sake! I can't make the man hold the train any longer . . .' He caught sight of Adam at that moment, and every vestige of colour drained fom his face. In the brief silence, in which all three of them stood as if turned to stone, the conductor's whistle sounded shrilly.

It seemed to release something in Adam, who leapt through the barrier and grasped Brenner's coat lapels. 'You baby-faced little hyena,' he said in a soft, deadly voice. 'Last time I hardly touched you. I didn't even spoil your pretty looks. This time, God help me, I'll kill you!'

Terror was printed on Brenner's face. His lips moved, but no sound came out. Then, with a superhuman effort born of panic, he tore himself free and and fled, racing headlong down the platform. The train was already moving away, gathering speed. He grabbed at the handle of one of the carriage doors, and when it was torn from his grasp, at the next. This time the door was insecurely shut and flew open.

'Come back there!' yelled the station master, suddenly aware of what was happening. 'Come back, it's too late!'

Even Adam had halted in his pursuit, and yelled, 'Leave it, man! You can't do it. I won't touch you, I swear!'

Brenner leapt.

As he did so, a great cloud of thick greyish-white steam flooded the platform, obscuring everything, people, train and the frantic scrabbling figure. In the fog, someone screamed. It was an inhuman sound, of neither man nor woman, a terrible, shrill, weird and despairing cry, echoing up among the girders of the station roof like the last distorted shriek of a lost soul hurtling down into the fiery depths of hell.

Even as it cut through the air, Adam launched himself forward, flinging himself headlong, and was lost to Gabriela's view in the cloud of smoke and steam. She peered into the cloud, trying desperately to see him, but the choking fog obscured everything. When, for a few seconds, it cleared, she had a brief glimpse of two figures on the platform. Rather, one was on the platform and holding grimly on to the other, who had slipped half over the edge and was clinging frantically to the hand reached down to save him. Then the swirling smoke flooded across again and robbed her of even this sight.

As it finally thinned and cleared, people came running from all corners of the station. The train itself had stopped further down the track, and she realised that the dreadful scream she had heard had indeed not been purely human in origin, but a compound of Brenner's despairing cry as he felt himself fall and the grinding squeal of the train's brakes and the metal rims of the wheels on the frozen steel tracks.

Passengers were leaning out of the windows, shouting to know what had happened, and the loose door flapped once and then swung slowly shut of its own accord. Gabriela put a trembling hand to her forehead. The old woman, sitting hunched by her basket, was crossing herself repeatedly and muttering prayers, and the girl's lips moved instinctively in unison with hers. People clustered in a group on the platform, including two stalwart members of the railway police in heavy great-coats and flowerpot-shaped peaked shakos, who had come lumbering from the quiet nook where they had taken refuge from the cold air. Between them, Brenner was borne away, and Gabriela closed her eyes as they passed by her.

When she opened them, Adam stood beside her. 'He won't die,' he said impatiently. 'So stop praying for him. Only the *good* die young, and Brenner doesn't qualify!'

'Is he hurt badly?' she asked in a strained voice.

Adam shrugged. 'A broken ankle, I fancy—and the worst fright of his mis-spent young life. He'll recover from both, well enough and soon enough to answer all the questions that a great many people are anxious to put to him!'

'You saved his life,' Gabriela said soberly. 'Though he wronged you, you pulled him back when he would have gone under the train's wheels.'

Even as she spoke, she was thinking, 'Adam is the finest man I ever knew. How could I ever think of leaving him?' She understood then, for the first time, how much she had grown to love him. She could not have said exactly when this love had begun to blossom within her. Perhaps the seeds of it had been sown long ago. With her growing love had grown her despair, and now she wondered if he would ever forgive what she had done.

In answer to her last spoken words, Adam said brusquely, 'Let's hope I don't live to regret it. However, he won't play any further part in *your* life, that I can promise!'

Gabriela had not realised how chilled she was until they reached the house. But by that time she was shaking, and the cold seemed to have eaten into her bones. She knew that shock contributed to this, but try as she might, she could not control the trembling, though she stood by the stove and held out her hands to its hot glazed tiles. She began to cry, unable to prevent herself, the hot tears trickling down her cheeks and stinging, because the cold wind on the station platform had chafed her skin. She rubbed at her face with her hand, stifling the sobs, not wanting Adam to see.

But he was close behind her. 'You needn't weep for him,' he said sharply. 'He's a poisonous little snake, and a threat to us all. I hope they lock him up and throw away the key. I'm already beginning to regret my good deed.' He pushed a glass of brandy into her fingers. 'Here, drink this. It will steady your nerves,' he added with rough kindness.

'I don't think Mischa knows how to be different, Adam,' she said quietly. She sipped at the brandy and spluttered as the fiery liquid burned her throat.

'I am sure you are right,' he agreed. 'But it doesn't make things any better, Gaby. He's totally amoral, like an animal, unable to envisage right or wrong, or any moral code or notion of honour. People like that do untold harm.' He paused. 'Evil is a very real force. Sometimes it's easily identified. Anyone meeting old Jetta knew at once in what presence he was. But sometimes evil is beautiful, acceptable outwardly, so that it even wins your pity and friendship. That is Brenner's kind of evil, and, believe me, it's much the worst kind.'

Gabriela put down the brandy glass and forced herself to look up into his face. It was difficult to interpret the expression on it, but he did not look angry, only a little sad.

'If you knew he was here,' she asked, puzzled, 'and I was seeing him, why didn't you stop me—or him?'

Adam avoided her eyes. 'My first instinct was to interfere. But then I thought, if I did that, there would always be a doubt between us . . . You accused me once before of doubting you, Gabriela. I knew I had to show you that I trusted you.'

Gabriela whispered brokenly, 'Oh, Adam . . .' and putting her arms round him, leaned her head on his tunic, unable to say more.

He hesitated, and then put his own arms about her and bending his head, kissed the tangled damp curls which clung to her temple. 'You said—back there at the station—that I didn't want you,' he whispered huskily. 'But I always wanted you, Gabriela, from the moment I first saw you, so bedraggled in the rain outside the Golden Fleece. At first I thought it was a kind of curse on me. A punishment for my pride, for condemning you unseen, for failing Max. I thought that you could never be mine. And then, Fate or heaven, I don't know which, put us into a situation where I could ask you to be mine. Perhaps I should be grateful to young Brenner, because it was he who made it all possible! Yet my situation was worse, not better, because you were both mine—and not mine.'

He stroked her hair gently. 'I was too impatient. The night I came to you in Vienna, you were not ready . . . It was much too soon; it was my mistake, and I knew it. So, I tried to give you time. But while I waited, I began to see other things which were wrong between us.'

Gabriela looked up at him questioningly. He disengaged her from his embrace and stepped away. Inside the tiled stove, some burning wood fell down. Adam stooped to hook open the little iron door and fed in another piece of kindling from the basket by it. The red light from the glowing embers was reflected on his face, casting shadows into the hollow and lines.

'I was born in this house,' he said very quietly. 'I've been away from it often. Sometimes for long periods. But it's always been my home.'

He pushed the little door shut and dusted his hands, and they sat together on the sofa by mutual accord.

'I suppose that because I loved it, and the city, I saw no fault in it. I wanted to bring you here, Gabriela. I wanted you to see it. I wanted you to love it, as I did. But when you came, I began to see it differently, as *you* must be seeing it, through your eyes. A dull, provincial backwater with little happening. A city of good solid bourgeois families, with everything reflecting their tastes. There was nothing for you to do but go down into the kitchen and get chapped hands and broken fingernails doing tasks a servant should be doing!'

'But I wanted . . .' she began.

He interrupted her. 'No, let me finish. I promised my uncle, and, what was much more important, I promised *you*, Gaby, that I'd look after you—and this is what I had to offer! Dull and dreary domestic tedium in a sleepy little city, struggling to learn my language, so that you could talk to the housekeeper! How could I come and make love to you, Gabriela?' he went on miserably. 'Though, God knows, I wanted to! It would be as if I used you, took, and offered nothing. You don't know what it cost me to walk past your door every night.'

In a strange way, Mischa Brenner had understood Adam very well. 'Dubrowski makes up his mind about all sorts of things,' he had told her, 'but he isn't always right.'

'You were wrong about me before, Adam,' she told him gently. 'And you are wrong now, if you think I don't love this city, and this house, and you.' She took his hand in hers. 'And you don't have to walk past my door any more, Adam.'

He lowered his head and kissed her fingers, and then, unable to control his pent-up emotion any longer, pulled her towards him and crushed his mouth fiercely against hers.

'Take me to bed now, Adam . . .' she whispered as soon as she was able.

Together they climbed the crooked wooden stair, Adam's arm about her waist. In her room, they paused and looked at one another, but neither of them spoke. Words were not needed. Adam stretched out his hand behind him, and turned the key in the lock.

SAY IT WITH ROMANCE

Margaret Rome – Pagan Gold
Emma Darcy – The Impossible Woman
Dana James – Rough Waters
Carole Mortimer – Darkness Into Light

Mother's Day is a special day and our pack makes
a special gift. Four brand new Mills & Boon romances,
attractively packaged for £4.40.
Available from 14th February 1986.